Praise for

But Not Forever

2017 Rossetti Book Awards Shortlist in Young Adult Fiction

"Doppelgangers separated by twelve decades exchange places in this deftly intertwined fish-out-of-water tale from debut author Jan Von Schleh. Magical and fast-moving, *But Not Forever* challenges social conventions, celebrates friendship, and demonstrates the resilience of love with an unflinching compassion which is sure to delight."
—Mindy Tarquini, award-winning author of *The Infinite Now* and *Hindsight*

"Lush, poignant, enchanting. Sonnet and Emma, and their intertwining stories, grabbed me from the start and wouldn't let me go."
—Julia Inserro, author of *Nonni's Moon*

"*But Not Forever* is a magical time-traveling adventure that captivates readers from the start. Von Schleh's sparkling prose sets the stage for the thrilling, intertwining journeys of Sonnet and Emma. Doppelgangers born into separate worlds, both are forced to face family dysfunction and reexamine societal conventions. Love and heartache cross over generations while universe forces and unbreakable family ties are clearly at work in this page-turning tale."
—Heather Cumiskey, award-winning author of *I Like You Like This*

But Not Forever

But Not Forever

A NOVEL

by

JAN VON SCHLEH

Published by SparkPress, a BookSparks imprint,
A division of SparkPoint Studio, LLC
Tempe, Arizona, USA, 85281
www.gosparkpress.com

Published 2018
Printed in the United States of America
ISBN: 978-1-943006-58-8 (pbk)
ISBN: 978-1-943006-59-5 (e-bk)

Library of Congress Control Number: 2018932730

Book design by Stacey Aaronson

For Kahlil, Nikolai, and Akio
My three reasons for everything

What's past is prologue.
—WILLIAM SHAKESPEARE

CHAPTER ONE

———

Sonnet
2015

The six of us stood before the mansion, dazed by what we had stumbled on, out of breath after chasing each other around the dark, tangled forest. I pushed past my sister and slid up close to Rapp as he leaned, panting, against a tree.

I pretended not to notice him, pretended not to see the shaggy, dark hair falling into eyes the color of the green ferns we had trampled on our way up the hill, or the long drip of pine sap worming down his tan leg. A beat-up messenger bag was slung over his shoulder, settling on his hip, a bulky thing between us. His finger looped through the leather strap, fiddling with the buckle, forcing a metal noise as if he was drumming out a song. *What was inside that khaki bag? Would it solve the mystery of him?*

Clicking, clicking, a *rat-ta-tat-tat.* Rapp stared straight ahead and watched as bits of August sunlight tunneled through branches onto the ancient structure, riveted on this long-dead, rich man's house, emerging out of the early morning fog.

My brother, sister, and two cousins chattered around us, their words like helium-filled balloons, floating away from the quiet of Rapp and me. I was so close I could see his chest move in a slow, steady beat, the soft air dancing against me, our bare arms almost touching. He was breathing normally now, breathing in the same mountain air as me, and for some strange reason that thrilled me, made butterflies flitter around my heart. I gave him another sidelong stare and caught his scent, warm and soapy. . . .

Dear god. I was acting like a wild animal in heat. A stalker. I squeezed my eyes shut. This place was doing crazy things to my head.

As if someone was slowly turning up the volume, my family's jabbering became a heated conversation. And heated conversation turned into an intense debate. The metal tapping stopped, and an invisible sword descended from the sky, slicing through the thick, sweet air between us.

Although neither of us had moved, Rapp and I were separated as suddenly as we had come together, and the four others in our escaping-the-adults fan club came tumbling back into view.

I sucked air as if I had been holding my breath—either in pain or in bliss, I wasn't quite sure which—and stepped away, still there, still standing on a forested hill above a ghost town called Monte Cristo.

In a place we probably weren't meant to be.

NOT creeped out in the least, my twin brother, Evan, and cousin Lia, talked up the merits of busting into the mansion as a *really great* history lesson, while my sister, Jules, and older cousin Niki shook their heads. Evan and Lia were always up for a little adventure, and just their wanting something triggered the opposite response from Niki and Jules who thought, being a year older, they were the authorities on pretty much everything.

I let them hash it out. At ages fifteen and sixteen, were any of us really up on the pluses and minuses of trespassing in an ancient, abandoned house?

"And, anyway," Evan said, with his please-can-we-just-do-it grin, "There's a reason why we just happened to find this old wreck of a place."

"Serendipity, with a capital S . . . right?" said Lia. On-board with Evan's breaking-in plan, she cast around her best smile.

Niki's feet were planted rock-solid on a carpet of crispy pine needles, arms folded tight across her shirt. "What's with you two? There're probably ghosts flying around in there, biting and scratching. This house is trouble with a capital T. I vote no."

"Ghosts don't bite and scratch. That's stupid, Niki," said Lia.

"They told us to stay away from mine shafts and old shacks," said my sister, her voice rising with each syllable. She joined up tight to Niki, her typical spot, no daylight between them. "I vote no, too."

"C'mon, Jules—no? This is clearly not a shack. It's a *casa grande*. Practically a palace." Evan turned to Rapp and me. "Step out from the shadows. Time to cast your ballots."

"I'm in," said Rapp, snapping out of his daze. He swung to me. "Sonnet?"

My cheeks scorched. Before I could open my mouth, an ink-colored crow, big and agitated, opened its beak and cawed insults from the shadows of the roof. Jules jumped, her perfect hair nipping at her face as she spun to me. "You're just standing there, Sonnet. Saying nothing."

"I'm weighing our options." I surveyed the mysterious patch of land around us, buying time. Named after the fictitious Count of Monte Cristo, who had plundered someone else's treasure and used it to unleash horrible revenge, this Monte Cristo was a deserted gold-mining town in the Cascade Mountains. And, here, preserved inside a ring of towering evergreens, sat a Victorian-era house that seemed to have been waiting, biding its time, just for us.

Except for the wind rustling through the trees and the occasional plop of pinecones falling around us, it was as quiet as the moon. I would have been happy just digging around outside. There were probably all sorts of lost artifacts hiding under the forest rot. But five sets of eyes were glued on me for the final tally. I turned off my brain and got off my usual place, straddling a decision. I took the plunge. "I'm in, too." I wasn't going to let anyone consider me a terrified ghost-believer.

Four against two. Trouble with a capital T had won.

We winners left Niki and Jules, with their dagger eyes, sitting on a mossy log, pretending not to care. Hauling away a snarl of withered blackberry vines that, like a locked gate, kept us from reaching our goal, we made our way up the stairs to the crumbling porch. A turret loomed over our heads, and loose gingerbread trim rocked in the blustery air. Rusty nails had disintegrated, bleeding coppery-red streaks down weather-beaten boards covering the windows. Evan yanked one off and threw it behind him. He pressed his face to the glass.

Sudden pops of splintering wood shot out from underneath his feet as the plank he was standing on cracked apart. Our leader fell backwards. Whirling his arms like a madman at the blackened doorknocker that stretched out its hand-and-ball toward his descending chest, he caught it and leaped. The old front door creaked open and swung into the house with Evan hanging on. With a thud, he landed on the grimy floor.

Niki and Jules, as shocked as we were, stomped up the stairs after the rest of us. We jumped over the spot where the rotten wood had caved in and ran howling through the dark opening after Evan.

My brother rolled off the floor, clawing cobwebs off his face and out of his buzz-cut. "See? Unlocked. It was meant to be. The door opened itself for us." He laughed and brushed off his shorts, gesturing his head toward a lonely piano in the corner of a vast, empty room.

I crunched over mouse droppings to the baby grand, feeling lucky to have chosen my red Converse high-tops over sandals earlier that morning. The cold air shifted, whispering, rumbling. *Was that thunder?* I glanced around to the door. Everyone had scattered. The piano and a jolt of *déja vu* tugged at me. Children's laughter and piano tinkling echoed around in my head . . . I couldn't quite catch it. I flipped up the fall-board, reaching forward to tap at a key.

Squeaking footsteps exploded my heart into my throat. The cover fell from my hand and—*crack!*—banged down over the ebony and ivory. "Geez, Lia, you scared me—"

"Just trying to find you."

Shrieks of laughter bounced around the ceiling as running feet skidded above us. Dust powdered our heads. I shuddered away the fear. "So, it turns out those two goddesses are just kids like the rest of us. Well, I just hope they don't get bitten by a ghost."

"Niki and Jules are so ridiculous," said Lia, laughing. "It's good they have each other."

I laughed with her, glad my cousin, my best friend, had found me.

Dusty shafts of light seeped in between window boards and lit our way to a hallway and another big room where a tarnished spike of metal pointed like a falling spear from the middle of the ceiling. "It's the old dining room in here. I thought Monte Cristo was just shacks, you know, for the gold miners. Rich people lived in this ghost town, too." I rubbed greasy dirt off fireplace tiles with the sleeve of my sweatshirt. Dull glaze turned to peacock feathers and, suddenly, a dazzling, blue bird. "Look, Lia. So many forgotten things."

"Hidden gems. I wonder what's in here." Lia attacked a drawer in the built-in cabinet. It grated and stuck and finally budged free. "A candle. Another forgotten thing."

"A candle and a piano—left behind. Like a message from the dead."

"Yeah, like a hologram, beamed in from heaven." Lia

waved the petrified stick of yellow wax around in the old air. "Isn't this the weirdest place? What's a fancy city house doing in the forest?"

"It probably wasn't a forest back in the day. It would have been logged and cleared when they built the place. Now it's just trees again. Like, full circle."

"Logged and cleared, huh? Whatever. You're the expert." Lia tossed the candle back in the drawer. "I don't want to take anything out of here. A spirit might follow me home and haunt me for the rest of my life. That's what happens, you know. I've seen stuff like that on TV. Real people getting haunted right out of their homes 'cause they piss off the ghosts."

"Let's go find everyone and get outta here, then. We don't want to make the ghosts mad."

Lia smiled. "Let's go find Rapp, isn't that what you mean?"

Rapp. His name whizzed against my ears, hurtled through my core and nicked my heart. The butterflies were back— *what was wrong with me?* I had just met him last night at my birthday party—the McKay Twins' Fifteenth Birthday Bash.

Instalove, that silly thing I'd always avoided, that drama I repeatedly accused my sister of, seemed to have infected me. "He's running around up there with Niki and Jules. Obviously, he wants to be with the goddesses."

"I'll bet he's crushing on you, not them," said Lia. "He was ogling you at your birthday party last night when you weren't looking, and then he stared at you over his bread pudding at the diner this morning. Seriously. I watched him."

I sighed. "I doubt it."

"Keep your nerve, Sonnet. You just need to talk about stuff that's interesting to the male animal. Like Niki and Jules do. Like, you know, sports. Or like that antique T-shirt he ripped off his uncle because he's into old rock and blues."

"How do you know that?"

"Because I asked him."

Even Lia had a relationship with him.

We shuffled through the house, whorls of black billowing at our ankles, back to the entry where the front door was still wide open to a cloud-covered sun. Thunder rumbled, again. It had started to rain, and the sudden dampness made me sneeze. "Ugh, my allergies," I sniffed. "Maybe I'll go back down to the river and pan for gold with the adults. This day is boring and . . . absurd."

"C'mon, you don't mean that," Lia pleaded.

No, I didn't mean it. The grand staircase wound around to the next level where the dark opening at the top gaped at us like open jaws—and he was up there. I grabbed Lia's hand. We tiptoed up the creaking stairs. On the second floor landing we heard muted laughter above us. "There must be a third floor," I said, thinking of my mom's favorite old-time British shows. "The maid's quarters—"

"Shhh." Lia yanked on my sleeve. "Someone's coming."

Rapp whipped around a corner, stumbling into us. He put his finger to his lips and motioned, towing me along with his big hand around my skinny wrist. He whispered, "They want to scare you. Evan's hatching a diabolical plan." He opened a door along the hallway and pushed us in.

I pressed up against a wall. Strips of brown-stained wallpaper curled down to the floor and lay in moldy piles at my feet. The charred corner fireplace still had chunks of old petrified wood from its last smoky fire.

"This is my favorite room so far." Rapp strode past us over his earlier footprints toward the boarded-up windows. "Come look. The view would have been epic." He banged and rattled on a window until it opened, knocking loose boards to the ground below. Outside, the storm had moved in and surrounded us with a vengeance. A piece of the house's dangling gingerbread trim blew past. "Yowza! Look at that!" He stuck his head out and closed his eyes, letting raindrops sprinkle across his face

I moved to Rapp's side. Tree branches loomed in my face, their shiny wet needles swishing at me. The hard splattering of rain hit the dirt below and sent the smell of damp earth back up. I narrowed my eyes and peered out and up at the sky through the tops of the trees. Dark clouds had bumped white ones out of their way and were quickly filling in the blue. Thunder boomed. I looked over my shoulder, but Lia wasn't in the room. I had missed her leaving.

"Something wrong?" Rapp asked, pulling his head back in and shaking the wetness away.

"I don't know, I just feel . . . weird. Maybe we should go."

Rapp looked at his phone. "Really? It's not even twelve. We still have an hour."

My mind scrambled for something interesting to say. But *interesting* failed me. The strap of his messenger bag crossed over the front of an old black T-shirt, ballooning letters blasting a tweet from the seventies—*Heart! Live at the Paramount!* His uncle's T-shirt, according to Lia, 'cause he was into old rock and blues, also according to Lia. Except for the fact that he was a year ahead of me in school and was staying with his uncle for some unknown reason, I knew nothing about him.

Another crack of thunder and a flash of lightning lit up the room. Rain began to pelt the windows, and a few random raindrops hit me in the face. Rapp closed the window. We heard Niki and Jules running and laughing through the crack under the door. I hoped they kept going. I didn't need my sister in here, sprinkling her golden gorgeousness all over Rapp. I raked my fingers through the dusty, red hair falling past my shoulders. Jules would win the beauty contest. She always did.

"Niki and Jules stick together like superglue, don't they?" Rapp said.

"You could say they're as bad as me and Lia."

"Cousins and best friends. Times two. That's convenient."

"Convenient when we come back home every summer. Sad the rest of the year."

"I'd take your life any day over mine, Sonnet."

Once again, a perfect comeback escaped me. The wind yowled and shifted, and rain hammered at the windowpanes. Another streak of lightning lit us up, standing close and facing each other. Rapp took my hand and turned my new birthday ring to the faint light. "Beautiful," he whispered. His smell, that warm soapy smell, paralyzed me once again.

I would give anything to have him kiss me. I stared at his hand holding mine.

After a moment, he let me go. "If you're not too scared, go hide in the closet. I'll tell them I don't know where you went," he said.

"No, thanks." I managed to smile. He thought I was a scaredy-cat.

"Come on."

I really didn't want to. My head told me I wanted to stay right there, right next to him. I teetered back and forth for a minute and then crossed the room. For once I wouldn't over-think it. It was just a closet. The rusty hinges squealed as the door opened onto shimmery air. "Do you see that?"

"Do I see what?"

"Like little shiny bubbles."

"No." He grinned. "You're crazy."

I put my head inside and wrinkled my nose. "It smells like death in here. Hide with me." I turned around to face him. An angry gust of wind banged the window back open. It whistled past his head, blowing his hair into his face. With that gust, the closet door slammed shut, dragging me with it.

I smashed against the wall and flipped around and around, my hair whipping at my face.

I tried to catch myself as the space grew and changed. I tried to hold on to something, anything, as the floor skated away.

Flying objects hit my head.

I felt my ribs crack.

Darkness opened its jaws and swallowed me.

CHAPTER TWO

———

Emma
1895

*E*mma heard her mother calling—what in heaven's name was it *now*? She gave herself a few more minutes of sweet Monte Cristo solitude before facing the onslaught.

Shutting out the shrilling, Emma savored the gift of warmth on this sunny August morning. A blackberry-scented breeze played against her skin and rattled pine-needle-glazed branches in the trees beyond where she lay. An eagle must have heard the incessant noise, too. With a sudden, strong flap, it lifted from the top of the tallest tree and flew in a lazy circle above her head before it left its forest lair on a winged journey to another, quieter part of the wooded mountainside.

Emma would have given anything to be that bird. And for a moment she pretended she was.

She closed her eyes and let an imaginary spiral of air catch her dress and blow her far away from her mother's relentlessness. She coasted above the house and the trees toward dark clouds gathering in the distance over Foggy Peak. She heard rumbling. *Was that thunder?* Perhaps a storm was approaching.

She tilted her body and extended her dark, feathered arms, entranced by the view back to earth. How small and insignificant everything seemed. Her mother had disappeared, and their house was nothing more than a colorful speck, the world beyond the mountains an open jewel box, waiting for her, wishing for her. . . .

And then again she heard that voice.

She plummeted from the sky and was back firmly on earth, mired, as always, in her mother's disapproval.

With a sigh, Emma stood and closed her book, shaking away bits of grass that clung to the back of her dress. She scanned the horizon for a last glimpse of eagle wings as she meandered through the meadow to where her mother stood on the porch, the immense, elegant mansion dwarfing her, an angry shadow crossing her face.

She was in her usual tizzy. "You disappear exactly when you are needed, Emma. I thought I told you yesterday I would require help with the tea."

"I thought that meant later today. I assumed I had the morning free."

"Well, you assumed wrong."

Before their tête-à-tête spiraled her mother from tizzy to fury, Emma smiled her learned smile and changed the subject. "How may I be of help?"

"Go find your brothers. Kerry took them for a nature walk over an hour ago, and she should have returned them by now."

"Which way did they go?"

"Toward the new barn construction. I want you all in the parlor in twenty minutes for further instruction. You know I am expecting the finest ladies of Monte Cristo society today. Has everyone forgotten the need for proper dress? Does everyone imagine they can just throw on any old apparel over an unclean body without thought or regard to the occasion?" With that, she whirled away in her pink frock and propelled herself through the front door.

The only words of significance Emma heard out of her mother's mouth were *new barn construction.* She turned back toward the meadow and the hiding spot she had just come from. Their secret meeting place.

He would be back any day now.

A smile spread like molten gold across her face, and a quiver of joy cleaved straight through her heart.

SHE found their nanny, with Jacob and Miles, near the riverbank. They had been piling rocks around on the grass to form what looked like a town ringed with a fence.

"Mother wants you to bring the boys back to the house, Kerry."

Kerry grimaced at the sky with a wobble of her head and a roll of her eyes. "Indeed? She had given me a full two hours to spend outside with the boys, miss. I imagine not even an hour has yet passed."

This slight, freckled nanny, sixteen, and only a year older than Emma, had a bold streak she often admired, though admittedly from afar and in silence. "She has changed her mind, and requests our presence in the parlor. Immediately."

"I would prefer to stay here, Emma. Right, Jacob?" said Miles, prodding at his brother.

"You can come back to your city, later," Emma cajoled, with the promise of another day.

"This is a fort. Not a city." Her younger brother looked at her with his pretty, pleading eyes. She stifled a smile. Miles could swindle a tough robber out of his booty with just such a look.

"No, dear, you must get up now. It's starting to rain"

Jacob glanced at Emma's face and got off the ground, picking grass off his knees. "Come, Miles. Better to mind Mother."

Already at five years old, Jacob had good instincts and would do what he had to do to keep their mother on an even keel. He leaned up against Emma, waiting for his year-younger brother, who was taking his time, hating to be parted from any sort of fun.

They walked in silence back to the house, all knowing they could be heading into a hurricane. Her mother, as promised, waited in the parlor.

"Well, you have returned them at last, Kerry. Now, after their midday meal, the boys must be sponged and powdered and dressed in their new white sailor suits and best black shoes. And make sure their hair is combed and curled properly around their faces and collars."

"Yes, madam," said Kerry.

Emma's mother beamed at her sons. "You will make me proud. And Jacob, your piano recital for the ladies will be ever so pleasing. Are you ready to be watched by female admirers?"

"Yes, Mother."

"And you . . ." She turned to Emma and frowned. "Not the blue linen today. It clashes badly with your hair. Although, everything clashes with your unseemly red hair. It is an unlovely color." She shook her head. "Wear the apricot silk. I suppose it will do."

Jacob took Emma's hand and squeezed. His small act of kindness brought a lump to her throat. Except for the occasional strike against her legs with a pine bough, her mother rarely brought her to tears anymore. But the constant love of her brothers, especially this one, often did.

Her mother dismissed her, keeping Jacob and Miles behind. Alone, Emma climbed the elaborate staircase and walked the long length of corridor to her room, all the while listening to her brothers' laughter and the ivory and ebony tinkling under Jacob's little fingers as he practiced his piece. She heard her mother's loving encouragement. For her brothers. It had always been this way.

Emma closed her door and removed her clothing and the bow from her hair. She put on her lace dressing gown and sat on her brass bed, breathing a sigh of relief, stilling her heart. She was safe in her private refuge now, an oasis of peace in this troubled home.

Her mother was wrong. Someone thought her hair was a lovely color. Someone even loved her. Desire ran up from her legs to her stomach, melting her insides, and the thought of his kisses and his hands on her made her gasp. A thrilling new life was opening in front of her, filled with a passion so great that the very thought of him nearly swept her off the bed and onto the floor.

This was her secret, his promise, something of her very own, and no one could take it away. She would disappear from this lonely house. Escape her mother. She had exactly two years and ten months to find the courage to leave.

Thunder rumbled again and brought her out of her reverie. It was never too soon to prepare. She was fifteen now, certainly too big for toys. She would store away her childish playthings.

She shrugged out of the dressing gown, not wanting to take a chance on tearing it. In her cotton knickers and chemise, she dragged a stool inside her closet and stacked her wooden horses, spinning tops, and picture puzzles high on the top shelf.

She piled six dolls on the next shelf. They had been her companions for as long as she could remember. Emma ran her fingers across fine china limbs, and smoothed their elegant gowns and lustrous manes. She turned their painted faces away from her and tucked a yellow baby blanket around their bodies as if she were putting them to bed. Next, she hung her hoops and ice skates on clothes hooks hammered into the pink painted beadboard.

The light in the closet dimmed. Emma watched dark clouds paint gray streaks across the sun outside the little window. She shuddered at a violent clap of thunder. A ferocious storm had arrived. Rain pelted the windowpanes, and a flash of lightning lit up her room. Emma leapt off the stool and glanced at the clock sitting on her bedside table. There was still time to finish up before Kerry came to help her dress for the tea.

She crossed to the open window. Black clouds had

pushed away all the white ones, and the texture of the sky was churning. Just like that, the sun disappeared, as if a shade had been drawn over it. Cool raindrops hit Emma's face, and the smell of loamy earth wafted up from the yard as she caught the knob and closed it. Thunder clapped again, followed by a flash and streak of lightning. Whispers of voices resonated in her head, a male and a female in conversation.

A rolling boom brought her back. The clock's hands had moved too quickly. It was now just before noon. *Where had the missing measure of time gone?* She shook herself and scanned the room. Emma would not let a summer rainstorm hamper her important work.

The biggest doll of all stood by itself in the corner. The doll's stony blue eyes, set in smooth, creamy porcelain, gazed at Emma in reproach. The extravagant Christmas gift had been from her father over three years ago. It had been a kindness from a father who was often distracted by his impressive job, but loved her in his own way. And she loved him back, mostly in silence, as was *her* way.

She looked the closet over to make sure there was enough room to prop the doll in against the wall. The air inside shimmered. *How peculiar!* Frowning, Emma moved closer and waved her hand in front of her, running it through what seemed to be tiny, glistening bubbles. A crash of thunder, and the tempest rattled the house, and rain beat like little pebbles on the glass.

She turned around again to the doll as a fierce gust of wind banged the window back open. With that gust, the little door slammed shut, snatching her like the devil into darkness.

Emma struck the far wall and screamed Kerry's name.

She twisted around and around. Her hair whipped and pricked her face.

The slippery walls tumbled away and a chilly wind scraped against her body.

She felt herself falling. . . .

CHAPTER THREE

———

Sonnet
1895

Small hands grabbed my wrists and dragged me forward. A jumble of broken dolls and toys and ice skates tumbled with me. A wooden stool with a yellow baby blanket coiled through its rungs had fallen over on my leg. I bent my knee and it toppled away. Every inch of my body hurt. I lay against the wall and felt something wet dripping down my face and off my chin. It hurt to breathe.

A voice standing over me whirred in almost indecipherable English, "Whatever were you doing in the closet? Sit still now. You have hurt your head. And what clothes have you donned? And these red boots?" She dabbed at my face.

"Ouch!" I tried to focus. "What?" I raised my arm and touched my forehead. White hot pain. I heard moaning. *Was that me?*

She grabbed my hand. "And what is this? A ring?" Her words floated out in a soft lilt. Worried hazel eyes skimmed across my face.

"Do I know you?" I asked.

"Miss Emma, it is I, Kerry!"

"My name is Sonnet. And I have no idea who you are." Drained, I laid my splitting head back against the wall. Even my teeth hurt. I ran my tongue around my mouth and tasted blood. I had bitten the inside of my cheek. "How did you find me? Have you seen the others?"

"Others? You are not making any sense."

Footsteps charged at us from outside the room. Kerry snatched a lacy thing off the floor and tossed it over my clothes. She threw the hem of her long dress over my red tennis shoes and clobbered her hand down on my hand and held on tight. The door burst open.

"What is this, Emma? What have you done?"

The woman's dress clenched her waist into a tiny circle hardly bigger around than her head, and poodle-dog bangs, falling from a loose bun, quivered in a blond mound above her eyebrows. She would have been beautiful, except for that hard face. I pushed back against the wall. She was calling me Emma, too. "I don't understand . . ."

"You have made a mess and broken your old playthings. The shelving has fallen. Kerry, get her out of that dressing gown and into bed. She is bleeding on the expensive lace. I will send for Doctor Withers—and no fighting me in this regard, young lady. You will see the doctor whether you want to or not. And now, between the storm and this, my tea is *ruined*." She left the room in a whirling haze of pink.

Crazy lady. Kerry lugged me to my feet and handed me a cloth to hold against my forehead. Swaying with pain, I held my sore ribs and tried to push away the confusion. Was I dreaming? Or was this a mind-altering concussion? Kerry appeared to be my age. A small, white cap perched on top of hair stretched back into a frizzy knob, a few red twists escaping from its sides around her flushed cheeks. A gray dress and white apron stained with blood hung on her tiny body. She had been using her clothes to catch the drips from my forehead.

"Is this a hotel, Kerry?"

"No, miss, a house, as well you know it." She led me to a brass bed and urged me forward. I watched through half-closed eyes as she ripped off my clothes and pulled a white flannel nightgown over my head. She gathered my things up, shoving them into a pillowcase, and tossed the white bundle under the bed.

"I must have hurt myself in that old mansion we were running around in and somehow ended up at a neighbor's. I didn't know people actually lived in this place. Can you please go get someone from my family? They're . . . down the hill through the trees. You'll see the cars parked by the river." I was babbling.

"You mean your mother? She is sending for the doctor. Lie still, Miss Emma."

"My mother isn't here. She went home yesterday. My aunt and uncle and another man are panning for gold. At the river. Close to a big boulder. They're probably setting up the picnic by now. And stop with the Emma. You're mistaking me for someone else."

Kerry ignored me. She sat down on the side of the bed and took my hand in hers. She eyed my new ring for a moment and then yanked it off my finger, dropping it into her pocket.

"Hey!" I leaned forward to grab at it. A searing pain in my neck knocked me back on the pillow. I glared at her. "My grandfather gave that to me for my birthday yesterday. Give it to me."

"Yes, yes. I will keep it for you today. You know how your mother feels about fripperies on young ladies."

"I don't understand a word you're saying."

"The doctor will be here soon. You lie still. You have a severe injury, and moving your head around does not help your condition."

I scrunched my face at her and turned away, scanning across the space. Pink-and-white wallpaper. A fireplace, stacked with books on its mantel. A row of windows covered in lace. A big doll standing in a corner. The room was girly, a kid's bedroom. I ran my hand over the bedcover's pastel softness and let a lemony smell and a ticking clock calm me.

I heard horses' hooves. Stamping. Horses in Monte Cristo?

And where were Rapp and Evan? Where were Lia and Niki and Jules? Why had they just left me?

A loud knock jolted me back to groggy consciousness. A man in a formal suit, followed by the woman in pink, scurried at me, sweaty and hot, as if he'd just stepped out of a sauna with all his clothes on. "Miss Emma."

"I'm not Emma."

Bringing himself and his large black bag to the side of the bed, the doctor moved the bloody cloth and bent over me. A bead of sweat rolled from his forehead down the side of his wet face and plopped on the pillow. He stood and unbuttoned his wool jacket, handing it behind him to Kerry, creating a strong waft of tobacco and cheese across my face. My stomach turned. I wrenched my head as far away as I could. He pressed hard against me while he rolled up his sleeves and unbuttoned his collar. "Seven stitches. Bring clean towels and a bowl of hot water."

"You can't just stitch up my head without getting someone's permission," I said.

He aimed his words at the pink dress. "I will give her a large dose of laudanum now for the pain and the accompanying bout of hysteria. Emma is not herself. The head injury has brought on temporary amnesia. Make sure she takes large doses of the remedy over the next two days. She'll be able to leave the bed by then if her memory returns."

"Hello! I'm right here! You can't do anything without talking to my aunt first. You need her permission. Please, bring me a cell phone."

"I have your *mother's* permission. I do not need your aunt's." He reached into his black bag and brought out a glass bottle. He popped the cork stopper and poured reddish-brown, dirty smelling liquid into a big metal spoon. "Open up your mouth."

"She's not my mother! You're mistaking me for someone else. All of you. What is this, a freak house? Get away from me!" I tried to slide out of the other side of the bed as he snatched my arm and dragged me back.

"Do not argue with Doctor Withers, Emma," said the woman. "Now, open your mouth and take the linctus. Do what you must, Doctor. We will tie her down if necessary."

The doctor was ready with the spoon. The woman held

my arms against my sides, pinning me. Doctor Withers pushed my chin down, opening my mouth, and poured in the liquid. I kicked my legs and gagged, but I swallowed the fiery, foul-tasting medicine. He put another spoonful in my mouth. And another. I bucked and screamed and choked while he caught my face and held his hand over my mouth until I swallowed. Flames singed my throat, and hot tears fell from my eyes.

Kerry appeared holding towels and a water bowl. She patted at my feet. "There, there, Emma. Hold still for Doctor Withers. His job is to help you."

"I don't know who he is," I wheezed. "I don't know who you are."

"I must clean off the muck first. And then some antiseptic before I stitch." Doctor Wither's hands darted out at me. His eyes snaked across my flannel-wrapped body. A tobacco-stained tongue slithered out past his teeth, licking his lips.

"Please . . ." I couldn't tell if my mouth moved. Faces melted. The room teetered as hands pulsated and dissolved. My nose tingled with the sharp odor of antiseptic. Another set of smaller hands appeared along with the doctor's. They slid away the wetness along my eyebrows. I heard my skin punch open and felt tugs of thread being laced through.

There was no pain.

I was spinning, spinning. . . .

Let me wake up at the river. Everyone will call me "Sonnet" again. I'll help pack up. We'll pile into the big, white van. Cruise back down this horrid mountain. To Seattle. Back to my life. My normal vacation.

I would have cried if I could, but as it was, I closed my eyes and fell into a reddish-brown-drug-induced stupor. . . .

⌒

WAKING with a start, I sensed someone in the dark room with me. A ghostly figure crept toward the bed with both arms outstretched. Hands reached for my neck.

I couldn't move. I strained to scream but no sound came out. One of the hands extended behind my head and lifted it up. The other hand slipped something over it, tucking it into the top of the flannel nightgown. The shadow leaned over and dragged something from under the bed. It backed away and slid out of the room.

The door closed with a soft and final click.

CHAPTER FOUR

⸺

Emma
2015

A foul odor swept across Emma's face, rousing her as it irritated her skin and stung her eyes. A doorknob ground and rattled, and a voice called out on the other side of the door. She raised her head and sat up, sneezing, and ran her hands along her arms and legs.

The little door squeaked open. The outline of a young man stood in the doorway, his face hidden in darkness, his dark, unkempt hair almost touching his shoulders. He was tall and strong and without a doubt, did not belong in a lady's room. "Please sir—have you no sense of decency?" Emma gathered her legs to her chest and threw her arms around her knees. "Please remove yourself!"

"Sonnet?"

"Surely you know my name is Emma. Now, *go!*"

The bedroom door opened with a blow against the wall and two more people ran in. "What's going on, Rapp?"

"Something's wrong with Sonnet."

Emma drew herself into a haughty pose and mustered as

much pride as possible. Three criminals had accessed her family's private quarters while she sat unclothed in her closet. "I am not Sonnet! Now, leave my room. As you can see, I still have to dress."

They stared at her without moving. Without speaking.

The lower body of the one called Rapp was an unwanted spectacle before her. His too-big trousers stopped at his knees, and a spot of tree sap dripped on his sun-browned leg as if he had just been cutting wood.

A lumberjack. In her bedroom.

Emma pressed her eyes shut to avoid his naked limbs and armed herself in self-righteous anger in case the vilest situation were to occur. Next would be a bloody scream if she opened her eyes and still found him in her room. "Leave *now*, Mister Rapp! How many times must I ask! I shall no longer be pleasant and will shout and summon the hired help, if you do not. My father will see you off this mountain for good."

"*Mister Rapp?*" He backed away shaking his head. "Hired help? She's gone flipping berserk. You handle her."

The dark-haired girl and the blonde reached in and hauled her to her feet. Emma was bruised and scratched, and her undergarments were dirty and torn. She blinked and tossed her head away from the eyes of her unexpected guests to the corner of the room where she had cast off her dressing gown. It was gone.

She blinked again. And again.

Emma's beautifully appointed pink-and-white bedroom had vanished. The two girls moved toward her. She clapped a hand over her mouth, eyes darting across the dark, empty room. "What's happened? Where am I?"

"Quit playing. Whose clothes are those?" The blonde reached for her arm.

She backed away. "Who are you? What have you done?"

"Sonnet? What's wrong with you?" The blonde lunged.

"I am not Sonnet! I'm Emma!" She pitched around to the bedroom door just as another dark-haired girl appeared.

"Rapp said you needed help. Here's Evan's sweatshirt." She held out the garment and then frowned, running her eyes down Emma's body to her bare feet and back to her face again.

Emma shrieked and thrust past this latest outsider, knocking her away hard against the wall. The three girls pushed and shoved each other in their hurry to follow as she staggered into the empty hallway and dashed down the stairs.

The air was suffocating her with dust and decay, and her heart thumped madly as she searched every corner, every surface, for something familiar. *What had happened to her home?* Her mother's piano hunched like a whipped creature, battled and worn, the only piece of furniture in the entire house.

Her imagination flitted to the implausible, the insane. Had she missed something terrible? A fire? A flood? That made no sense. None of it made sense. She must be dreaming. *She must be.*

They forced themselves around her like small beasts in a terrifying nightmare. She pressed her back against the side of the piano and wiped across it, inspecting her hand. Her fist clenched. She moaned and eyed the knot of three girls—their short, tight trousers and manly shirts and shoes as foreign to her as jungle garb. They gabbled like monkeys, pointing at her and waving their heads around. She heard the names they called each other, but their diction was appalling.

She understood nothing of their back and forth. *Nothing!*

The one named Lia glided to her in slow motion as if trying not to startle a wild animal. "Here. Let me help you with the sweatshirt," she whispered, and attempted once again to dress her in the lumpy garment. She laced it through Emma's arms and over her head, and then backed away just as a very large male, topped with short, clipped hair the color of her own, joined them.

He pushed his face close and stared down her body to her knickers. "What the hell? What's wrong with you? What're you wearing?"

"She's found some old clothes and gone stark raving mad, Evan," said Niki.

Emma reared away from his collarless shirt and short pants and glowered, slapping at him. His legs below his knees were also naked. "The only thing wrong with *me* is your unwelcome presence in my home." She lifted her chin and hardened her face at this interloper. "I am Emma Sweetwine, and *you*, sir, are trespassing!"

His mouth gaped opened. He moved even closer. "What in the world?"

"Hey! I just found something!" Mister Rapp rushed in, the last to join the smothering circle crowding her. He brought a badly damaged photograph from his bag and held it out, positioning it in a channel of light. "Look. This is too weird."

Emma snapped her eyes at the worn brown-and-white photograph. "There we are. My parents. My brothers, Jacob and Miles. My father is a *very* important man, and my mother has a temper . . ."

"*Monte Cristo Ice Caves Fair*," Niki interrupted, reading

the banner that hung across a mountain in the photo's background.

"Yes, the Ice Caves Fair is the weekend after this one." Emma frowned. "But how can that be? I haven't been to the fair, as yet. But here is the photograph." Her finger skimmed across it. "Why am I wearing that dress?"

"No!" Rapp brandished the photo at them. "Look at the date on the banner."

Lia lifted her head. "August twenty-first to August twenty-third . . . 1895?"

"1895? *1895?*" Jules wailed.

The house grew quiet. The rain had stopped. The front door was thrown wide open to the outside world. A bird called out something evil, something dangerous, running shivers down Emma's spine. Her head throbbed with the horrendous smell and the strangeness of the day. She was sick with confusion. And when her mother caught sight of the wretchedness that was once their home, hellfire would reign down on them all.

"What happened, Rapp? I left you and Sonnet in the bedroom," said Lia.

He ran his hands through his locks and tugged. "The closet, Lia. Up there in that bedroom. That's what happened."

"The closet?" Evan slowly turned toward the staircase. "Up there?" One by one they all looked.

"Rain was coming in the open window," Rapp continued. "So, I closed it, and we heard Niki and Jules in the hallway. I told Sonnet to hide in the closet. She opened the door and the wind blew the window open and the door knocked her inside. I couldn't get it open. When it finally budged, Sonnet sat there with different clothes talking all proper like she didn't know me." He nodded at Emma. "It was her."

Lia grew silent, transfixed by Emma, who was still jammed up tight to the piano. She poked her head at Emma's, inches from her face. "She's paler, her freckles less prominent, like she's never in the sun." Lia held the ends of Emma's hair, pulling it straight. "And her hair's longer than Sonnet's. At least five inches longer. Show me the photo again, Rapp."

He held it out. "Look," she whispered. Lia held Emma's wild hair back behind her head and brushed it forward, letting it fall over her left shoulder in an identical style. "The girl in the photo has shorter hair by about five inches. Now, how do we explain *that?*"

Evan paced around, cracking his knuckles. "She's my twin sister and this girl isn't her. I should know. Something has gone terribly wrong." He stared at the ceiling. "*Think, Evan.*" Walking the perimeter of the room again, he stopped suddenly. "Could they have switched? Could it be possible? But why?"

The others huffed out their disbelief. But Evan marshaled his body and moved toward the staircase. "I'm gonna investigate!"

Lia grabbed Emma's hand. They thundered after Evan amid the grime, rushing up the stairs on each other's heels.

Rapp led them to Emma's room. "This one. It happened in here."

Evan strode to the closet door and opened it, the rusty hinges crying out like a wounded animal. "What if . . . what if . . ." He held up his hands and stood still. "What if they switched because they look alike and, and . . . god, I don't know what the reason would be."

Evan swung around, a final reckoning spreading across his face. "This is going to sound crazy, but what if this closet is . . . some kind of portal? Some kind of time travel highway, right?"

Portal? Time travel highway? The foreign words were ominous, spitting out of Evan's mouth as fast as the lightning that had crackled across the sky. Emma's heart began to sink. He was right. Something was terribly wrong.

"What year do you think it is?" Niki narrowed her eyes and crossed her arms at Emma, challenging her.

"It's 1895, of course."

"Oh, god," Lia groaned "A *really great* history lesson. What have we done?" She looked as if she were going be sick.

"Told ya there were ghosts in here," said Niki.

Jules pressed her fist to her mouth and whimpered.

"I forced her to go," said Rapp. "She didn't want to. She asked me if I could see the bubbly air. I thought she was kidding around, and I told her she was crazy. Oh, man, I feel terrible."

Emma saw Rapp, finally, his face illuminated clearly for the first time by the dim light of her bedroom window. Her heart lurched to a stop. *On top of everything else, now this?* She held herself and swayed, willing herself not to faint, and wondered what was in the canvas bag that crossed over his body. Hammers? *Lord, help her—his eyes . . .*

"This is our reality. We just have to deal with it." Evan held out a small, slender box, a white arc of light casting a lit path onto his face and into the gloomy room. "And we have to find our way back to the picnic before they come looking for us. It's almost one, and they'll kill us if we're late." He dropped the object back into his pocket.

Kill us? Emma tore her eyes from Rapp and fixed on Evan and the light shining through his pants. At any moment, a fire would surely engulf this person who spoke of attending a picnic with potential murderers as calmly as if he were discussing a game of poker with friends.

She was going insane.

"So . . . Emma," Evan said. "You'll have to come with us and be Sonnet until we can figure this thing out."

Jules gasped. "Seriously? We're going to pass her off as Sonnet?"

"What else can we do? Look at her. She's helpless. She doesn't even have clothes. And anyway, how will we explain losing Sonnet? Think about it, Jules."

"Absolutely not," Emma said, holding on to the last of her dignity. "I will not be passed off as someone named Sonnet. I know nothing of you people."

"Evan's right, Emma. You can't stay in this empty house. We'll take care of you. We're all you've got now." Lia held her arm and gestured at the boy who had, thus far, not caught on fire. "Look. That's Evan McKay, Sonnet's twin brother. Jules McKay is Sonnet's older sister. Niki Macadangdang is Sonnet's cousin and my sister. I'm Lia Macadangdang, Sonnet's cousin and best bud. Rapp Loken there—he's our friend. Now you know everyone. We're not strangers."

"Your family name is *Loken?*" Her mouth dropped open. She dragged her attention away from the mystery of Rapp and took measure of her other four guests. Sonnet's cousins, the long-haired, dark-skinned Macadangdang sisters, stared back, Niki in brashness and Lia in anguish. They were both as exotic as gardenia blossoms, odd in this cold light, more belonging in the environment of a hothouse. *Tahiti,* Emma thought. *Maybe Tahitians had come to Monte Cristo.*

Sonnet's older sister, Jules McKay, was lovely . . . a magnificent, golden orb attached to Niki's side as a barnacle would be to its ship. She had made the greatest attempt at some semblance of flair. At least her clothing matched in color. And their leader, Evan McKay, twin of Sonnet, was muscular under his tight, white shirt. Where Rapp's dark hair hung too long, Evan's red hair bristled too short.

"It is a difficulty to understand you, Lia. I don't know what a 'best bud' is. And even your names are uncommon. Whatever is a *Macadangdang?*"

Lia nodded. She spoke slowly, enunciating her words as if she were speaking to a child. "Emma, I know you don't understand much of this, so I'll just say it. We think what's happened is that you are from our past. And we, for you, are from the future. It's not 1895 here. The year is 2015. One hundred and twenty years in the future. And somehow you've switched places with my cousin who looks just like you."

"That's why the house is a wreck," said Jules. "It's been abandoned for probably a hundred years. Monte Cristo is a ghost town. No one lives here anymore."

"Ghost town . . ." Emma shivered.

Lia clasped her hand in hers. "We want Sonnet back here with us as much as you want to go back to 1895 and your family. You have to trust us to come up with a plan. We'll take care of you in the meantime . . ."

"Okay, Emma," interrupted Niki. "Chop, chop. If you're coming, we gotta get back to the river *now*. We all brought extra stuff, so we can swing by the cars and fix you up before you're around the adults. We'll stick your hair into a baseball cap until we get home and can cut it. Mom has eagle eyes. And then you just need to keep your mouth shut."

"Cars?" Emma frowned. She turned her battered shoulders to the empty space that had once been a stunning room with all the latest amenities. Furniture, carpets, and knickknacks had all disappeared. Her family and the hired help had vanished, leaving her alone with strangers. She wiped dirt from her face with the long sleeves that hung down past her hands, her awful fate sinking in. "I'm not dreaming this, Rapp Loken? The future is here?"

He smiled. "The future is here."

"And someone named Sonnet, someone just like me, has gone away, and I have replaced her. And you will help me. You will all be my friends." Emma gripped Lia's hand, exhausted and ready to buckle. She was numb to it. Too tired to fight. She would have to accept their offer, even with the possibility of losing her life on account of tardiness. She had no other choice. She rolled her eyes down the fuzzy garment to where her knickers gathered with a pink ribbon around her knees. Her dirty legs and feet were bare beyond the cotton material.

Rapp handed Jules his bag. "You can climb on my back, and I'll carry you down the hill, Emma." He tossed his dark hair and sent her a reassuring grin. "I'll be your packhorse."

All Emma had was faith. She ignored the violent thumping of her heart and the tears threatening to fall from her eyes again, and wished her visitors to see her as brave. She dropped Lia's hand and took hold of Rapp's as they made their way down the staircase and out the doorway to the porch. They jumped over a splintered hole. Rapp kicked away blackberry vines and stood two steps below her. Emma said a quick prayer, not much more than a *keep me safe*, and leapt up on his back for the trek through the forest to the river.

In the lead, Niki and Evan were already forging through the dense stand of trees that stood where once grew a manicured lawn. Rapp followed Jules, her smaller but identical sweatshirt blazing AMERICAN INTERNATIONAL SCHOOL OF CAPE TOWN across the back. Emma twisted around one last time and watched as Lia banged the front door shut, closing her home off from this astonishing new world.

CHAPTER FIVE

———

Sonnet
1895

A door cracked open, and with it came giggling. I poked my head out from under the sheet. Dull mist parted, and agonizing misery receded along with my fuzzy dream. Finally, a morning without that wretched medicine forced down my throat.

I ran my finger under the loose bandage where seven knots of thread lumped up across my tender forehead. The sweaty flannel nightgown had twisted around underneath me. I stretched out my legs and arms and said good morning to the room with a groggy yawn.

More giggling and feet scrambling. Two little heads ducked behind the foot of the bed.

"Who are you?" I asked.

"You know who we are, Emma."

Emma again. I sighed. "Who am I, then?"

The brass curlicue at the end of the bed had four small hands wound around it. "Our sister."

"Emma's your sister . . . and you think *I'm* Emma?"

Two children stood up and bobbled their little heads at me.

"Come over here, let me see you. What're your names?"

The smallest one sprinted across the room, crossed behind the life-size doll, and circled back. He jumped up on the bed. "I love guessing games, Emma! I'm Miles. You know who I am. There stands Jacob." He pointed his tiny finger at the other one. Silky blond curls hung to their shoulders and their eyes were as clear and blue as the sky out the window panes behind their heads. They were beautiful. I had mistaken them for girls.

Jacob walked from the foot of the bed around to the side where I lay propped up on pillows and took my hand. Wrinkles creased his brow. "Mother said you are sick and we are not allowed to bother you."

They were dressed in baby-blue sailor suits with navy buttons and navy collars. Their little black ankle boots were polished to mirrors. "You're welcome to bother me. You're both adorable. Are you guys going to a party with those fancy clothes on?"

"No," said Miles. "We are being sent outside to play on the swing."

"Well, you have really nice clothes on for just messing around in the yard. Like matching uniforms."

Jacob ran his palms along the buttons on the front of his shirt. "Mother has us dress every day in this play apparel. You know that."

"How would I know, silly? Climb up here on the bed with Miles. Where are we?"

"More games?" Miles jumped three times on the soft mattress with the last fall ending in my lap. "*Oof!*" He caught his breath and squealed with both of his little hands on my cheeks. He pressed his face to mine. "We are in the biggest house in Monte Cristo!"

Growls from my stomach ricocheted around the room, sending Miles tipping off me and into hysterics.

"Kerry is seeing to your breakfast tray," said Jacob, patting my hand. Concern for me rippled his brow again.

"Good. I'm starving." I patted him, returning the favor, and set my throbbing head back on the pillow. Jacob and Miles sat against me and held my hands as if it were the most normal thing to do with a visitor. The bedroom door swung partway open and Kerry pushed it the rest of the way with her elbow, coming toward us with a tray of food. She fixed the tray and a big cloth napkin across my lap and opened the window, letting woodsy smells drift in with the warm breeze.

Tantalizing breakfast aromas mixed with the clean air. I untangled myself from the boys and picked up the toast with one hand, glopping lumps of jam across it with the other. I held it up, taking big bites and licking the sides before the jam could drip down my arm. The milk spilled down my throat in three big gulps. I finished the toast, nabbed the hardboiled egg, cracked and peeled off the shell and devoured it. I licked the jam bowl clean.

"Yum, that was good. I haven't eaten since Snohomish— bread pudding. Kerry, can I use a phone? I don't have my cell with me, and I want to call my family and let them know I'm okay. They have to be totally frantic about me by now."

Kerry, Jacob, and Miles stared. Of course they did. I had made a pig of myself. I wiped sticky jam off my fingers and face.

Kerry closed her mouth and then opened it again. "You seem well this morning. I . . . I am pleased you had an appetite for your breakfast. The madam will allow you downstairs today, but only if you have your memory back. You mustn't continue to speak of odd things, or Doctor Withers will be summoned. You do not want that now, do you?"

"Absolutely not. No more Doctor Withers. And no more Emma. I just want outta this house."

Kerry sighed. "You would be best off to *pretend* you are Emma, then."

"Is this a name game?" asked Miles.

"No more games," said Kerry. "Master Jacob and Master Miles, please remove yourselves from the bed and leave the room with haste. The miss must dress."

"God, you're so freaking formal with them. They're just little kids," I said.

Kerry's mouth dropped open again.

"I have to go to the bathroom, Kerry . . . I have to pee. And a shower would be nice."

Alarmed, she pushed the wide-eyed boys out of the room.

"*No comprende?*" I asked. "I feel like we're speaking different languages. How about . . . toilet?"

She narrowed her eyes at me for a moment and then walked behind a screen. She rolled out a wooden box on wheels with a shallow white bowl rattling around inside. Worry lapped across her face. "She's waiting for you in the parlor. You need to be well, now. For your own sake, please stop this peculiarity." With that, she followed Jacob and Miles out the door as I blinked down at the makeshift toilet squatting in the middle of the room.

⌒

MY own things were nowhere to be found, and my ring now hung from a gold chain around my neck. The mysteries in this house just kept piling up. With no other choice, I put on the white dress Kerry had left out. It choked me around my neck and squeezed me around my waist. Maybe this family belonged to a strict, no-jewelry sect that oppressed females and small boys with uncomfortable clothing and unusual toilets. Whatever it was, I ignored the boots with the pale buttons and left the room. I wanted out of this place. But first, I had to find a phone.

I put one hand on my sore ribs and the other across my forehead and moved down the staircase. Something felt off. The smooth oak floor in the entry stared back at me. *What was it . . . what was wrong?* I turned around. The dark opening at the top of the stairs gaped at me like open jaws.

Twisting back, I stared at the front door. I had seen Evan swinging into an old house on that same door. And land in an entry on his back—the very entry in front of me.

Only it had been old rotten wood.

Covered in old rotten dust.

And now it was new.

I pushed at my heart. It skipped a beat, skidded with a thud, and raced in my chest. "Oh, my god, no, no, no . . ." My whimpers started small and rose up like a tornado.

I tripped across a red carpet, stumbling into the first room. It was crowded with dark furniture. And little things. On every surface. On every shelf. On every wall.

Heavy drapes stretched across tall windows, strangling

the light. I zeroed in on a grand piano in the corner. Beautiful. Glossy. New.

Someone's hot breath chafed my neck. "Why are you whining?" she said. "Are you listening to me?"

An arched doorway—the dining room. I wheeled in a circle, herky-jerky. Red velvet drapes hung too thick, too heavy. A chandelier hissed, its tiny gas lights illuminating green and blue iridescent fireplace tiles. A preening peacock.

Yes. I knew that peacock.

The top left-hand drawer in the cabinet held candles. I didn't need to see inside to know this.

The woman stalked me, stabbing at my shoulder. "You are a terrible girl after that tomfoolery in your closet. I will not have this, not again."

I swung to the voice. Her finger aimed at my feet. "Where are your shoes and stockings? And where is your sash? Your hairbow?"

I reeled away.

Kerry's arm stretched out to mine. I slapped at it and ran past the piano. I crossed back over the red carpet toward the door. I yanked it open. The porch railing rose up in front of my clutching hands.

Tree stumps dotted the landscape beyond a rolling green lawn.

Logged and cleared. Logged and cleared. Logged and cleared.

A swing hung from a tree next to a barn. A large stuffed pony and its bright blue cart stood in the dirt. Jacob and Miles waved their arms at me. They called out Emma's name.

I hurtled down the stairs and turned around to face the house. Shiny new colors. A shiny new mansion.

Porches. Turrets. Gingerbread trim.

No one I knew would be hunting for me at the river—or anywhere else in this place—

"Emma!"

The ground rushed at my body. Gravel bit into my knees. My hand came at me, slapping my mouth. Smothering my scream.

KERRY darted in front of the woman and ran down the stairs. "Up with you, miss. Let us go get your shoes on." She hauled me to my feet. "She's fine, madam, just chilled. We will be down properly dressed. This is my fault. I should have assisted her in her dressing today. She's still a might unsteady."

Anger flooded off the woman in waves and dripped straight down her dress to my bare feet.

"Make sure she stays in her room until supper, Kerry. See that she is bathed and dressed properly this time. I will have the tub sent to her room. And do something with her hair. I will not have it hanging down in her face. She is a wild animal. Repulsive."

"Yes, madam." Kerry took me away from the woman and dragged me, like a limp doll, upstairs. She pushed me into the pink room. Backing up tight against the far wall, her face was as horrified as mine.

The egg and toast and jam churned in my stomach as the awfulness of my situation bubbled up inside. I was swirling down to crazy-town. "I'm going to throw up. I swear I am."

I held my arms out. The bedroom slowly stopped gyrating. The floor stabilized. The nausea was passing.

"Who are you?" she whispered.

"I'm Sonnet," I whispered back. "Who are you?"

"Kerry. Your nanny."

My nanny. My *nanny.* My heart sank. "What's the date today?"

"August fourteenth."

"The *year*, Kerry."

"1895."

My mind glittered shards of glass. Pieces as distinct as my own fingers and toes. I saw everything as it was. Finally. How could I have not understood? "The clothes, the language, the stares. You had no idea what I was talking about. Cars and phones and showers . . ."

I paced back and forth, panting like the animal I had just been accused of being. "Stupid. Stupid! My life is supposed to be in front of me. Not behind me. How did this happen? How?" The doll standing in the corner mocked me with her stony eyes and old-fashioned dress. A dress I hadn't really seen until just now. I hadn't seen anything, anything until now. I wanted to kick the doll over, smash her perfect, jeering face.

I couldn't breathe.

I pushed the lace on the window to one side. The same window Rapp had pried open a few days ago was still open from breakfast this morning. The wind blew the mountain air across my face. I gulped it deep into my lungs. My hands stretched out in front of me.

Still mine. Still my hands.

"How long ago did the accident happen, Kerry? When did I hurt my head?"

"Three days before this day," she whispered.

"No one here knows they're living in a place that will go bust eventually and turn into a dark, scary forest for people like my family to chill out in. You have no idea what's in store for this mountain. But, of course—how could you?" I crushed my fist against the windowsill. "What family in their right mind has a summer picnic in the middle of a damn ghost town?"

I wrapped my arms around myself and faced the poor girl still squashed against the wall. I may as well have been blabbing in Pig Latin. "Kerry, my name is Sonnet McKay. I'm from the year 2015. One hundred and twenty years from now. I know how impossible this sounds."

"You haven't been the same since your injury."

"You believe me?"

She swung her head back and forth, her eyes pasted to my face. Bits of red curls popped from her white cap and her mouth was frozen into a silent gasp. "What has happened in this house of late? My mind reels from hearing you speak on this distressing subject."

"I don't blame you. I'm acting like a crazy girl who looks like someone named Emma who plays with dolls in this pink room, sleeps in this bed . . ." My throbbing head sank like a sack of potatoes into my hands. Tears slid through my fingers. My side hurt every time I drank air into my lungs. "How do I just turn into some identical person from 1895? No one will believe me. I'll be trapped here forever with that, that witch—"

"There are differences. Things that make no sense."

I spread my fingers and peered at her. I lifted my head. Encouraged.

"Where did those clothes come from? Such odd red canvas boots with bouncy bottoms, more likely for a man than a girl. And your hair. How could it be shorter? I cut your hair. You have no scissors! And your undergarments, no more than silky ribbons . . ." Pink flushed up her neck and onto her cheeks.

"The ring," she went on, talking to herself as much as to me. "Emma would not have dared wear a ring in this household. She would have known the punishment. Where Emma would have acquired a ring like that I do not know. It's impossible. You wanted it back, so I slipped my cross off its gold chain, and put in its place your ring. I set it around your head and under your nightgown while you slept. I could not imagine what else to do."

"You were the one who brought my ring that night? You put it around my neck?"

"Aye. Keep it hidden from her." Her eyes had slowly let go of the horror. Light trickled in. "I had my doubts, but this morning I saw. With my own eyes, I observed you. And now I know. You are not Emma. I know Emma. I have known her for almost four years. Your voice is different. Your spoken language. Your movements and manner. You are not her."

"You believe me?"

She nodded.

Kerry believed me. My knees crumpled under the white dress. I made it across the room and dropped onto the bed.

Kerry moved from the wall she had been leaning up against to the window and the view of the trees and river beyond the house. Her hand touched the windowsill I had just wacked with my fist and ran along it, smoothing its slick, wooden surface. "What does this mean? How will you find your way back again? It's too much to be borne. I rightly should be afraid of you, but curiously I am not."

"I don't know what's happened or why. But I'll find my way home again if it's the last thing I do."

"I will help you. You have my word on it. But you mustn't act like anyone but Emma now. I will school you. Nothing odd anymore. Emma is quiet. She acts meek and docile—at the very least with her mother. I have no idea what the madam has in store for her, but whatever it is, it will be accelerated with your behavior."

"What do you mean?"

"I believe she wants Emma out of this house and far away from her husband and the wee ones. Yes, I am sure of it. I have been listening and watching. She's just waiting for the right time to convince her husband. And your actions have now given her cause to initiate her unholy plan."

I shivered. Unholy plan. "Why does she hate her daughter?"

"There is no earthly reason for it. She's a good girl. Her father loves her very much and has no ill will toward her. And Jacob and Miles are devoted to her, much to their mother's dismay. The madam dotes on her boys, but toward Emma, something is wrong about her heart."

"What're their names?"

"John and Rose Sweetwine."

"Rose Sweetwine? Oh, that's a good one, Kerry. A pretty rose. A delightful tasting wine. The irony . . ."

Kerry smiled wide and giggled. "Aye, incongruous it is, indeed. She should be called 'Thorn.' Thorn Sourwater for the despicable way she treats Emma."

There was a knock on the door. Two men hauled a steaming tub of water into the room as Jacob and Miles ran by in the hallway, laughing and bouncing a ball between them. Kerry took towels and a bar of soap out of a dresser drawer.

"You take a bath. I must go see to the boys. I will return and help you dress for seven o'clock supper. We can speak on how to survive in this grand house then."

"Where are my clothes, Kerry? My bouncy-bottomed boots?"

"They are safe with me. I gathered them from under the bed the night I brought you the ring. I was afraid Bess might clean and find them."

I caught her hand and hugged her before she could leave. "Thank you."

"Can you do this, miss? Can you be her?"

"I can do whatever it takes to get me home."

"Then I swear my allegiance to you and your mission." She stood on her toes and kissed me on the cheek. And with that our pact was made.

I waited until the door closed and then folded the tight material around my arm up where an African leather and silver bracelet wound around my wrist. I loosened the knot and rolled it over my hand. Kerry had missed it. I would keep it with me for good luck. I stuffed it deep between the feather mattresses and then patted at the ring hanging under my dress. A temporary fix to hide who I was.

Yes. I could do this. But not forever.

⌒

A magnificent grandfather clock stood tall and mighty in the study across from the dining room and gonged seven times. A flaming log burned in the peacock fireplace. I slid the bulky dress into Emma's chair and hunched over, meek and docile, exhaling my nervousness away. I secretly took in the formally dressed Sweetwine family dinner. Rose—or Thorn, as Kerry had branded her—sat at one end of the long table, her husband at the other. The boys sat across from me. Like a faux family in a high-end magazine, the matched set of four were flawless. I stuck out like a wild, red-haired, freckled-skinned, genetic throwback.

Heavy silverware surrounded an exquisite gold-rimmed plate. I tried to remember what to eat with which fork as a large woman wound around the table with a steaming platter of food. My rumbling stomach greeted her as she held the platter close so I could stab at chicken and potatoes. Her round face gleamed down with goodness. I smiled up at her. "Thank you—"

"Emma. Did you hear me?"

The serving fork clattered to my plate. I jerked my head over to Emma's mother. "I'm sorry, no."

"I said we will picnic at the river tomorrow with Missus Rodgers and Miss Olive, and Missus Jenkins and Miss Pearl. I expect you to converse nicely with Miss Olive, unlike our last visit to their home. I heard back you hardly spoke a word to the poor girl, and her mother was immensely disappointed. The report back from Missus Rodgers was unacceptable."

"Yes . . . Mother."

"I do not need to remind you we are senior in this society. And with that seniority go certain responsibilities and duties. You shall be decent and observe the niceties and standards of our station, at all times. That means conversing politely with someone, whether you want to or not . . . and that includes Olive Rodgers. Do you understand me, Emma? Or will you find it necessary to tax my patience during our picnic outing?"

Her words scratched at my brain. "Yes, I understand. I won't tax your patience."

"Do you feel up to this? Are you quite well now?"

"Yes, I am quite well, thank you." I lifted my chin. The dead chicken on my plate was a friend compared to her. I took a small bite and forced myself to swallow.

Thorn leaned from me toward her oldest son. "Would you like to go with us, my sweet? You are almost a big boy now that you will begin school next month. And Missus Rodgers is bringing William. He is just your age and will be in your class. It would be nice for you both to play together at the river. Missus Rodgers will be quite pleased if I bring you. She is aware of the status you bring her son."

Jacob shifted his eyes from his mother to me and back again. "Yes, Mother. I would like that very much. Can Miles come along?"

"No. He still needs his afternoon nap."

"But, Mother . . ." Miles's joyful little face wilted.

"My love, you must take your daily nap. Next summer, when you are no longer four, you may go out with us in the afternoon, and not until then."

Case closed. Miles turned back to his gravy-drenched potatoes.

She called down the length of the table to her husband.

"We will pick blackberries for Cook, John. You know her delicious pies. Would you like that, dear?"

His voice rumbled out to the lump of peas and chicken his knife had just smushed up onto the back of his fork. "Yes, Rose." The perfect male mouth, almost buried by a thick, blond mustache, opened, and the upside-down fork with the mash went in.

Rose ran her gaze across the top of her husband's bent head as he took his silverware and prepared another bite. "And if we find enough berries, I will have Cook make jam for some of the miners," she went on. "Perhaps Emma can deliver the jars. This will be a godly endeavor—so many are without wives. Emma, are you listening?"

Jacob flinched at his mother.

"Yes, I'm listening," I said.

"Fine, then. You will finish your peas tonight before I allow you a slice of chocolate cake. And sit up straight. Slouching does not become a lady."

I sat up. A gooey cake perched in a cut glass stand on the sideboard behind her poufy, blonde head. The heavy glass sparkled rainbow colors next to flickering candles and dangling gaslight. From where I sat, the cut edges on the stand appeared sharp.

I would have to keep that in mind.

CHAPTER SIX

———

Emma

2015

*E*mma awoke with effort, as if pulling herself out of thick, black molasses. She found it difficult to open her eyes. Her limbs felt as heavy as tree trunks and her skin seared with cuts and bruises. She felt something next to her move. She sat up, blinking at a pair of small, devilish eyes across the room. Her heart jumped. She heard quiet steps advancing, steadily, stealthily, wickedly.

This was *not* her bed. Had she been captured?

As if of its own volition, her voice shrilled out of her tight, strangled throat, "Help!"

A body rolled over and clapped a hand over her mouth before she could cry out again. Emma struggled to escape, but found her wiggling body pinned to the mattress. An arm swung out and around her, igniting a white ruffled light.

"Shhh! Emma! Are you cracked? You'll wake up my parents."

The lamp illuminated a girl with dark tousled hair. With

a jolt, Emma remembered where she was. In Lia's bed. In Lia's room. In another world. "I saw a demon with yellow eyes—beyond the bed, over there. A terrible vision! I heard it clacking and clicking at me—"

"Quiet down! That's just my owl nightlight. And my cell phone. I probably have text messages coming in." Lia held out her pointer finger at Emma for a moment, shaking it. "Stay put." Sliding out her side of the white-canopied bed, she tapped her finger on the owl and held up a similar item as Emma had seen emitting light in Evan's pocket that first day.

"See?"

Emma reached out and touched the slender box. It felt cool, like a china plate. She sat back against the pillow and clutched the neck of the pony-covered sleeping garment. Sonnet's pajamas, borrowed for the night. "There are many things to educate myself on in this new life."

Lia yawned and joggled her hair, clawing it with her fingers, as if that would fix the snarled mess. "There are, and lucky for you I'm a good teacher. I'm just glad you finally woke up. You've been asleep for over twenty-four hours. We had to make sure someone babysat you during the day. We didn't want you to wake up and get scared and go running through the house like a demented lunatic, scaring my mom and dad to death."

"I have never slumbered for two days!"

"We just figured it was a major case of jetlag." Lia smiled. "Time travel lag."

"You are speaking in riddles."

"Yes, well, I'll tell you everything as we go along. I have one day to bring you up to speed on our modern life you know nothing about. And then we're all meeting over at Rapp's tomorrow, to come up with a switchback plan."

"Good. I am ready to go back. But right now, I'm famished. Would you mind ringing for a breakfast tray?"

"Yeah, just ring for a tray of food. I wish." Lia laughed. "But there aren't any servants at this house. The sun's coming up. Let's go down to the kitchen and grab some breakfast. Then you can take a shower. You still have black gunk between your fingers and toes."

"Riddles, again. *Shower?*"

"Sorry, I promise I'll explain. Now, don't forget who you are when my parents are around. They probably thought the person they knew as Sonnet was acting kinda goofy at the picnic. Just sitting there, tired, not saying a word and stuff. You'll have to remember to call them Uncle Vince and Aunt Kate, okay? And act normal. There's no formality around here."

Emma nodded. "Speak directly to adults. Act normal. I can do that." She noted Lia's rare beauty again. She had never met anyone as foreign as the Macadangdang sisters. It was as if she and Lia should be sipping tropical juice together on a hot, steamy beach instead of sitting on a bed in their sleeping garments somewhere in the modern city of Seattle. "Lia, are you and Niki and your father Tahitian?"

"Tahitian?"

"Are you Siamese?"

"Huh?" Lia shook her head.

"Oriental?" Emma felt her cheeks burn.

"Are you trying to say *Asian?*"

She had blundered. "I am not sure what I'm trying to say."

"My dad is Filipino. Which makes me and Niki half Filipino, half white."

"What is Filipino?"

The smile disappeared from Lia's face. In its place came a furrowed brow and something close to pity. "I can only imagine what's going through your head right now. It's like you've landed on the moon, isn't it?"

"I'm having a difficult time understanding much at all. I have never met the likes of you and your sister. The races are not known to mix in my time. We are not allowed to even speak of such a thing in polite company, and your family would certainly be banished. But I believe you and Niki are quite lovely with your darkened skin and golden olive eyes. Your mother and father have created a unique combination."

"Unique and lovely." Lia's smile returned. "Get used to diversity, Emma—it's everywhere. And thanks for not banishing us."

Lia sat down on the floor and opened the lid of a slim trunk. "Now, what do you feel like wearing today? You can decide for yourself which of Sonnet's clothes you like."

"Why does Sonnet have her apparel in a trunk?"

"Trunk? You mean like a suitcase? Luggage? They don't live here. Jules, Evan, and Sonnet are just here for the summer. A vacation from their lives in South Africa."

Africa? Emma stared at the clothes for a moment, processing the information. Perhaps their father was a missionary. She had heard of such a thing, religious men and their families traveling around Africa, bringing the word of God to the people. Jules and her brother didn't strike her as the religious types, but this new world was topsy-turvy. Not wanting to appear naïve again, she swept her hand through the pile, and brought up a handful of clothes. "I should like this pink shift under a pretty dress."

"That's not a shift to go underneath a dress. That *is* a dress. Considering, it's probably way too short for you, though. But you could wear it as a top with jeans or shorts or leggings. We could even make it work with yoga pants, I suppose. We'll start you slow so you don't feel too crazed."

Emma had no idea what *too crazed* meant, but whatever it was, she was sure she was feeling it. She knew nothing of the words Lia had just rattled off regarding Sonnet's wardrobe. But she would pretend to understand, and soon she just might. As if she were learning an expressive foreign language. Like Italian. "Yes, that will do. Are these Sonnet's books?"

"Yeah, you could say she's a committed reader."

"Would she mind if I read them? I would handle them with care. I adore the written word. I spend much of my day reading."

"No, she wouldn't mind a bit. If I know Sonnet, she might be reading your books right now. You should start with this one, though." Lia slid *Meth Zombies* out of Emma's hands and replaced it with *Up a Hill with Thérèse Du Plessis*, reading off the back cover. "Let's see. This is about a French girl traveling around Vietnam in the late 1950s before the war breaks out, and she becomes a nun. A stranger traveling in a strange land, trying to figure it all out. Just like you. You can move on to the more lurid books as you get used to this place. I don't want you to be freaked out."

"You are very thoughtful. I appreciate you not wanting to

see me upset because of a frightening story. I assume *freaked out* has the same meaning as upset. I am learning!" Emma thumbed through the book before setting it aside. "Because of the black gunk, perhaps I should tend to my bathing now and then breakfast afterwards."

Lia led her down the hall to the bathing room and rummaged around in a drawer. She took out a pair of scissors, slicing the air with them. "It has to be done. Like Niki said, my mom has eagle eyes. We'll cut your hair after you wash it."

"All right." After what Emma had been through, losing five inches of hair seemed minor.

Lia took a wall lever behind a smooth, slippery curtain, and pulled. Warm water from a round metal disc above their heads shot out in a perfect, steady stream into the porcelain tub. Emma would stand upright under the spray and wash herself, with the used water running down a drain to some unknown destination. It was a marvel.

Lia instructed her. "Keep it mostly in the center here so that the water temperature is medium. See these red and blue marks? If you want it hotter, edge it toward the red. Colder, the opposite way toward the blue. Just do it incrementally, though. It doesn't take much effort at all. When you're done, push the lever back toward the wall like this. Here's shampoo." Lia put the container under Emma's nose and flexed the soft material a few times, letting sweet coconut air dance across her face.

And Emma knew, without a smidgen of doubt, she was sniffing heaven. "Divine!"

AFTER a quick breakfast of toast and blackberry jam, standing like thieves at the kitchen counter, Lia and Emma strolled out to the sunny backyard in a quest for Lia's mother. They found her kneeling on a cushion in the rose garden trimming away unruly shoots like a common gardener. Her own mother would be horrified at such a display of coarse pedestrianism coming from the lady of the house. But here sat Aunt Kate without a hat and in the dirt, casually pruning as if it were just one of her many female duties around the Macadangdang household.

"We're gonna go mess around today, Mom. Probably go downtown, maybe see a movie. We'll be gone all day," said Lia.

"When will you be home? I was going to make tacos tonight. I'm just working a half-day."

"We'll be back after dinner. But save some for us. We'll be starving by then."

A daughter telling a mother what *she* was going to do. And they would be allowed to wander the city alone without a chaperone or escort. What a fascinating world Emma had been dropped into.

"How about you, Sonnet?" asked Aunt Kate. "You're awfully pale. Will you be okay?"

"Yes, I will be . . . okay." The sun's rays shined directly on the rose garden and its gardener. Emma was struck by Aunt Kate's coppery hair and familiar eyes. With a twinge, she realized the similarities between them and had to stop herself from reaching out and touching the freckled face.

I will look like her when I am older.

"Your arms are all bruised," said Aunt Kate.

"She fell in a ditch," countered Lia.

Eagle eyes, thought Emma.

Charging down the wooden deck stairs beyond Aunt Kate's head, a black ball of fur charged over the lawn toward Emma. It yipped and pawed and sniffed at her shoes. She stepped back, fright flooding her veins.

As if she were an ax chopping down on firewood, Lia fell over Emma's feet and gathered the writhing animal under her arm. "Silly dog."

Aunt Kate had turned back to a particularly long sprout. "Lia, put Peetie in the house before you leave. And grab a couple of apples and some breakfast bars to go. You girls will need something to munch on along the way. Have fun!"

Lia's unoccupied fingers reached out to Emma's arm and tweaked, breaking into the chaotic moment. "Let's go."

THEY spent the rest of the day on foot, touring landmarks and places Lia deemed important for Emma's modernity lessons. Their first stop was a grand science building, entered through arches and pools and fountains, where Emma gawked at bewildering new gadgets and walked in a daze through a butterfly exhibit. They battled the masses and made their way further down the street, entering large tiered buildings and ascending levels on moving staircases, ambling through shops with every kind of clothing and shoes. To all this, Emma remained almost mute, so startled by the immenseness and noise and humanity pressing against her.

In an old part of the city, Lia thought it would be fun for Emma to see how Seattle looked in her time. "These were probably important businesses in 1895. Just think, if you had come here, you would have seen these buildings when they were new."

Emma imagined the old buildings had most likely held saloons and whorehouses and nefarious gambling operations. She changed the subject by pointing at a totem pole sitting in a small grassy park in the middle of the street. "That object, there, is especially fascinating. Last May, I saw the same type of carved poles in an Indian encampment during a long carriage trip to a stallion farm. In fact . . ." She smiled. "Our horse and carriage driver is an Indian of the nicest sort."

"You need to say *Native American*. Not Indian."

Emma had tried to impress Lia with her understanding of diversity, but had failed. Would it take forever to learn the language?

Their last stop was the Cinerama Theater, where they sat in the dark, ate buttered popcorn, and watched the film, *Mockingjay*. Instead of being "freaked out," Emma kept her eyes and her ears open to the sensory assault, telling herself this lesson was a necessary example in understanding the future of the world.

As she came out of the theater with her ears still ringing and her heart still breaking, the sun had set, and Emma had thoughts of the white-canopied bed. "I am generally driven in a carriage. Walking from place to place is frowned upon for someone of my class. In other words, Lia, my feet are weary."

Lia nodded. "That's fine. We'll head for home. You're up on it now. Immersed and ready to go."

Emma had nothing to judge her readiness by, so she believed Lia and let her put them on a bus and lead the way back to the Macadangdang house under a darkening sky and an almost-full moon.

Lia walked straight to the kitchen. "I'm *so* hungry. Let's get those tacos." They rooted around in the refrigerator and found the leftover food from the evening meal.

At the kitchen counter again, but *sitting* on it this time, they ate the strangely spiced food directly off the platter Lia had placed between them. Finished, Emma jumped to the floor behind Lia and tottered upstairs where she promptly put on Sonnet's pony pajamas and climbed into bed. It was good she was getting her sleep. She had a big day tomorrow with the rest of her new friends. They would search for a way to get her home.

"Good night, Lia. Thank you for the extraordinary day. My head is stuffed full of all your lessons, and I believe I will do just fine now. Immersed and up on it. Ready to go."

And just maybe, she would get to see Aunt Kate again. Aunt Kate, who noticed her pale face and bruised arms and worried that she might be hungry.

Yes, if she was lucky, she would see her again tomorrow.

Emma reached for the white-ruffled lamp on her side of the bed, found the little black button, and pressed it, extinguishing the light—just as she had seen Lia do earlier that morning.

CHAPTER SEVEN

—

Sonnet
1895

"Now, for the picnic outing today," said Kerry. "You cannot just choose your clothing willy-nilly. I must select what you will wear until you have learned how to dress yourself properly. You must be impeccable or the lady of the house will notice and take it out on both of us. Here is a light shawl in case the wind picks up."

I ran the softness through my fingers. "I hate wasting my time on a dumb picnic when I could be scouting for a way home."

"Everything must remain ordinary. You have no choice but to go." Kerry stood in front of the carved oak wardrobe with her hands on her hips. She reached inside, her arms flying in and out of drawers and off wooden hangers. "The green linen and matching bow for your hair. The high button shoes with the dark bone buttons will do. These are the undergarments to go with the picnic costume. And I implore you to not forget this handkerchief. You may need it to wave the flies away."

"High button *shoes?*" Sonnet held one out in front of her. "They look like little boots to me."

"Heavens no! Boots are for working men and women. For the hired class. The inside help like me and the woodcutters and miners you see out the window." Kerry held up her dress and flashed her scuffed brown boots. Dirty laces braided through small holes up the center and were tied in small bows at her ankles. "High button shoes are for the civilized class, not for the likes of me. When the snow flies, women of society would have their feet turn to blocks of ice rather than be seen in mannish foot apparel."

"Too many rules around here."

"Yes, there are many rules. But there it is. We must live with it, and you must call things as they are or risk being found out. Now, another rule. It shan't matter how ravenous you are. A small sandwich or chicken wing, some lemonade, and perhaps a bite of cookie is all you are allowed, no matter how bulging the picnic basket. Any more and you shall be thought of as a repulsive animal."

"She already thinks I'm a repulsive animal."

Kerry laughed. "You were a rampaging fiend in both our eyes yesterday. Fortunately for me, I know now why. Unlike her." She laid the pile of clothing out on the brass bed. "Here you go. You must dress yourself and I must go see to Master Jacob. Will the buttons on the shoes be too difficult? Can you manage without my help? Here is the buttonhook."

I slid the hook out of her hand and hugged her in thanks before she went down the hall to the boys' nursery. She hugged me back.

"You're starting to like the relaxed ways of one hundred and twenty years from now, aren't you, Kerry?"

"Well, I must admit you are rather demonstrative. Except

for the boys, I haven't had so much blessed attention since I left my Ma and Pa when I was twelve."

"Why did you leave?"

"In honesty . . . there was just not enough money to feed all the children in my family. My father was often sick with the black lung disease. Being the eldest of seven, it was high time for me to go to work and find my own support."

"Go to work!? Support yourself? You were twelve!"

"Don't feel bad, miss. No tears for me. I am in America, away from that sorrowful country of Ireland. I eat well, surely better than the wee ones I left behind. With the kindness of others, I have taught myself to read and write and speak like a lady. So much good is mine. I believe everything happens for a reason. I am here, right now, because I'm supposed to be. And as mysterious as it is, I believe that about you, too. Just as you are meant to go on the picnic today."

"I've been so caught up in my own troubles, I hadn't even considered yours. I hadn't considered you at all, Kerry."

She smiled. "Get on with you. You would be advised not to keep Thorn waiting."

"Thorn." I laughed and rubbed the tears from my eyelashes. I would cry for this heroic girl on my own time. "How old are you now?"

"Sixteen," said Kerry.

"The same age as my sister, Jules, and cousin Niki."

"You are rich with family. Hold them tight," she said, as she left the room.

Kerry might never see her family again, which made her an expert on missing people. I thrust those excruciating thoughts out of my head and surveyed the complicated clothes laid out in the order of putting them on.

I started with the long, satin-trimmed knickers and chemise and the stiff petticoat. I rolled cotton leggings up around my thighs and pulled the green linen and lace dress over my head, tying the sash in the back. The shoes slid on easily but the buttons fought the hook for twenty minutes. I brushed out my hair and tried a dozen times to style it like Kerry had the night before. The bow flopped and sagged.

At last the oval mirror reflected a hot and sweaty child covered in ruffles and lace. Sonnet had disappeared under the picnic costume disguise. I flapped my arms around and fanned myself with my handkerchief.

A horse whinnied. I stuck my stifling body out the open window as far as it would go and let a cool breeze wash over my face and neck. Below me, Cook loaded up a red-and-gold carriage with a large basket. One of the workers who had brought me my tub yesterday tossed in blankets and umbrellas.

I gathered up the parasol and shawl and wandered downstairs and out to the front porch, determined not to let that woman destroy my day. The sun felt delicious on my face, after my three-day imprisonment. I twirled the parasol out in front of me and watched pink and green blend and swirl.

A pair of spotted Appaloosas, hitched to the carriage, waited in the driveway. I stood in front of them and cooed, stroking their muzzles. "Wish I could ride you, pretty girls." They nuzzled my shoulder and then dipped their heads to where a pocket would be if I had a jacket on. "No, I don't have any sugar for you," I murmured, and nuzzled them back.

"Starlight stands there on the right and Moonbeam on the left, miss," said a quiet voice behind me. "They fancy you."

Moonbeam nudged my shoulder while I laughed and turned toward an ugly squawking noise. *Thorn.* I had already forgotten myself and the picnic hadn't even started.

"Get into the carriage, Emma," she said. "We are late." She shoved in front of me.

I took the offered hand and climbed in after her onto the tufted red leather bench next to Jacob. Thorn sat across from us.

"Precious little boy," I whispered at Jacob as he scooted closer to me across the seat.

Chaos reigned out the window as we wound down a lane through the miners' cabins and outbuildings. Tough men with bushy beards and dirty clothes trudged on the side of the road and in the fields. Some held pickaxes on their shoulders or maneuvered wheelbarrows. Others led donkeys piled high with gear. Human odor, mixed with the smell of animals, blew in the open carriage windows. The men tipped their stained leather hats our way.

"Those dogs," I said to Jacob. "Where in the world did they come from?"

"They belong to the miners. They chase away the bears and the cougars. You remember, Father told us when we first moved to Monte Cristo."

A gurgled harrumph came at us from Thorn's throat. I turned away. "Of course. I knew that." I smiled at him. "Do you want to play a game? It's called 'I see.' We both yell out what we see and whoever says it first wins. Like, I say, 'I see five dogs.' and then you yell out, 'I see a man with a red coat!'"

Jacob eyed his mother's pinched face. "I would prefer to sit quietly, Emma."

"You would be correctly advised to follow the boy's instruction. And your language is especially atrocious today." Thorn smoldered, shaking her head. "Really, when a five-year-old knows proper comportment while riding in a carriage and a fifteen-year-old does not . . ."

Her laser-like focus on me was a nonstop tsunami, boring down, pounding and pounding on the shores of my new life. Mean. Just plain mean.

I swiveled my body away from her to the window and laid my head back against the leather. I crossed my arms and narrowed my eyes at the bushy, sun-dappled evergreens along the side of the narrow dirt roadway. They rushed backwards away from the carriage—green-colored blurs through my eyelashes, as hazy as this mysterious world.

A dark red horse stood in a curve of trees. The rider sat still in the saddle. *Rapp?* I sat up and craned my neck to look. Sun flashed in the window. He disappeared as we rounded a curve in the road.

No, I scolded my jumping heart. *Impossible.* I was seeing things. No way.

THE carriage crunched to a stop in a large meadow. The driver jumped from his perch and held out his hand as I stepped out into the light. *Ahhh . . .* The sun hovered hot and the woodsy, shredded-bark scent was intoxicating. It was good to finally be out of that dreary house. I held the parasol over my head and walked to the cluster of waiting females and one small boy who wagged their hands at us. A wooden table stood next to the river with eight matching wooden chairs and a wildflower-filled vase.

Olive, Pearl, and I sat next to each other as the bows in our hair, each in a different color, blew around in the river breeze. The two girls gossiped while china and crystal clinked and tinkled and my half-eaten cream cheese and pimento sandwich sat stewing in the sun. I stared at my plate and slowly counted to one hundred.

"I've been requested to pick blackberries today for pies and jam. I should get started. Would you girls like to join me?" I veered away from the table and avoided Thorn's eyes.

Pearl's mother tied white aprons over our dresses and Jacob and William waved goodbye from the riverbank. I blew sweet Jacob a kiss. Pearl struck out toward the clearing and the trees beyond the carriages, and Olive and I followed her lead, the mind-numbing picnic receding behind us.

As we passed the three carriages and headed into the woods, Pearl twirled around with a smile, her pink lacy dress covered in the white apron ballooning out from her knees. "It is good to be momentarily freed from the restrictive environment of our mothers. Now if only a swashbuckling pirate might ride by."

"Pearl, you read far too many racy books. And the restrictions are for our own good. What do you say, Emma? Please do, join in," said Olive, with a smug face.

She was setting a trap. "I have no opinion on this topic because I'm concentrating on finding blackberries."

"Really, Emma. You are very vocal today. And Pearl, if your mother only knew, she would lock you up. I find your independent nature offensive. Pirate, indeed."

Oh, brother. I pivoted toward a clump of blackberry bushes before anything could escape my mouth. The pine-scented forest edge, still and cool as a wet cloth on my hot forehead, dried the sweat running down my back under the layers of clothes. I waded into a small, girl-sized depression in a large bush and nipped the soft, fragrant berries from their thorny nests. They hit the tin bucket like summer rain striking a tin roof. Pretty soon the berries found a soft landing on top of each other and Olive and Pearl's voices ebbed away into the distance. Making up for the dismal lunch, I popped a few fat berries into my mouth and thought about warm and sugary pies.

I filled the first bucket to overflowing and placed it back on the trail behind me. I started filling the second bucket and ate every seventh berry. Why not? The juicy lumps burst with sweetness and their smell was heaven. *Ping-ping-ping* sounded as the blackberries hit the tin. Olive and Pearl had wandered far away and freedom felt wonderful.

I reached to the top of the bush and strained for some big ones. A bee buzzed close by, attracted like me to the sweet taste. Humming, I fell into a leisurely rhythm and thought of all the times my family had picked wild blackberries together.

Huh? I peered over the top of the bush and behind me. I was sure I had heard twigs snapping. From the corner of my eye I saw something move. A boy's head behind me. Or a man's head? It disappeared.

And then it appeared again. He came bobbing down the path. Standing in the middle of a blackberry thicket, the only way out was the trail where I had placed the first bucket. And that was where he now stood. I slid off the heavy apron to make it easier to run.

"I have not come to harm you, miss."

"What do you want? I'll scream—"

He took a step backwards. "Please, you needn't scream. I just want to speak to you." Coarse dark hair hung under a red-and-gold-checked cap. Eyes, with long black lashes, sat in his light brown face, wet and soft like drops of melted chocolate. He wasn't much older than me. "My grandfather and I are trying to understand why you are here among us."

"What do you mean why I am here among you?"

"Why are you here in this time? You are not from this time."

I froze. His eyes betrayed nothing but curiosity and concern. "I don't know why I'm here," I whispered, afraid Olive lurked within striking distance. Afraid she would hear and report back to her mother. "I banged into a closet in an abandoned house in Monte Cristo. I woke up one hundred and twenty years earlier in the Sweetwine home. That's all I know."

"My grandfather saw you in a vision. Said you are not from our age, our time. You are not Emma. What is your name, miss?"

I could have dropped to my knees and kissed his brown mannish working boots. For the second time in two days I said my name out loud to someone who believed me. "Sonnet McKay."

He nodded, as if he ran into time travelers picking blackberries in a forest every day. "My grandfather wishes to meet you, Miss McKay."

"Who are you? Who's your grandfather?"

"I am Maxwell. My grandfather is Simeon. I have seen it

now and know for certain. Emma is skittish around horses. Not you."

"Can you help me? I'm desperate to get home. I don't know what to do—"

"Nature and spirits keep their own timeline. Whether we want them to or not, a bear slumbers all winter and fireflies appear to us only at night."

"Do you mean I should I just sit back and wait for something to happen instead of searching for an answer? You're confusing me."

Olive and Pearl's nattering voices coasted toward us through the blackberry bushes. Maxwell backed away and crossed the trail.

"Wait! Don't go, Maxwell. Please."

He tipped his cap and disappeared into the forest. My brain did cartwheels.

"Is that you in there, Emma? We have two large buckets filled to the brim apiece. How many do *you* have?" Olive and Pearl stood on the trail where Maxwell had just been.

I hated that they had interrupted us. I stopped myself from shoving past their linen and lace covered bodies and fleeing into the woods after Maxwell. "Almost two buckets, Olive."

"Is that all? And where is your pinafore?" Olive narrowed her bulging gray eyes at my thrown-off apron lying crumpled at my feet and then turned them on my blackberry-stained lips.

"I was hot." I ripped the apron off the ground and put it back on. Olive was insufferable. Emma hadn't wanted to talk to her and neither did I. "Wait, let me just fill this last bucket.

I can't go back to . . . my mother without as many blackberries as you both have."

"We can help," said Pearl.

With the bucket filled, the girls continued their silly conversation about boys and pirates as we walked back to the river. I followed silently in their shadows.

Jacob threw his arms around my waist and hugged me as if I had been gone for days. I kissed the top of his head.

Missus Jenkins fussed around our heaping buckets. "Superb blackberry-picking, girls."

Throwing my dirt- and blackberry-stained apron on the empty picnic table, I walked away and sat under a tree next to the riverbank with Jacob by my side. I listened to picnic gear clank around as the drivers heaved it back to the carriages waiting in the meadow.

Jacob's little hand stretched out to mine, and together we watched the cold, crystal water gurgle and swirl as it ran over smooth gray rocks. A fish swam by with speckles on its side, dotting a silver, shimmery casing. If I stared long enough, I might see gold glittering in this mining town river. I bent forward and dipped my fingers into the water and brought them to my hot face. I let river water drip down my cheeks—

"What are you doing?" Thorn blocked the sun.

I twitched.

Jacob squeezed my hand.

Her finger struck out at me. She caught my chin and turned it toward her, blue eyes sweeping across my face. "Where is your parasol? You are as brown as an Indian."

She snatched Jacob's arm and walked her beautiful high button shoes up to the others, leaving me by myself.

I shuffled behind, kicking at the rocky dirt and shrubby grass. Tall trees beyond the carriages called my name, lured me to keep walking, begged to swallow me up, hide me from her. I wondered if it would be possible to just disappear, camp out, find a hollow tree trunk to live in, survive on blackberries and speckled fish and river water until I could figure this thing out. Maybe Kerry could bring me blankets, maybe Maxwell and his grandfather could guide me.

The horse and carriage driver held his hand out as I hopped up to take my place on the red leather seat. A red-and-gold checked cap sat at a jaunty angle on his head.

"Maxwell?" I opened my mouth to say something else but he shook his head at me. I sat in silence, my face turned to the open window, my hand holding Jacob's little one. I had learned my lesson.

AT the house, I held back and let Thorn and Jacob out of the carriage in front of me. Maxwell helped me down. I stalled for a minute and then whispered, just loud enough for him to hear, "Kerry's our friend. She knows who I am and who I'm not."

He nodded. I walked across the gravel path and entered the house.

"Emma."

I whirled around.

"Go to your room now and stay there. I do not want to see you again until supper."

"Fine with me."

Thorn took my arm before I could bolt. Her voice softened. "Teaching you to act like a lady is my job. When you are willful, I must correct you."

My eyes skated over her thin, taut neck. Being with her was like being on a dangerous roller coaster. I nodded, extracted my ensnared arm, and ran up the stairs.

Halfway down the hallway, piano chords and laughter suddenly made me turn around. I had heard those sounds before. I crept back down and peeked into the parlor. Thorn sat on the piano bench with Jacob and Miles on either side of her, running her fingers over the keys. Miles turned to her and said something with a chortle. She laughed her answer back to him and kissed the top of his head. Jacob had his arm around her waist and she turned to kiss him, too. And there she sat, a loving mother, between her boys.

She was a certified Jekyll and Hyde.

I tore the loathsome green bow out of my hair as I scooted back up. Shoving the bedroom door shut, I dragged off the layers of Emma's stifling picnic costume and batted them away. With vicious stabs, I took the buttonhook to her shoes and kicked them across the room. I marched to the closet in the old-fashioned underwear. A small high window let in light. The shelves were empty and the pile of broken junk had been swept away. I shut the door behind me.

Was this the way back? I sat on the floor and squeezed my eyes shut, my muscles taut with the intensity of my wish.

I wanted to go home. I had never been hated before. I didn't know how to behave—how to be meek and docile. Mom and Dad treated me as if I was one of the three most remarkable kids that had ever been born. Cliché Jules, with her cheerleading and club-joining and popularity. And almost as cliché Evan, with his sports and good grades and multitudes of friends. Then there was me. Lacking in their social skills, but with a brain that made pretty much everything as easy as snapping my fingers. Until now.

Nothing. I banged back against the wall and cracked the closet door open—the stupid little closet door I never should have opened in the first place, that day. I should have listened to my head. Not the siren sound of Rapp's voice.

And now here I was. Broken into a million pieces. Shattered.

Why? *Why?*

There was no logic to it. Nothing made sense.

My body felt hollow, emptied of anything special. Wonderful, smart me, the girl who went out of her way to minimize mistakes, was now gone, replaced with something alien, someone who was *only* making mistakes.

Someone even I didn't recognize.

I ran my palm down the smooth pink bead board and thought about Emma, who had been sentenced to live out her life in this beautiful, lonely bedroom. My sanctuary . . . a gilded cage.

CHAPTER EIGHT

—

Emma

2015

*E*mma took up a quilt from where it had fallen off the end of Lia's bed and wrapped herself up in it. She drew the gauzy curtains away from the open window and watched the brand-new morning sky cast its emergent light across the backyard and through the tall trees beyond the large wooden porch. Lia had called the porch a *deck.* Lia had called many things words she had never heard before.

Yesterday had been a cascade of colors and an opera of sounds. Hordes of humans, of every creed and color, wearing bright apparel and calling out to each other, had dashed from place to place with no notice of a girl from 1895. Lines of *cars* blasted and rushed, and shiny, winged cylinders of metal roared overhead. Emma's ears had rung with the noise, and her heart had raced with the pandemonium. But she felt she had educated herself on more things yesterday than she had learned in her entire life. She was ready for this unexpected education.

She took a deep breath. The air was salty like a beach and fragrant with the scent of Aunt Kate's roses. Quiet morning sounds came from other rooms in the house. She smelled brewing coffee. Lia's family gently stirred. In her Monte Cristo life, the inside of her parents' home clanged with a silent bell of danger. Little Miles didn't notice much . . . but dear Jacob did. She wondered if he was searching for her. Searching every nook and cranny. The thought brought a sudden sob to her throat.

Stop, Emma. Worrying would help nothing.

She took another breath of roses. Still and calm. She knew she had nothing to be afraid of here.

She brought Sonnet's book from the bedside table and sat down on a small white chair to wait for her new friend to awaken. The tale of a French girl wandering in a Vietnamese jungle teeming with slithering snakes, crouching tigers, and snapping crocodiles caught her attention.

THE door opened a sliver. Aunt Kate put her head in the room and observed Lia's sleeping form. She crooked a finger, bidding Emma to come.

Emma put the book down. Excited and frightened all at once, her time on stage had arrived, and she would go alone without Lia. She hoped she was a good actress. And she wished more than anything that snarling Peetie dog wasn't around.

Aunt Kate, in a hurry like all these people, held Emma's wrist and drew her through the hallway and down the staircase to the kitchen in a fast clip.

"I'm just finishing up the cinnamon rolls. You can be my assistant. Then I want to show you something. Get your advice."

She bustled around, busy-busy, and poured a pink colored liquid into a large blue cup festooned with sailing boats, pushing it at Emma.

"What is this?"

"Are you still asleep? Hot pink lemonade. Your favorite."

Emma took a sip. Delicious. "Thank you."

Aunt Kate whirled like a ballerina from counter to appliance to counter again. She brought a small tin of cinnamon and a bowl of sugar to Emma and rolled out a layer of dough on the stone tabletop in the middle of the room. She smoothed butter over the thin membrane.

"Sprinkle, honey."

Emma held the tin and shook it over the dough, sending a layer of cinnamon showering down. She tried out a new word. "Okay?"

"Perfect. Now the sugar."

This was fun. She had never assisted in Cook's kitchen. Helping the help was not allowed. Emma found a spoon and sprinkled sugar. Aunt Kate rolled the brown-and-white sprinkled dough into a long spool and sliced it into pieces. She helped put them on a baking tin. The tin went into a small heated closet in the wall.

"Come with me."

Emma took the liquid gift and followed her back up the stairs to the master bedroom. Sleeping smells drifted in a room still messy with clothes from the day before. She watched from the doorway as Aunt Kate sat on an unmade bed and patted the spot next to her. She leaned over, taking a catalogue off the bedside table.

"Come, Sonnet. Sit. I need your opinion."

Emma sat, mortified, her cheeks on fire. She had never been invited into her *own* parent's bedchambers. Not once. And now here she was in an adult stranger's room. She crossed one leg over the other and balanced the hot cup in her lap. She wished she were dressed in something other than Sonnet's bedclothes.

The bright catalogue thrust at her had pictures of matching beds and desks and dressers.

"I like these two sets," said Aunt Kate. "What do you think? Will she like either of them?"

Would *who* like either one of them—did she refer to Lia? After a moment, Emma pointed at furniture painted a robin's egg blue. "This color is beautiful. I would even like it for myself."

"Thought so. That's the one, then. Won't she be surprised on her birthday? She's had that banged-up white set since she turned seven. Now don't tell her. Promise?"

"No, of course not. I promise." Banged up and white. The bed she had been sleeping in and the chair she had been sitting on. The furniture was for Lia from a loving mother who thought of her and wished to please her. She clenched her jaw and swallowed, but too late. A fat, hot tear slid down her cheek.

"Ahhh . . . sweetheart." Aunt Kate put her arm around Emma's shoulder and hugged her close, rocking and humming. She kissed Emma's hair. The same hair her own mother turned from in disgust.

Emma relaxed and let herself be lulled and petted as if she were a baby bird dropped out of its nest. Her body draped into maternal curves and creases and her arms stretched around the ample waist and hung on tight as her tears shed away like liquid drops of sadness into the sweet woman's lap.

How many days filled fifteen years? How many hours, minutes, seconds? Emma had waited that long to feel her head on a mother's soft shoulder. She had waited that long to have a mother kiss her cheek. She lay still in the warmth of Aunt Kate's arms, not wanting to break the magic.

Emma had longed for this moment her entire life.

LIA, Niki, and Jules, all still in their sleeping clothes, skated toward the bed, matching looks of alarm on their faces.

Jules towed her out of Aunt Kate's arms. "We couldn't find you. We've gotta get ready to go to Rapp's this morning. Remember, *Sonnet?* Evan's gonna be waiting."

"What's wrong, Mom?" asked Niki, wrinkling her face at Emma.

"Just a bout of homesickness, I think. Oh, god, the cinnamon rolls!" She ran from the room toward a buzzing sound.

Lia closed the door behind her mother. "You scared us, Emma. We didn't know where you went. We've been searching the house and the yard and everywhere."

"What happened?" Niki asked. "Whatever possessed you to hang out in here with Mom?"

Emma's quavering breath plumbed the very depths of her soul. She felt peaceful, somehow. As if her tears and that woman's loving arms had joined to chip off a few years of mistreatment at the hands of her own mother.

"Aunt Kate came and found me in Lia's bedroom. She made hot pink lemonade. Just for me. I helped her make cinnamon rolls. And then she brought me in here to discuss—odds and ends. Nothing important." Emma wiped across her cheeks. "Besides our family cook, Niki, your mother is the kindest person I have ever met."

"Well, *your* mom must be hell," said Jules.

Lia glared at Jules and flicked her hard with a finger. "She's having a moment, here."

"Oww!" Jules looked ready to flick Lia back.

"God, Jules, she's been through a lot," said Lia. "Think about your words. Be nice."

"Actually, my mother *is* hell, Lia."

"See?" Jules gloated.

"Okay, okay," said Niki, getting between them. "Emma, just go with Lia and get dressed. We have to get ready. Meet us in my bedroom in forty-five minutes. We'll go to the kitchen together, have something to eat, and then walk to Rapp's for our meeting. We told him we'd be there before noon. And just remember, Emma, Sonnet wouldn't be acting like this. She doesn't get homesick. She loves it here. You need to be more careful."

"Perhaps Aunt Kate will assume I am still unwell." Emma gazed into her blue cup. She wasn't sure she could be more careful. She was drawn to that dear woman like a bee to a lilac tree.

She wanted nothing more than to follow Aunt Kate back into the kitchen and be her special assistant for the rest of the day.

CHAPTER NINE

——

Sonnet
1895

Kerry stood over me. "Get up, miss. Why do you slumber in the closet? 'Tis time to ready for supper."

Still half asleep, I crawled out and reached for the green picnic dress I had flung off earlier. Kerry smiled and took it from me. "You mustn't wear that again. You wore it earlier in the day. Here, this dress will do for supper." She put the petticoat back over my head and covered it with a light pink dress with vertical white stripes.

Running from me to the wardrobe and back again, she dressed me and fixed my hair while I yawned and shook myself awake. "What would I do without you, Kerry? What took me over an hour today has taken you only ten minutes."

"I have had many years of practice . . . you but a few days. From the way you have described, in your time you need only set a wrinkled item of clothing on your body and a shake of your hair to be presentable. If that is the case, not even a child would need a helper to get dressed."

"No, children practically dress themselves by the time they're three. You have to learn fast or get left behind—especially in big families."

"That is a wonderment, indeed, although it would certainly hasten the end of my working days." Kerry stared out the window, thinking about that. "Well, I must go see to the boys. They could never manage without some help, sweet darlings."

I realized after she left that I hadn't told her about Maxwell's surprising message from his grandfather and opened the door to call her back. She had disappeared. I lay on the bed and watched the clock. At four minutes to seven, I pushed my heavily clothed body downstairs to the dining room.

The air was stultifying in its muggy stillness. The big clock in the next room bonged seven times as I slid into my chair, its reverberations pulsating across the table. Without small talk, the Sweetwine family quietly dug into the food.

After a half-meal's worth of silence, the only sounds being the clinking of forks and knives on china, John cleared his throat. "Did you enjoy yourself searching for berries and picnicking today, Emma? I heard you and your friends had great success."

I popped up from my plate and stared directly into his eyes for our first-ever conversation. "Yes, I enjoyed it very much. Pearl, Olive, and I got two very large buckets of blackberries each."

"Very good. There will be pies and jam aplenty." He swallowed hard, his Adam's apple bopping up and down. "Well, how would you like to have lunch with me tomorrow at the Gold Nugget Hotel? We have not spent any time together lately, dear. I thought it would be a nice idea if we dined in town. Something special. They have a very nice restaurant—"

"Can I go, too? I would very much like to eat out with you," said Miles, batting his eyes at his father.

"No, my pet. Your mother is going to take you and your brother for a pony ride instead. Would you like that, Miles?"

"Yes!"

"How about you, Jacob? You are very quiet tonight."

"Yes, I would like a pony ride, too, Father."

John said, "Well, Emma?"

"Of course."

Out of the corner of my eye I caught Thorn's triumph. She fit her hands into the shape of a steeple in front of her, tapping her thumbs together. "You will need to be ready at half past eleven, Emma. Wear the yellow silk day suit and the matching yellow shoes. Important people will see you and take notice. You will honor the Sweetwine name with your virtuous appearance."

I nodded and gulped down the rest of my dinner, the roast and potatoes and green beans glopping together in greasy lumps as I stuffed them down my throat. "Can I please be excused?"

"No dessert, Emma? Cook baked a nice coconut cake. You love that." Thorn smiled at me.

The roller coaster was chugging up to the highest peak before it would certainly plunge straight down. "No, thank you. I'll just go to my room."

I changed into the white flannel nightgown and lay on Emma's bed, as stiff and tight as the doll in the corner, and waited until the house quieted. I opened the door and listened. Not a sound. I slipped down the hall in the opposite direction of the grand staircase, certain there was a second staircase up to the third floor leading to the maid's quarters. It couldn't be far.

There it was.

I climbed up the steep stairs into darkness, holding out my arms and skimming my hands along the walls as I went. A small lantern glimmered on a table at the end of the hallway. Six small, unpainted doors, three on each side, lined the narrow space. I tiptoed to the first one on the right and listened with my ear pressed up against the door panel. Snoring and whistling sounds streamed out from under the door. I opened it a crack to let in a touch of light. A bulky mound splayed out under the covers. Cook.

I glided across to the first door on the left. No sound. I peered in. Bess, the housekeeper, had her back to me and was dragging an old, ratty nightgown on over her naked back. I quickly shut the door. My heart reeled as I pressed up against the wall, hoping against hope she hadn't heard me. A minute passed before I moved to the next door.

A light shined under it. I clicked it open a crack. Kerry sat on a little bed, a book in her lap, a small gaslight on a table next to her. A mess of red hair fell to her waist. I darted in and shut the door.

She gawked up from the page. "Miss?"

My hushed words burbled out. "I had to talk to you, and I was so sleepy. I forgot earlier—this just can't wait until tomorrow. I met Maxwell today while I was picking blackberries. He secretly found me—he knows I'm not Emma. And his grandfather Simeon wants to meet me. Simeon had a vision about me and knows I don't belong in this time. They want to help, but Maxwell spoke about it in a way I didn't understand. Something about sleeping bears and fireflies . . ."

"This is good news. They say old Simeon de la Croix has the sight. I have also heard it said Simeon's mother was full-blood Salish Indian and his father a French trapper. He lives as a recluse on top of Foggy Peak."

I sat down on the end of Kerry's narrow bed and tucked my bare feet under the white nightgown. "There's something else. John wants to take me to lunch at the Gold Nugget Hotel tomorrow. Alone. I think something's up. Thorn smiled at me at the dinner table tonight. She was gloating."

"The Gold Nugget! Well! If Mister Sweetwine is taking you to dine alone at a fine hotel . . ." Kerry paused and tapped her fingers on the bed. "He has something to tell you or something to ask of you. Something important. The madam would never allow Emma to be alone with him in town, or anywhere else for that matter, but especially for something as special as dining out." She shook her head. "No, she wouldn't miss it. Or allow her sons to miss it."

"She has agreed to it. In fact, it seemed like it was her plan."

"Unholy plan," we whispered in unison.

"I wanted to talk to you about something else, Kerry. Something I've been thinking about. We haven't really talked about Emma. Like, what happened to her? What if we switched places? And if I'm here in Monte Cristo as Emma living her life, is she in Seattle as Sonnet living mine? Is she with my family? If that's the case, my family would know what happened to me. And is there something about this we can use if they're searching for a way to get me back there and to get Emma back here?"

"Use? In what way? I'm not sure I quite understand."

"Clues. Something they might find if they go back to the house and dig around. I'll hide clues and try to communicate. Let them know I'm okay and trying to find a way back."

"Yes, of course! Tell me what to do. I shall help you—"

There was a sharp knock on the door. "Kerry! Is that you talking?" Thorn's voice bleated through the thin wood, inches from where we sat. Panic swept over us. The bed was too low to the ground for me to crawl under. There was nowhere to hide.

"Yes, madam. I sit quoting the Bible."

I pressed against the wall where the opened door might hide me. Kerry crammed the book she had been holding under the covers and snatched a Bible off the bedside table. She rolled off the bed and stood as far from me as she could get, clutching the black, leather-bound book out in front of her, her face a blank. "Please enter."

The door punched open. Thorn stood on the threshold, so close to my trembling body, I could taste her perfume. I held my breath and prayed I wouldn't sneeze.

"Maxwell will take the boys and myself down the mountain to the Miller Farm tomorrow, Kerry. Jacob and Miles are going to ride ponies and have lunch with little Wendell and Walter while Missus Miller and I take tea. I want them ready at quarter past ten, after their porridge. Have them in their new brown-and-tan summer riding gear. After we have been safely delivered, Maxwell will return and take Mister Sweetwine and Miss Emma to dine in town. Please help her dress in the yellow silk day suit."

"Yes, madam."

"Jacob seemed diminished at the table tonight. Did you notice anything amiss with him today?"

"No, madam. He seemed fine to me."

"He is so sensitive to people's feelings. He seems eternally upset about his sister, and that infuriates me. She is a bad influence on my sons."

"I will let you know if I notice anything out of the ordinary."

"Yes, do. Report anything she does that you feel is affecting Jacob. She is morose and melancholic, and she inflicts her mood on him."

"Yes, madam, I certainly will."

"One more matter. I have instructed Bess, as well, but I want you to give her assistance. Emma's apparel, shoes, and sundries must be gone through and either repaired and cleaned for keeping, or set aside if too worn or small. I will need a detailed list of everything she needs for the coming school year, including warm outer garments, coats, and hats. Also footwear. I suppose some of her things are worn through."

"Why, madam?"

"What do you mean, why? How *dare* you ask me why? That is none of your business."

"I'm sorry, madam. I . . . I thought it might make it easier to make decisions about the clothing and such—"

"Just do as you are told. Do not forget your station. I am not opposed to using the switch on hired help that require it. You know that, do you not? And you know I have already let several people go since you started with us. Do you consider yourself immune?"

"No, madam."

Was Kerry going to be hit? My flapping heart was a bird with a hundred pairs of wings. I shut my eyes, squeezing, squeezing, and counted backwards from one hundred, ready to explode.

"*Now.* You may continue quoting the good book, Kerry. Do it quietly. The rest of the house is sleeping."

"Yes, madam."

The door closed with a loud crack, tossing my lungs a life jacket.

I slurped air as Kerry and I faced each other, expressions frozen in mutual dread. I waited long minutes until my heart settled down and the sound of Thorn's clacking footsteps had disappeared into the night. Then I, too, left the room, my shocked legs shunting me back down the dark stairs and hallway to the safety of Emma's bedroom.

Just as I opened the bedroom door I heard what sounded like crying. The quiet yelps and snuffling didn't come from the nursery. The noise came from the direction of the front staircase. I followed the sound. Around the corner and up a short flight of stairs was the inside of the tallest turret. *Was that Thorn crying?*

I heard a man's voice growling out a plea for silence.

John.

The mewling stopped.

I slunk back to Emma's room and shut myself in for the night.

CHAPTER TEN

—

Emma
2015

Rapp's uncle opened the front door and sent the Macadangdang, McKay, and Sweetwine gang plummeting down old wooden stairs to the lower level. Rapp waited at the bottom and led them to a large room. Evan banged the door shut behind them, ready to seal off their secrets between pine-paneled walls.

Couches and chairs circled a low table. Sooty ashes from a brick fireplace filled the room with a spent gunpowder-like scent doing battle with the aroma of clean laundry emanating from a mound of folded clothes. A stringed instrument with wires and knobs coming out of its red body and wooden neck lay across a small bed. Next to that was stacked luggage with a lamp balanced on top. Beside the lamp was a tower of books.

Suitcases casually flung on the floor of a sleeping room once more. *Had Rapp also come from somewhere far away?*

"Glad to see you finally woke up."

Emma looked toward the voice. There he was. Tall and

striking. With a face as known to her as her own hand. She had not dreamt it. He wore pants that came to his knees again, and so did Evan. After her jaunt downtown with Lia, men's baggy clothing and naked legs no longer startled her. She understood, now.

"Hello, Rapp. Yes, I finally woke up. As Lia says, I had time travel lag." Emma laughed along with her new companions and reveled in the attention. The speed with which she had become intimate with these people was astounding. They had only met a few days ago, and she had already been invited into four of their bedrooms.

She patted her tight jeans. "I'm developing a love for Sonnet's clothing. And Lia has shown me many ingenious things. We live a rustic and difficult life compared to you."

Evan said, "Good coach, Lia. Emma's just part of our team now. She'll definitely pass as Sonnet until we can switch them back. 'Team Switch.' That's what we'll call ourselves."

"Team Switch," said Emma, trying it out. "I love it. Our surreptitious enterprise captured in your two perfect words."

"*Your* words are perfect." Evan laughed. "You increase our lame vocabulary every time you open your mouth."

Niki had been talking into her slender box. Her cell phone. "Hey, are you ready to go to a party later today, Emma? We've all been invited over to my friend's house on Fairweather Bay. Sam's family has a speedboat, and we get to take it out. It'll be pretty exciting for you. You're gonna literally fly across Lake Washington."

"Truly, it will be my first ride in a boat, Niki! Am I ready for a party on Lake Washington, Lia? Am I ready to fly across the lake? It sounds like a marvelous outing."

Lia smiled at her. "As far as I'm concerned, you're ready for anything. You're the best pupil I've ever had."

"The *only* pupil you've ever had," said Jules. "And, really? Old-fashioned Emma in a bikini. That's a joke, right?"

"I'll show her some options," said Lia. "She can decide what she wants to wear. It's not like she's a baby, Jules. We don't need to coddle her."

"*Bikini?*" Emma glanced back at Lia, her source for answers to all things confusing.

"Oh, this is gonna be good," said Evan, laughing.

"Hey, Team Switch. Focus. We need to ramp this thing up." Rapp sat down on a chair and leaned toward a thin metal box. He opened its lid. "Has anyone come up with any ideas?"

Emma watched him touch around on it, like they had all been doing with their phones. Another amazement to catalogue in her ever-expanding universe.

"I found a couple time travel experts," said Evan. "I want to call and see if someone will believe our story and see us. Hopefully tomorrow."

"Excellent," said Rapp.

Evan said, "Anybody else?"

"Doppelganger. A mirror image of someone. I don't know if it will lead anywhere but it seems like maybe we should consider it. Jules and I will take it," said Niki.

"Have you fortunetellers here? Someone who can read the future? Or perhaps read my palm?" Emma blushed. "Am I being too forward?"

"Actually, that's not a bad idea at all," said Niki. "We can't discount anything."

"Uncle Jack used to be into all that," said Rapp. "Horoscopes and tarot cards and stuff. He would know someone. I'm not sure I want to bring him into this, though. What do you guys think?"

"We need all the help we can get," said Evan. "I want my sister back. Can he keep a secret?"

Rapp nodded. "He won't give anything away. He's like this old hippie, you know? If I was to ask him to get me some pot, he'd probably go out and try to score me some. That's just the kind of guy he is. Helpful." He looked over at Emma. "Not that I do drugs."

"*Do drugs?*" asked Emma, shaking her head.

Lia said, "You may as well be speaking Russian, Rapp. Your words are just gibberish to her."

"Note to self . . ." He tapped his head. "*1895.* Anyway, Uncle Jack can drive us around if we need rides, since he's not doing anything else right now. Let's wait and see if we need him for something. We can keep him as backup."

"Emma and I will take the fortuneteller idea," Lia said. "I'm pretty sure they're called psychics. We can find out as much as possible first. Maybe we won't need your uncle."

Evan dragged his chair closer, nudging Rapp. "Let's go. Google 'time travel.' Let's see what we can learn."

"Wow. Look at this," Niki said, reading the laptop's lid over Rapp's shoulder. "'Time travel alters the reality of present, past, and future, upsetting the equilibrium and balance of universal existence. Extreme risks and potential disaster . . .'"

Evan elbowed her away before she could read anymore and glanced around at Emma. "Geez, Niki, I changed my mind. We already know what time travel is. Let's just stick with finding people who can help us."

BUCK *Swan*, it was called, and true to its name, the speedboat sped across the smooth-as-glass lake with the power of one thousand reindeer and the grace of a magical swan. Hanging on to a taut rope attached to the end of the boat, Evan, their leader, jumped his wooden board up and through and over the bubbling water, leaving two churning trails of white froth in his wake, sailing and spinning behind them. Emma, in Sonnet's shorts, T-shirt, and bikini hidden underneath, shrieked with glee over the roar of the engine, as if she, herself, were bouncing over the foamy curls atop Evan's shoulders.

After the initial realization and utter shock at the expected attire for the day, Emma had taken the challenge and agreed to it. Years of being browbeaten and banished to her bedroom fell away, and exquisite liberation exploded across her, as powerful as the wind that whipped her hair, as bright as the sun that burnt her cheeks. She had never in her life felt so alive, and she thought she might just jump in the water later with the two pieces of cloth covering only a tiny bit of her body. Or maybe she wouldn't. Maybe she would leave her outer clothes on with the bikini underneath and jump in that way.

In this new life, she could choose. She could decide for herself. No one would tell her that she was right or she was wrong, or that the color of her clothing clashed with her hair. The notion of free will electrified her, streaming through her body like the power systems generating modern light and machinery.

Niki's friend, Sam—*a girl!*—sat in the driver's seat and piloted the boat, as strong and capable as any man. Rapp sat in front with her and pointed his face into the wind and into the sun. His long, dark hair covered his face as he cast his attention back at Evan, eager for his turn to be towed. Niki, Jules, Lia, and Emma sat crowded in the back of the loud, vibrating vessel with several nearly naked boys.

Next to her sat her favorite. Loyal and generous and kind, Lia made her feel safe and loved, no matter how difficult it must have been for her to lose her best friend, Sonnet, and how trying it must be to now contend with her.

With happy, windy tears in her eyes, Emma mouthed "Thank you" to Lia, the ear-piercing engine making it impossible to talk.

As long as Emma lived, she would never forget this day.

This feeling. This freedom. As free as the eagle Emma had watched with envy, from the confines of her old life. And now here she was, as free as that bird.

Her new friends had captured her heart. And so had this life.

CHAPTER ELEVEN

—

Sonnet
1895

Feeling trapped, I leaned back against the black tufted cushion and inhaled the leather smell, using the deep breaths to drive out thoughts of Thorn's overly pleased face at the dinner table the night before.

The open window framed the Sweetwine mansion as John's black-and-blue carriage jolted down the hill, hurtling us to the Gold Nugget Hotel for lunch. Pink, yellow, and white painted surfaces stood in contrast to the green trees and brilliant blue sky. The house's dazzling exterior decorated nothing but a lie. It hid a cold, unhappy interior—much like Thorn, the lady of the house. If it weren't for Miles, there would never be laughter in that home.

"Where does the Sweetwine money come from?" I asked John.

"An odd question, Emma, but I suppose with your advancing age, you are developing a curiosity about such matters." John folded his arms across his chest and fluttered his fingers on his suit-covered biceps. "Mister John D. Rockefeller, to be exact. He is bankrolling the gold mining operation. Good breeding discourages bragging, Emma, but I am Mister Rockefeller's first agent and manager of business and mining affairs of Monte Cristo. Money is a private matter, dear girl. We do not discuss personal dealings with anyone outside the family. Remember that."

"Mister Rockefeller must like you a lot to trust you with such an important job."

John beamed across the carriage at me. A big version of Miles, his neck was squeezed in a tight, stiff collar, and his chiseled face and bright blue eyes made him look like a Viking.

I turned back to the window and fidgeted, my hands twisting around in my yellow silk lap. A parasol in the same color sat on the bench next to me. I reached over to it and ran my palm across the honeyed softness.

Hats tipped at us as we wound around Dumas Street through the commercial center on our way down the hill. In front of a backdrop of soaring, cloud-covered mountains, we passed a church, a school, and a post office. Tidy businesses operating out of new wooden buildings ran down the incline beyond horses carrying coarse riders and cargo-piled, horse-drawn wagons.

The carriage crossed over a railroad track as the road bent downward into another more dubious section of booming Monte Cristo. Saloons and boarding houses butted up to a long wooden boardwalk, where scruffy boys and men leaned against hitching posts and smoked and laughed. Railroad offices, mining companies, and general stores advertised with large painted signs over their buildings. It rolled to a smooth stop in front of the biggest building in town. The brown-uniformed doorman booted a straggly black-and-white dog, causing it to yap and limp away. I wanted to slap his face. Instead, I knifed him with my eyes.

"Welcome to the Gold Nugget Hotel, Mister Sweetwine. Let me seat you and lovely Miss Emma near the window." The small man chatted us up in his heavily accented English as he ushered us from the lobby into the dining room. Heavy crystal and silver decked the tables, and gold velvet drapes obscured most of the view out the windows. A candle flickered between us, and smoky oil fumes hung in the air above our heads. I held the menu in front of my face and skimmed the room over the top of it. Well-dressed people filled the tables around us and gawked—taking note of my yellow silk day suit and matching yellow shoes.

"What would you like, my dear?"

I sighed, scanning the menu. I wanted French fries and something fresh like a big green salad. "Chicken?"

"Very good. We will both have the chicken cordon blue. And Waldorf salad." John handed the menus to the waiter. "A glass of sherry for me, iced lemonade for the girl." He twirled the greasy end of his mustache at me.

"Dear, I have—"

"Hello, Miss Emma, Mister Sweetwine. I hope I'm not causing an interruption?"

More accented English. I turned in my chair and traversed up a male body to his face. *Oh, my god!* I grabbed at the edge of the table, stopping myself before I could pitch over and slide onto the floor. It was *him*—the one I had seen flash by on the dark red horse the day of the picnic. My knuckles turned white as I hung on. I was Alice in Wonderland. I had tumbled into the rabbit hole.

"Miss, how are you this fine day?" He shoved his hat off his head and grinned at me. Dark blond hair revealed the difference. But those were Rapp's eyes, Rapp's face.

John said, "Young Mister Loken. Good to see you. What is it, lad?"

"I'm sorry for bothering you, sir. I saw your carriage out front and thought to speak to you. I'm done at last with my weeklong commitment at the fairgrounds, and the crew and I are ready to start again on your barn project. I would like to finish the work before the fall snow sets in."

"Yes of course. Please tell me where we are in the process."

"The old fishing cabin has been demolished and the new framing erected. Finishing the structure can now begin."

"As you can see, I'm dining with my daughter, but please come 'round to the office this afternoon. We can discuss the project and timing then."

He bowed. "Good day then, sir. I will present myself at your office after three o'clock."

I hadn't moved. Another grin and a long intense stare lit up my cheeks. He made his exit with my eyes still on him, my heart still grinding. Rapp's body. Rapp's walk. Through the looking-glass, I had met Rapp Loken's long-ago relative—it had to be—young Mister Loken.

I watched through the window as he slapped his hat back on and mounted his horse—strong and tall. His tan face cocked in my direction. *Was that a wink?* My heart leapt.

"What's his name? Mister Loken's first name?"

"Such odd questions from you today, Emma. Are you sure you have recovered from your head injury?"

"I'm just a curious girl."

"I can see that." He tapped his chin. "His first name is Tor. I was sure you had met him before this."

"Not really."

"Mister Loken is working on our land, constructing another barn—or motor garage I hear them called. I want to be ready. There's a new invention called a motor car, and I hope to have one here in Monte Cristo, although the carriage will never be replaced, as horses are more dependable than a motor. And I assume the carriage interior is much more comfortable for the weaker sex."

He stroked the arm of his brown leather chair. "However, the motor car will be a convenience to get me back and forth to work on occasion, when the weather allows. I will learn to drive the contraption, and this will free up Maxwell to devote his time to your mother and the boys as they get older. Respectable men are starting to acquire them, and a man in my position cannot be last."

I dragged my mind from the impossible coincidence of Tor. "Motor cars will replace the horse and carriage. It's just a matter of time."

"Well, we should stay with a subject we both know something about. I apologize for boring you with talk of a new-fangled invention."

"It doesn't bore me at all."

He spun a spoon around on the table. "Dear, we have more important things to discuss than construction projects and new inventions. Serious things." He took a breath. "Emma . . ."

He brought the spinning spoon to a standstill. A ray of sunshine from the window behind his head hit it just right, almost blinding me with its mirror-like finish. It was the shiniest, most ornate spoon I had ever seen in my life. I waited with clenched teeth.

"Your mother and I have decided to send you to boarding school. This town is too rough-and-tumble for a girl of your breeding. You are a young lady now. We must consider your eventual match, and it certainly will not happen with someone from Monte Cristo. The men here are brutish, really, even the better reared ones."

John looked down at his plate, miserable with the job of springing this news on his daughter. "I realize that just fifteen is generally younger than the usual age to be sent away."

Marched off to boarding school.

Forced into marriage.

Unholy plan.

I unclenched my teeth. "Where?"

"Your mother has found you very nice accommodations. The Oldfield's School for Ladies. Only the best families send their daughters. And there is an opening available. We sent for literature several months ago, and it arrived by post last week. It seems a very enjoyable place." He hesitated. "This fine school is in Baltimore."

Baltimore!

A line of sweat formed in the narrow strip of skin between his mustache and nose. He fumbled around for his napkin and wiped his forehead. "They have even introduced the subject of chemistry for ladies. I know you will like that sort of advanced curriculum. Just imagine all the books they will have in their library. You can read and read to your heart's content. And their choir is one of the finest. It will be very stimulating, Emma. The school here in Monte Cristo is lackluster to say the least. We may have to hire a private tutor for Jacob—"

He was rambling now. "When?" I croaked.

"We will send you by train. We have purchased a ticket for next Monday. The boys will not be told until you and I depart on Sunday for the Everett Station. It will be upsetting to them, and that is the real issue right now, although your mother believes they will forget you quickly—they are so young. Do I have your word you will not say anything to Jacob and Miles?"

I bobbed my head. My heart hurt. The boys would be more than upset. They would be devastated. And I somehow knew the way back home was here. Right here in Monte Cristo. Not Baltimore. I had a week to find it.

"Thank you for not making a fuss, my dear Emma. I knew I could count on you. Now, here is our chicken. Splendid." John nattered away through the rest of the meal while I took my fork and pushed the apples and walnuts from my Waldorf salad around on my plate, choking down a few bites.

AFTER lunch, John had Maxwell drop him down the street at his office. The carriage turned and started for home. When we reached a vacant area of the road, I took the lovely yellow silk parasol and used it to hammer on the window frame. "Maxwell!"

The carriage swayed to a stop. Maxwell had switched to a

black-and-blue-checked cap to match John's manly rig and had set it, once again, at a jaunty angle. He held on to it and leaned back, peering in the window. "Are you quite all right?"

"They're sending me to Baltimore. Forever! I have to see your grandfather."

Maxwell thought for a minute and nodded. "Tomorrow night the moon will be full. I will let Kerry know after I've determined a plan to get you further up the mountain to my grandfather. She will deliver the message to you. Don't contact me yourself, miss. That will only lead to trouble." He nipped at the horses and got us back out onto the bumpy road.

Trouble.

Trouble tore my forehead and bruised my ribs and scratched at my arms and legs. It hissed at me across the dinner table and snatched sweet children out of my lap. It banished me to Emma's bedroom, alone and scared. And now Trouble wanted to haul me off to Baltimore, away from Monte Cristo and my only way home.

Trouble. With a capital T.

CHAPTER TWELVE

———

Emma

2015

*E*mma watched as Rapp's uncle drove the white van away from the curb and back onto the congested road. He honked the horn and put a fist out the window with his thumb pointing up. Once again, they were on their own without adults, and Emma was getting used to her independence.

Her friends shouted and laughed and talked over each other about the latest goings-on as they strolled in a happy troupe to their destination. Emma loved their openness, their uninhibited, friendly banter. Just any old thought originating in their minds landed in their mouths and rolled to each other's ears. Nothing was strained through a sieve, picked apart, and checked for merit or effect before being spoken. She listened to the unvarnished truth of their stories and smiled down at her bare legs, scandalously exposed to the world in Sonnet's short skirt. Her sun-reddened skin was turning a light shade of brown, and her long strides and swinging arms were indistinguishable now from theirs. Emma was thrilled beyond measure to finally look like she belonged with the rest of the group.

It took an hour to walk to Professor Kapoor's Montlake home, a brick, timber, and leaded glass dwelling that appeared ready-made for an old-fashioned Englishman rather than a modern University of Washington professor. Evan bounded up to the porch and lifted and *thwopped* a bronze pineapple knocker against the rounded oak door as the rest of them stood behind him on the crooked walkway.

Professor Kapoor opened the door wide and led them to a cozy room. French doors opened to a small garden packed with fruit trees and pots of herbs, not unlike Cook's walled garden off the side of the Sweetwine house. The professor poured mint-adorned iced tea while his birdlike wife, dressed in a sumptuous Indian sari, hefted a platter of cookies to a low table, warm sugar and chocolate aromas trailing in from the kitchen.

"Well, now." Professor Kapoor beheld them each, one at a time. "Evan tells me you have a situation? Even though I'm a theoretical physics professor who believes in the concept of time travel, I remain skeptical of those who seek me out. That's the scientist in me. But curiosity won, and I wanted to meet you and hear about your intriguing problem."

"Professor, I told you all about us in my email. Here's Emma. She's the one who traded places with my sister." Evan handed him the old photo from the Ice Caves Fair. "We're pretty sure that's Sonnet standing there."

The professor stared at it and back at Emma through his gold rimmed spectacles. He wore a gray suit of clothes, not unlike what her father would typically wear. He was as properly dressed as any man Emma had seen so far in Seattle.

"This isn't you?"

"No, sir."

"Well, you have traveled here from a very long distance."

"Yes, I . . . departed . . . unexpectedly. Mercifully these good people were there to find me." She smiled at them all, strung out like a row of lustrous pearls across the professor's long couch, and felt enormously blessed by her good luck.

"Departed . . . from 1895. I like that." He handed the photo back. "There is a theory about time travel. Boiled down, it works something like a fissure in space that allows someone to get carried through a crack-like substance. As in an earthquake when tectonic plates move and crash into each other, one rises and one falls. There is space between them that allows gas and air to escape from the earth's interior. This time travel theory works something like that. Only it's out there." He gestured to the sky. "And not down here." He tapped his feet. "Different timelines bumping up against each other and shifting open to let material—or in your case, two girls— escape."

He added, "Some areas are thought to be more active than others. Like the Bermuda Triangle. Have you heard of that?"

"I have," said Rapp. "It's where all those ships and planes disappear."

"Yes. There have been different theories for those unexplained mysteries. Traveling through a crack in time is one of them. What's interesting, though, is the fact that an actual switch took place. Someone from the past moved to the future and someone from the future moved to the past. Two identical humans. I've never heard of this before."

Lia said, "It happened in exactly the same spot, at exactly the same time of day—on the same day—to two people who are like exact copies. Exactly one hundred and twenty years apart."

"Yes." Professor Kapoor took a sip of his ice tea and sat back in his chair. "Have you heard of a doppelganger?"

"Niki and I researched it," said Jules.

"Well, there is a theory—and this may or may not have anything to do with your situation—that everyone has a twin. A mirror image. Someone from the same time or even a different time—past, present, or future. There are legends of these beings in ancient cultures and myths as diverse as Nordic, Egyptian, French, and Native American. They are known as double spirits or even time travel harbingers of life or of death. Over the span of hundreds of years, writers, poets, and even monarchs have written or spoken of their own experiences or tales of someone they knew involved in these unusual occurrences."

Evan reached for a second cookie. "Do you think Emma and Sonnet are doppelgangers?"

"Maybe. And just maybe they're the same person. Another theory out there is when you die you are someday reborn and are yourself again without the memories of a previous life. Except for a feeling of *déjà vu* at times, you remember nothing. There are actual religions based on this belief. Sonnet may be physically but unconsciously living a past life. In this same way, Emma is here living a future life. And if this is so, they are both feeling a very strong connection to everyone they encounter."

"Okay. This is getting weird," said Niki.

"You were all right with the time travel theory but not with a past life theory? You have to keep your mind open, Niki. It could be that and some sort of doppelganger thing, too." Evan swung around at everyone. "We all have to keep our minds open."

"And stay upbeat," added Lia.

"Well, these are just possibilities to reflect on—it's all vague theory at this point," said Professor Kapoor. "I'm just ruminating. These spheres really aren't my specialty. Time travel is. What it is doesn't really matter. What matters is that you switch these two girls back."

"We don't know what to do," said Jules.

"You don't want Sonnet and Emma in the same dimension. You must switch them both back—or neither. You will have to somehow time this, somehow coordinate this. Just as it has already happened. Do you understand?"

"How?" asked Lia. "Can you help us with that?"

"I'm not sure." He turned to Evan. "Is your sister considering these things?"

"Knowing Sonnet . . . yes."

"Good. That's half the battle. I'll discuss this matter with my colleagues and call you. I have to tell you, honestly, this is a critical situation." He got up from his chair and made his apologies. "My wife and I are expected at a reception today. We must go now."

With the professor's nudging, Evan helped himself to the rest of the cookies and spilled them into a paper bag the professor's wife held for him. Out on the sidewalk, Rapp called his uncle who agreed to pick them up in front of Husky Stadium in twenty minutes.

Emma had listened intently to Professor Kapoor and had many questions. There were twenty short minutes to get answers from Team Switch before they were herded into the white van and had to shift their conversation to small talk.

EMMA stood her ground. She would stay home tonight instead of going to a party. It was what she wanted with every fiber of her being and she would not let Lia convince her otherwise.

"You'll meet some of our friends, Emma. There'll be lots of guys there. Wouldn't you like to meet a cute guy?"

"Cute guy?"

"Handsome boy."

"No, frankly I'm just not interested, Lia."

"You'd rather stay home with my parents then go to a party? What's wrong with you?"

"I would just rather not go."

"Why?"

"I have a beau to whom I will remain true."

"A beau?"

"A suitor."

"You mean a boyfriend?"

"Yes, a boyfriend."

"I don't know if I believe you. Really, Emma, this is the first you've mentioned him."

Emma hardened her heart and clamped her jaw. She would answer any question and be as open and truthful as they, except for this one thing. She would say no more about her sworn secret. "Aunt Kate is making popcorn for me and displaying a film about a girl and wizard in a city called Oz."

"Well, Mom has finally found someone to watch that old movie with her. You know this is weird, don't you? Sonnet would never stay home if she'd been invited out to a party. Never."

"This is what I want. And I am not Sonnet. You do realize that, do you not?"

"You're starting to worry me."

"What more must I do? Give me this gift, Lia. Please share her with me. My relationship with my own mother is unlike what you have with yours. I just want . . . her attention a little longer. If you met my mother, you would understand. She is fonder of my brothers than she is of me, and Aunt Kate makes me feel special. There. I've said it."

"She's here, isn't she? She followed you. You let your mother follow you and sit in your head." Lia's face melted with pity. "Okay. I'm telling Niki you're sick, then, and going to bed. If she knew you were making excuses to stay home just to watch a ridiculous movie with Mom and Dad, she would come drag you out of here."

Emma kissed Lia on the cheek. "Thank you."

"You'll be careful, right? No crying. You need to really channel Sonnet, tonight. There'll be no one around to rescue you."

"You needn't worry. I know just how to be Sonnet now."

She watched from the porch as Lia ran down the stairs and joined Evan, Niki, and Jules, who were standing out in front of the house on the sidewalk. They would walk up the street and fetch Rapp at his uncle's and go to a party with cute guys. Emma had no need for a cute guy.

She made her way to the family room where Aunt Kate sat waiting for her with a big bowl of popcorn on the low table. Emma wiggled in against her warmth. Uncle Vince was already asleep in his big chair, legs and feet stretched out, softly snoring. Peetie, now accustomed to her smell, settled down across her thighs. She ran her fingers through the dog's soft fur.

What a sight she must be. Short shorts. A clingy sweater. Bare feet. An un-brushed tangle of wild red hair cascading down her back and shoulders, as if she were nothing more than a woman of the night. And most surprising of all, an animal curled in her lap.

She had never felt so at ease.

The lights were low, and the room was still and soothing. She immersed herself in the tale of a young girl and her dog being transported in a revolving house to the colorful Land of Oz and only happy-cried a little bit at the end along with Aunt Kate. It was the perfect movie. She liked this many times over the frightful *Mockingjay* film. She had watched Lia in the dark theater love *Mockingjay*, but she still had work to do when it came to observing people die in bloody terror. A house landing on a bad witch, deserving of death, but spouting no blood, was much more enjoyable.

Emma urged Peetie off her lap with a few pats on the couch, stretched out her legs, and said goodnight to her new family.

What a wonderful evening. Niki and Lia worried about her giving their secret away, but all she wanted was to be swept up in sweet motherly attention, and yes, love.

Was that so wrong?

CHAPTER THIRTEEN

—

Sonnet
1895

Bess and Kerry woke me up early. It was time to finish the clothes inventory, and Bess was in charge. She pursed her lips at me, ready to head into battle over Emma's wardrobe. "No lying about today, Miss Emma. You would best get your breakfast and go pick wildflowers. We will be in your room until lunch seeing to the madam's tasking."

"I'll help, Bess."

"Why in heaven's name would you do *that*? Help? Mercy me! Kerry, get her up and dressed. I will return at half past the hour. The madam will have our hides if this is still undone when she returns later today."

Kerry waited until the door closed. "Well? Tell me about the Gold Nugget Hotel."

"They're sending me away to boarding school in Baltimore—on Sunday!"

Kerry nodded and whistled softly. "Yes. Yes. Of course. There it is. The unholy plan. I knew the madam had been scheming on something. And the mystery of the sudden inventory is now solved."

"Maxwell is going to help me get up to Simeon's tonight. He said he would contact you about the arrangements. How will that happen if you're in my room working with Bess?"

"I'll find a moment to be alone with Maxwell. Put your mind at ease."

"I found a pen and a bottle of ink. You can show me how to use them. Can you get me three envelopes and three sheets of paper?"

"Aye," said Kerry, pointing. "You will spot them in the writing drawer later today. We must get you dressed now. Bess will return at any moment, and she's in a state of distress because of the sudden tasking. You must stay out of her way."

FROM my vantage point, sitting low in a field of wildflowers and blackberry bushes, I watched Maxwell help Thorn, Jacob, and Miles into the red-and-gold carriage. He climbed up and gently tapped the horses into action. The carriage shades were drawn down to keep the low morning sun from the eyes of the passengers. As it passed, I stood and gave Maxwell a steady gaze. He nodded, bobbing his red-and-gold-checked cap. He hadn't forgotten about our midnight plan. I heaved a sigh and sat down again.

A flower caught my attention, and I plucked it from its house of dirt. Orange and fragrant, I twirled it through my fingers and wondered about its botanical name. The rising sun felt warm on my shoulders and I lay back, my body cushioned on the spongy ground. The smell of coffee and cinnamon from Cook's kitchen found me where I lay. I closed my eyes and thought about my family.

Lights had glimmered in the tall trees around Uncle Vince's and Aunt Kate's quirky Queen Anne Hill house on the night of Evan's and my fifteenth birthday party. Yellow balloons bounced around in the breeze, and a picnic table on the deck held presents and the birthday cakes Mom had made for us that morning before she and Dad left for the airport, and their long trip home to Cape Town. Carrot cake for Evan and raspberry whipped cream on cinnamon sponge-cake for me. A tradition I could count on.

And that's when Rapp showed up out of nowhere.

And that's when the trouble started. I had taken one look at him and been struck by love-lightning. And now his ancestor lived here, today, right this minute, in Monte Cristo.

It was too much.

Under the collar of my dress, I located Kerry's chain with my ring hanging from the end. A small rectangle of black onyx held a row of three tiny diamonds planted down the center and sat on a thin platinum band. I swung it around above my head and watched the diamond chips sparkle in the morning sun.

I had been expecting money for my birthday. As usual. Like Evan got. Like we always got from Grandpa. Lia said he had combed through Grandma's stuff and chosen the ring himself. He was crushed that I didn't act excited about his present. But I was still mad at Grandma for dying, leaving Grandpa sad, leaving him to rattle around that big house by himself. I didn't want her ring, but I took it out on him. I acted like a jerk. And I hated myself for that.

I wrung the picture of Grandpa's crestfallen face out of my mind. I would just have to make it up to him when I saw him next. Have a do-over. It would be the motivation to get me home.

Clear blue sky towered above me, and little red birds twittered and chirped in the gnarled tree twisting down the slope from where I lay. The tiny feathered things hopped from branch to branch singing their song for me, unaware I was a fifteen-year-old freak of nature, not of their world. They might flap away, frightened and in a hurry, if they only knew.

Vibrations from the ground rattled through my shoulders and back. Galloping horse hooves brought me back to the bright Monte Cristo morning. I sat up and saw a lone rider hurtle up the road. Jumping to my feet, I stuffed the ring back inside my dress.

A horse came to an abrupt dusty stop and its rider hopped from the saddle. He caught me around the waist, the smell of horses and leather lifting off his shirt. And just like that, Tor Loken had his arms around me.

"How grand to find you in your flower nest."

I knocked his hands away and took a step back. "What are you doing?"

"You needn't worry. I saw the red carriage pass by just now. Your mother is away from the house and your father is at work. There is no one spying across the landscape, looking for you in our hiding spot."

"What?"

He frowned. "Have you forgotten our sworn secret?"

I exhaled—*Tor and Emma.* "No, I . . . bumped my head a

week ago, and I'm . . . still recovering." I brushed my hair away to show him the stitches.

He took my hand and tugged me back. He pressed his lips to my forehead. "Is that better?" My breath caught. He was staring at my mouth. He wanted to kiss me. I pushed closer, my body buzzing as he ran kisses from my cheek to my lips. His skin smelled like sunshine. My heart swelled and landed with an excruciating thud in my throat. He slid his arms around my back, and with his possessive hands he pulled me tight against his body. I'd never been this close to anyone. But my body knew what to do. I raised my arms up around him and pressed my frantic heart close to his. I let him kiss me. Deeply. I let his tongue play with mine. He tasted like honey.

He thought I was Emma.

I broke away before I burst, stabs of heat gushing in quick beats through my body, air not quite making it into my lungs.

When my eyes slid back to him, he devoured my face with his fern-colored eyes. They crinkled along with the sides of his mouth from the enormous smile he rained down on me. I hugged my arms around myself. It was like I had known him forever.

"The rest of the crew will be here soon. Your father wants the barn project finished by October, before the weather turns. I will see you every day until then, even if it's through a window."

His face, so like the one I had left behind, was etched with love and desire and care for the person standing in front of him. Tor was a friend to Emma, so he was a friend to me. I took my chance, pushing through my shyness, and blurted out my troubles.

"I have to talk to you about something. The lunch yesterday at the hotel? They're sending me to a boarding school in Baltimore this Sunday. John . . . my father . . . took me there to tell me. The plan is for me to never come back here. They want me to find a husband and stay forever."

Tor paced to his horse and back to me. And then back to his horse and back again. He kicked at a flower. He looked like he was going to explode. "No!"

"I know. I won't go. I'll run away before I get on a train to Baltimore."

"I want to marry you *now*. I can't wait any longer. This is torment, Emma."

Marry? Their romance was more than just a fling. Tor and Emma were secretly engaged.

A funnel of dirt and thunder churned up the road. A large wagon carted by a team of four horses barreled toward us. Tor caught the reins, before his red horse skittered away. "I must think hard on this, and now the crew has arrived. Your father plans on meeting me here at ten o'clock and he mustn't see me with you."

"Tor, wait. I want you to go with me tonight to see Simeon. Maxwell and I—"

"Simeon the recluse?"

"Say you'll go with me. I'm in a desperate situation. I'll explain then."

Dust from the wagon's wheels curled around us as it passed in the road. Gravel shot out and fell at our feet. Men's voices called out to Tor.

He yelled over the noise. "Yes, of course. I would follow you to the moon if asked."

"Talk to Maxwell when he comes back later today. He's making a plan."

"You're confusing me . . ."

"Trust me."

I glided on air through the brilliant wildflowers toward the house, still with the feel of his mouth on mine. I licked my lips and tasted honey. My first kiss. With a guy from 1895. Who looked just like someone I had been wishing, more than anything, would kiss me a week before.

You couldn't make this up.

Suddenly starving and craving something yummy, I headed to the kitchen and Cook's warm cinnamon rolls. I would sneak one upstairs into Emma's room and eat it there. Alone, I would think about what just happened, replay it again and again in my mind until it made sense.

And I didn't want to see John when he came home. I didn't want to see him, and I didn't want to talk to him. He let himself be pushed around by that woman. He had gone along with Thorn's unholy plan.

"I'M going with you," Kerry whispered. "You shan't travel to Simeon unescorted. I'll not allow you to spend the night alone with three men."

"I'm a very modern girl," I whispered back. "I can handle myself. Anyway, if you get caught, you'll lose your job, and how do you think that would make me feel?"

"You may be a modern girl, but you'll be riding through

an old-fashioned forest with old-fashioned men. And I'll not lose my job if caught. A thrashing is all it will be. 'Tis my luck—no one in Monte Cristo is good enough to replace me. Even she knows that."

In the distance, the grandfather clock bonged eleven times. Kerry had taken off her apron and carried a long wool coat and my jeans that I had asked her to bring me. She was going to be stubborn. And I was anxious to go.

"Okay, you win. No problem, Kerry." I took the jeans out of her hands and drew them up under my dress. They hugged me tight, a familiar feeling of home. I put on Emma's warmest shoes and wrapped myself in her long wool coat.

We snuck out the front door and climbed through the meadow. Maxwell and Tor waited behind the new barn construction on the bank of a curvy river. Tor tried to put me on his horse as if I was a lady, but I threw my leg over its back and straddled it. I smiled down from my perch, jeans-covered legs hanging out from under my dress. "Am I still confusing you?"

He rubbed his palm across my knee and down to my ankle as if confirming what his eyes saw. "What is this you're wearing? And where did your fear of horses go?" He jumped up snug to my back and put his arms around me.

Maxwell, with Kerry sitting sidesaddle, led the way through the moonlight. Riding along the edge of the clearcut meadow, we forged across the shallow river. Our horses threaded carefully through trees and waded into dense timberland. We found ourselves on a narrow horse-width trail heading up a steep incline. The sheer rocky face of the mountain plunged to another, more violent river, below. Wild, thundering water swirled and crashed against boulders and boomed up to us as we hung on above the sharp peaked forest.

The cliff turned into the top of a mountain. And the top of the mountain turned into clear, thin sky. We rode with the moon and the stars at our side. I breathed in the cold air, white clouds coiling back out, and snuggled closer into Tor's arms.

The smell of smoke and a barking dog welcomed us as we entered a valley. A log cabin, lit by moonlight, emerged out of the shadows. It sat in a clearing and backed up to a bend of evergreens. Light flickered in a window.

Maxwell whistled and called to the dog. "Kani!" He opened the cabin door to the smell of coffee and pungent chunks of fir burning in a stone-faced fireplace. A powerful man with long, white hair coursing over wide shoulders turned to me. His face was as creased and tan as a golden raisin.

"Sonnet."

I walked to him and he held my hands in his. "Thank you for letting me come, Mister de la Croix."

A white film lay across his eyes. So I took his big hands and ran them over my face. He stroked his gentle fingers against the lump of stitches on my forehead, and rubbed my hands as if he could hear them speak.

The crackling firewood and the steady purr of a small black cat warming itself on a rocking chair were the only sounds. He motioned his visitors to sit at a human-sized hobbit table, a polished slice of log for its top, thick, trimmed branches for its legs. A rustic sideboard held tin plates, cups, and pots and pans. Maxwell passed cups around and poured steaming coffee from a kettle hanging from a hook pounded into the wall of the fireplace.

"Grandfather, four of us have come tonight. Besides Sonnet, Tor and Kerry are here as well," said Maxwell. He turned to us. "And this is my grandfather, Simeon, Tyee of the Mountain People."

Simeon smiled at Maxwell's voice. "Chief, yes, long ago. Alas, not many people . . ."

"Why is he calling you 'Sonnet?'" Tor pulled his eyes from Simeon and stared at me, hurt and confused, as if he were the only one not in on the joke. As if he had an inkling of the trouble ahead.

"Please just listen, Tor," I said. "I'm sorry I couldn't tell you. Kerry is the only one here who knows the whole story."

I focused on Simeon as if he could see me and spoke about everything that had happened since the day my brother, sister, cousins, friend, and I had entered, through an unlocked door, an abandoned house in Monte Cristo. I told them about the closet, my gashed forehead and two-day delirium, and my "mother's" mistreatment of me.

And then I talked about my real life. My diplomat dad and British-born mom. My family's nomadic existence living around the world and our visits to Seattle every summer. I spoke about my grandfather who loved to cook and sing and make home-brewed root beer. I told them about me, Sonnet McKay, born in the year 2000, lover of books and horses and world civilization. Budding scientist, hopeful journalist, and wicked softball pitcher.

Tor sat, stunned, as if he had just been hit over the head with the blackened frying pan that sat on Simeon's sideboard. He had listened, he had frowned, his face sliding through the first three stages of grief—denial, anger, bargaining. He looked to be descending into the fourth. Depression. And the fifth, acceptance, wasn't even on the horizon. He shook his head, belief not in the realm of possibility.

"You say your name is Sonnet McKay? You live in Africa and you are from the year 2015? These things you describe, you ask me to believe? This is lunacy, Emma. You have been acting differently of late, yes, but this is utter madness. Your words are frightening, intolerable."

"The reason she has been acting differently is because she is different," said Kerry. "This girl sitting here in front of us is Sonnet, Tor. Ponder it, if you must, and then believe her—she is not Emma. But if Sonnet can find her way back to her time, it seems possible that Emma will return to us."

"It be the truth, boy. Your Emma will be back when Sonnet leaves this time and place," said Simeon.

"How will that happen, Simeon? And when? What can I do? I'm so confused. I'm feeling frantic about my situation now that I know they want to put me on a train to Baltimore. I don't understand much of anything. But I know I need to stay in Monte Cristo. I can feel it. If I leave, I won't go back. Ever."

Simeon nodded. "You listen to that voice inside you, Sonnet. If it is whispering to stay in Monte Cristo, then stay you must."

He tapped the table with his fingers and stood to reach for a piece of crystal on the fireplace mantle, clear white streaked in bands of purple, radiant from the dancing fire. He sat again, turning it in his hands. "I found this high in these mountains when I was just a lad of eight—many, many years ago, when not a soul lived in these parts but native people. I hiked with my mother that day. My rootless father had left us alone by then, never to return."

He sighed, running somewhere far beyond us with his thoughts. Somewhere years and years ago. After a minute, he joined us again.

"I took this rock before me and saw tales that spoke of unseen dreams. Even now with these blind eyes, I set it into these old hands, and my mind foretells of living. Of dying. Of life to be in the future and life once lived in the past. The understanding is not under my control. What is told to me resonates from the mountains and the water and the sky. It was meant to be that I found it. Over seventy years ago, by now."

He raised his head to me. "I saw you seven nights ago, Sonnet. I saw your fair, freckled face, your fiery hair, and your green-and-gold eyes. I saw the magical storm you came by, and I see a magical storm you must leave by. The same storm. Hear me now. You and Emma must not be together in the same place. As you leave, she must come. As she comes, you must leave. This is the law of the spirits, of the great universe, and time-and-time."

He paused, running across the translucent object with his thumbs. "I now see that you have come for a purpose. A purpose that will show itself in the future. A purpose that will affect lives. I have seen this tonight."

"I thought this was just a huge mistake me being here. A terrible, awful accident."

"There are no mistakes," said Maxwell.

His grandfather nodded toward Maxwell's voice. "There are no mistakes—my grandson speaks the truth. I cannot see when you return, or where you go in Monte Cristo to find your way home. I cannot see the reason for your visit to our time. But I know now there is a reason and you must leave by the same storm that brought you to us. I am sorry, child. You want more than I can give you. But even the hot Chinook wind knows not which way it will blow, and there is no need to push the mighty river—it flows by itself. You must find the truth of these words in your heart and believe. Believe you will find your path home when the time comes."

I wanted him to give me something more. Something real I could hang on to.

Simeon smiled and nodded, as if he heard my thoughts. "Faith does not make things easy, Sonnet. Faith makes things possible."

Out the window, the dark night sky had a sliver of brightness on its edge. The dying logs sizzled, and the black cat reared and stretched and jumped from the chair. Simeon's chin dropped to his chest, and his old eyes closed, his long white hair hanging down to his waist. Maxwell unwound the icy crystal from his gnarled fingers and placed it back on the mantle. He held his grandfather's long arms and gently steered him to bed.

Tor stood and took my hand. He led me out to his horse and put his hands together to give me a leg up. I flung myself over the horse's back, straddling it, jeans-clad legs hitched in tight against its warm sides. Tor climbed up behind me and put his arms around my waist, holding me close. He put his chin on my shoulder and murmured into my hair. "I promise I'll believe the words I have heard tonight. Just not this night. I need time."

———

CHAPTER FOURTEEN

Emma
2015

$\mathcal{E}$ mma counted and stacked bills on top of each other and piled the coins that spilled across the coffee table. Most of the money came from what remained of Evan's birthday gift from his grandpa. The rest, babysitting money from Lia, and lawn mowing money from Rapp, completed their loot. The other members of Team Switch were penniless. Even with a discount, seeing a psychic would cost close to seventy-five dollars.

Niki lifted her face to the ceiling as Rapp's uncle ambled around in the kitchen above their heads. "It's time to bring him in."

"Will he believe us, Rapp? He won't freak out, right?" asked Jules.

"No, he won't freak out, except that we didn't talk to him sooner." Rapp thumped up the wooden stairs. Muffled voices reached down to them for ten long minutes and then two sets of footsteps pounded back downstairs.

Jack Loken dropped onto the couch between Niki and

Jules. Thick dark hair, woven with gray, fanned out down his back from a leather tie at the base of his neck, and a tiny gold hoop glinted from his ear. "Which one of you is Emma?"

She stood up. "It is I, sir."

Evan handed him the photo. "We're pretty sure that's Sonnet. My sister."

Rapp's uncle scanned back and forth from the photo to Emma like Professor Kapoor before him. "I remember you. You were the one who slept all the way home from the Monte Cristo picnic in the back of my van. Well, Emma, you've journeyed a long way to us here in Seattle. No wonder you were conked out."

He glanced around at the rest of them, weighing their comprehension and commitment. "Do you guys understand how critical this is?"

"Oh yeah, we understand it," said Evan.

"I just called a good friend of mine. She's a world-renowned intuitive psychic who just happens to live on Vashon Island. She'll see you this afternoon. We can make the one o'clock Fauntleroy Ferry if we leave now. And bring something of Sonnet's that hasn't been worn by Emma . . . like a sweatshirt or sweater."

"World-renowned? She sounds expensive, Mister Loken." Niki nodded at the pile of money. "Sixty-one dollars and some change is all we have."

"Keko is gratis. She gets how critical this is, too. And you can all call me Uncle Jack. I'm not much of a 'mister'—" He turned to Emma. "And definitely not a 'sir.'"

"You are a noble man to come to my assistance, Uncle Jack," said Emma.

"There's that. But mostly I'm an out-of-school-for the-summer teacher angling for something to do," he said, winking at her. "So, let me thank you."

"IT'S a sign!" Uncle Jack could hardly contain his excitement. He bobbed and pointed, his arms wigwagging around like a windmill. Off to the side of the dipping and rolling ferry, two mammoth black fish with spots of white raced beside us through their watery kingdom. Lined up against the railing, Team Switch howled and clapped.

"Woo-hoo!" Lia twirled Emma around in a circle. "Having an orca whale follow us is good luck. Having *two* orcas follow is double luck. Our mission is now stamped in the heavens."

Tar-dripped wooden piers grew larger. A blast of horn sent seagulls crying and flapping in a circle above their heads. The black-and-white twins ducked under the waves and disappeared into the dark waters of Puget Sound.

Team Switch ran down the narrow metal staircase to the rows of cars as blustery gusts turned their hair into whirlwinds. They folded back into the white van, one after the other. Uncle Jack steered off the ferry onto dry land, the vehicle chugging up the incline on a two-lane road leading to the psychic's Vashon Island home.

Good luck. A sign. Emma held on tight to the mystical message.

LONG strings of turquoise and silver beads hung from Keko Kim's neck and swayed and clicked as she walked across the stone floor in bare feet to greet them. Her multi-colored orange, magenta, and black hair was piled high like a volcano on top of her head, and two gold enameled sticks pointed out from the loose knot that somehow kept the messy mound in place.

Keko smiled at Emma, but spoke to the rest of them. "You can cool your heels out on the patio and wait for us. This won't take long. I want to sit with Emma. I feel strongly that the time to be with her is right now." She caught Emma's hand and carted her away from Lia.

Lia moved with them. "I'll go with her—"

"No, it's better if it's just us." Keko made a second attempt at separating them. "Don't worry. I'll find you and let you know what we discover."

"Well . . . Okay." Lia handed over Sonnet's sweater and stood rooted to the same spot as Keko walked Emma down the corridor. Emma waved back to her as she entered a small room. Keko closed the door, invited Emma to sit on a couch, and held the sweater, shutting her eyes.

Lia had wanted to bring Sonnet's old blue sweatshirt, but Emma had insisted on the pink-and-white cardigan. For Emma, her color choice spoke of home. Her room. The color of the walls and the pretty, striped dress hanging in the wardrobe. A brass scale across time with both plates dangling at the same level. The coincidence of harmony.

Another sign, she hoped. Another good luck signal to the heavens.

⤳

KEKO called them in from the patio. "Who wants to help make lunch? We'll take it down to the beach and talk there."

"Me!" Like a red-furred cat, Evan leapt to Keko's side and wrangled a package of bread from her hands. If it had to do with food, Evan was a committed warrior.

Team Switch carried sandwiches, thin crispy potatoes, and drinks in metal cans down the sandy path. They sat with their backs against an immense piece of bleached driftwood, dried seaweed crunching at their feet. Seagulls danced in the marine wind above their heads, positioning themselves to dive for the bits of bread Rapp tossed up into the sky. They ate in silence and watched as waves swooshed against the shore.

Keko finished her sandwich and threw the last of her crust up in the air for the brazen birds. "So, I'm glad you came to me. I think I can be of help in your quest. Monte Cristo is the site where Emma and Sonnet traded places, and Monte Cristo is where you must return with Emma to send her home. I feel strongly that Sonnet is doing well and is searching hard for clues to her own return and maybe leaving clues for you. In fact, I seemed to get a double reading. Two direct streams of consciousness at the same time. One was clearly Emma's. The other, Sonnet's. As if the two people were one—split into two locations. Extremely interesting. And a first for me."

"Leaving clues? In Monte Cristo?" Jules brightened.

"Yes. I must tell you if you decide to pursue this, it'll be difficult."

Rapp sat up straight and flipped his hat sideways. "We can handle difficult. Uncle Jack, can you take us on an emergency camping trip to Monte Cristo?"

"I was just going to suggest it. It sounds like we need to get back up the mountain pronto, Keko."

"Yes, this can't wait. If Sonnet finds a way to get back while Emma is still here . . ." A look passed between them. "Well, let's just say we can't let that happen. How does tomorrow sound? I can be at your house in the late morning, Jack. We'll all ride up the mountain together."

Emma heard the tightness in their throats. She understood they were trying to give the moment a sense of levity. Calling it difficult instead of dangerous did not change the reality of her situation. Professor Kapoor had noted the danger as being "critical" and it appeared Uncle Jack and Keko knew it to be critical, too.

Together they would sit now in the sand and make a plan to return her to her world. She would steel herself for whatever came. Like the tide, mysteriously orchestrating the dark water in front of her, Emma's stretch of time in this glorious place seemed to be ebbing away.

CHAPTER FIFTEEN

—

Sonnet
1895

Tor had called me "Sonnet," and in this way, I knew he had finally come to believe the unbelievable. He was now a willing participant in our secret rendezvous, demanded by me in my mounting desperation as the hours slid closer to Sunday.

With Kerry at my side, I moved the lace curtain away from the glass and peered out as Maxwell drove the carriage away. Thorn and the boys were off to the Miller home for another Victorian-style playdate, and with Kerry feigning sickness as an excuse not to go, Tor, Maxwell, Kerry, and I had a short window of time to meet and make a plan.

Kerry looked at the clock on the nightstand. "Forty minutes until Maxwell returns."

I bounced onto Emma's bed and grabbed Kerry's wrist, pulling her down next to me. "Hey, you!"

"Hay is for horses," Kerry laughed.

"Not in my world." I giggled, feeling almost normal. How

I loved this funny girl, my lifeline to sanity. We lounged around, talking and talking, and laughed and howled, as if we were best friends, while we waited for Maxwell and Tor to join us in the barn.

WE were back at the window. Tor came down the slope and crossed the side meadow with his leather tool bag hung casually over his shoulder. We watched as he wound through the boys' abandoned toys and ducked through the barn's big opening to join Maxwell, who had clattered back with the empty carriage minutes before.

Kerry left the bedroom.

I counted to sixty and then tiptoed down the staircase and out the front door. I joined my friends in a back corner of the barn behind the horse stalls. Bales of straw hid us, and hens and their yellow, fluffy babies clucked and scratched around at our feet. A cow gawked and mooed, unsure why a bunch of humans had moved in on her territory.

"Kerry heard them talking," I whispered, as soon as I felt sure we were alone. "John is going to take me for the long carriage ride to Everett, without the rest of the family. We're leaving Monte Cristo Sunday morning and will stay the night at a hotel. The train leaves Everett Station Monday at noon."

"The Ice Caves Fair starts Friday night and continues through Sunday," said Tor. "If nothing else, the Sweetwine family will go on Saturday. That will be the big day. You can't come back to the house that evening. We'll have to make you disappear from the fair."

"She surely must be in disguise," said Kerry, running her

eyes over my hair and down my fancy lace and linen dress. "Everyone in town knows Emma."

Like Kerry, Maxwell checked me out from my head to my toes. "Would you be opposed to wearing men's clothing?"

"I would give anything to take off this dress and put on men's clothes."

"I have an idea then."

We stood close in the hay and came up with a plan. A simple plan we could pull off. With a grateful sigh, I felt the dark cloud lift off my shoulders.

I smiled at Kerry and Maxwell and took a big breath. "I have one more request. When it's just us, will you please call me Sonnet like Tor does? You are my friends, my only family here. I don't think of you as anything less."

I watched a look pass between them. Years of servitude, raising its ugly head.

Kerry finally spoke. "Calling one's superior by their first name is not done here. Whether Emma or Sonnet, your station is above ours."

"Have I just been a placeholder for Emma then? After all this time of knowing who I really am? We just hung out, Kerry! That's all I want. You have to understand. Where I come from, we would all be friends. We would all be family. There would be no reason for us not to be. That's my world."

"But not their world. You make this awkward for them," said Tor.

"I'm not Emma, and this isn't my house, and they're not my servants. This is something I want, Tor, from the bottom of my heart. I need family right now. Not hired help."

How could I make them understand? How could I explain

how important this was to me? "In my art class last year, we studied painters. My favorite was one called Hopper. Our teacher talked about how his work portrayed loneliness. I remember really liking his paintings but not understanding them. As hard as I tried, I couldn't conjure up the lonely feelings for Hopper's work like some of my classmates did. But I understand now. I understand loneliness. I really don't know what I would have done, trapped here in this house with that woman, without you, Kerry."

I turned to Maxwell. "And if—when—Emma comes back, she'll have known another way to live, and she'll need your help and friendship, too. You can be her secret family. Like I'm asking you to be mine. I don't want to be your 'miss' anymore. Please. Call me Sonnet."

Maxwell shoved his hands in his pockets and dropped his head to the little chicks pecking around his boots. He watched the mother hen chase after them for a moment, his always-sunny face gradually streaked in waves of grief. "I might understand this Hopper's paintings. I have ached for my parents for as long as I can remember. Even with all of Grandfather's devotion, I have had a lonely hole in my heart, a place as sad as the roiling river that took them away. In all honesty, Kerry might understand being left alone, too."

"Yes, I understand loneliness, certainly."

"Then let me be Sonnet when no one can hear."

Kerry slowly nodded. "Family. Being together and speaking on any topic without fear, as we have already done. Connecting without formality. It signifies how we feel about each other, not our stations, correct? As if you were my wee sister from Ireland, come to visit."

"Yes, all of that. Right! You're totally getting it."

"I haven't forgotten your blackberry-stained hands and face the first time we met in the forest," said Maxwell. "I think you ate as many berries that day as found their way into your tin pail. You will be my sister, Sonnet, lover of blackberries. Just as I am fond of them, a sister might be as well. If I had a sister."

I laughed, my heart almost bursting in my chest. They had given me a family and made this the best day of my life. "I am sister, then, to you both. This means everything to me. Thank you."

Tor took my hand and lifted it to his mouth. He kissed it. "Our Sonnet, then. Our family. You are very persuasive."

We parted ways one by one and snuck back out of the barn, back to the business of the day. I was the last to leave. I stayed in the shadows for a moment longer, my heart still big, and watched Tor stride up the hill, away from me, back to his construction site.

The domino ring felt smooth between my fingers as I made my way up the grand staircase to my gilded cage. I raised it to my nose, imagining the smell of home. Taking a chance, I would wear it for just a little while today. Put it on my finger where I could see it. A treat.

I peeled off my layers of clothes, able to finally breathe in just Emma's chemise and knickers. I reached between the mattresses and wriggled out my leather and silver bracelet and put that on, too.

Settling down on the brass bed, I crossed my arms above my heart and stared at the spot on my hand where Tor had just kissed it. The pink-and-white bedroom would be Emma's again as soon as we found a way to switch places. Unless she got shipped off to Baltimore, she would live in it, sneaking around and seeing her boyfriend when she could. The promise of a life with Tor would be the only thing that would keep her sane in this house with her crazy mother. I was happy she would have that. I couldn't be jealous. I couldn't want to go back and want to have him, too.

I just couldn't.

And, anyway, he was hers.

Stuck here until I found my way home, I would be a wee blackberry sister come to visit. Nothing else.

A sigh swept out of me from somewhere I didn't know existed. Out-of-kilter real life was hard. Emma's leather-bound copy of *Little Women* sat on the bedside table where I'd put it earlier. I would lose myself in something imaginary.

I turned to page 102, where I'd left off earlier that morning. Things were just starting to get good. Skating furiously down the frozen river after Jo and Laurie, Amy had fallen through the ice. . . .

CHAPTER SIXTEEN

—

Emma
2015

Uncle Vince frowned at Emma as he flicked egg shells into the kitchen sink. He was leaning against the counter, as seemed to be the dining habit of the entire household, eating hardboiled eggs and gulping coffee before he left for his prominent position at a big Seattle company that sold books and other things.

"I thought you didn't really like Monte Cristo, Sonnet. Why this sudden interest to go back up the mountain and camp?" He turned to Lia. "I wanted to take you all to Water Waves Park tomorrow after work. I thought that might be fun in this heat."

"It turns out Sonnet actually loves Monte Cristo, Dad. And the river is so fun to swim in, we thought we'd beat the heat that way. Right, Sonnet?"

"Yeah, I love swimming in the river, Uncle Vince."

"We might find gold, Dad." Lia graced her father with a beguiling smile.

Aunt Kate wiped at a few bits of wayward shells and toast

crumbs and then hopped up on the counter as if she were the same age as her daughters. If Emma ever caught her mother doing that in their kitchen, she would surely sink to the ground with a fatal heart attack. But being as it was Aunt Kate, Emma found she only adored her more.

"Why don't you guys wait until Friday when we can all go?" Aunt Kate asked, swinging her bare legs. She put a piece of jam-smeared toast into her mouth.

"Rapp's uncle wants to go today," said Lia. "He's bringing his friend Keko Kim from Vashon Island. Today works best for her."

Uncle Vince turned on a spray of water and whooshed egg shells into the drainer. "You need to be careful and have an adult with you every time you swim in that river. Things happen out in nature to city kids when they aren't paying attention. Understood? And I want phone calls from you and Niki twice a day, morning and night." He shouted behind him. "Did you hear that, Niki? I know you're listening!"

Niki shouted back, "Yo, Dad! Loud and clear!"

"Tell Jack to call me before you take off, Lia. I want to make sure this isn't something you've forced that nice man to do."

"Thank you." Emma put her arms around Uncle Vince and kissed him on the cheek. She turned to Aunt Kate and took her jam-sticky hands. "I love you dearly . . ."

"C'mon, Sonnet. We don't have all day." Lia seized Emma's arm and towed her through the house and out the front door.

Lia and Emma, with Niki, Jules, and Evan, walked up the street to Uncle Jack's house lugging sleeping bags and backpacks full of clothing. Keko arrived, tooting her horn. Uncle

Jack jumped down from the top of the van where he had been packing the tent and supplies into a big box.

"Seven bags of groceries, Keko? We'll have enough food for weeks. No one will go hungry on this camping trip," said Uncle Jack.

"Seven bags may only last a couple days. Your visit to Vashon reminded me teenagers are hungry beings after all that food disappeared from my kitchen in less than an hour yesterday."

Lia nudged Emma away from Uncle Jack's and Keko's banter and moved to the shade of an old crabapple tree.

"Sorry, I didn't mean to jerk your arm off, but I had to get you outta the house. I thought you were going to start sobbing and drooling over Mom again. And that would've been a disaster."

"I *was* going to cry. You were right to take me away. Sever me quickly from Aunt Kate's loving arms."

Lia sighed. "I would share my mom with you forever if I could. You know that, right?"

"I know you would. You are the best friend anyone could ever have."

"Now *I'm* gonna start crying."

Emma laughed and shoved at Lia's shoulder like she had seen her friends do to each other. Lia giggled and shoved her back. Emma was learning how to take her share of playfulness and joy. Just as the scarecrow in the Oz movie needed straw to be whole, when the straw fell out, or when it caught on fire, his friends would stuff him full again. Just like Lia's pokes and jokes with her.

∽

THE packed van careened into the camping area next to the river in the afternoon. They found a flat, grassy area and pitched a tent.

"Is there enough room in here for everyone?" Jules had stacked her belongings in a corner next to Emma's sack of clothes.

"Rapp and Evan can sleep outside under the stars and be on the lookout for bears. Or if they're pansies like me, hunker down in the van. The girls can have the tent—there's so many of them," said Uncle Jack, inhaling the woodsy air and stretching his arms over his head, happy and in his element. "Perfect. Negative ions. Just what we all need to keep us steady and focused on our plan."

Evan and Niki set up chairs around a large fire pit and sat down. Niki extended her tennis shoe to the edge of the bricks and flicked off a piece of old charcoal with her toe. "Where did Keko go? She needs to wear a bright orange hunting vest so we can keep track of her."

"Here!" Keko stood still in a swath of ferns beside an enormous tree. She stared off into the universe, her army-green tunic melding with the landscape. "My, my. I'm picking up sensations from days gone by. The vibes I'm getting are literally out of this world. I'm so glad I came. This should be good."

"Please tell us," said Emma.

"I certainly will. There were many people here at one time when the town was booming, and then hardly anyone after the mining operations shut down and everyone moved away. So, there is no interference, no confusion for me to have to override like there would be in a big city with continuous civilization. Just a clear path to a specific time and place when you lived here in the late eighteen hundreds. This is good. Do you understand?"

Emma turned to the dimming sky, seeing things in front of her only she could see. The giant cedar trees swayed and groaned in the wind and the nearby river gurgled and rolled against rocks. A sharp green odor hung in the air. It smelled and sounded and looked like home. It was her home. "Yes, I understand. I only wish you could hear their voices distinctly and tell me what they are saying. I would like to know if they miss me."

"You're just homesick, Emma," said Niki.

"Yes, I am sick for my loved ones. My brothers. My . . ." She sighed. "Being here makes me melancholy. This was the place of my life, as unrecognizable as it is now."

"Well, I know what cheers me up." Evan opened the cooler and prodded around. "Are we gonna have fire-toasted hot dogs for dinner? I can get everything started. Someone start finding some good, sharp sticks and firewood."

Keko joined Evan and dug through her grocery bags. "Let's see. Graham crackers, marshmallows, and chocolate bars. S'mores later around the campfire, anyone?" She held up the packages as if they were important prizes as Team Switch screamed out in delight.

"Oh, man, Emma," said Evan. "Just wait until you try the best camping dessert in the world—you'll never want to go back."

Emma wandered over to Evan's side. "Let me help, Evan. Please, give me something to do. Being with you can only make me happy."

"Sure, Emma. If helping me makes you happy, let's do this thing." Evan handed her bags of lightweight utensils and plates. "Set this up on that table over there. Niki, can you help? Maybe try to wipe off the table first. Here's the buns and mustard and stuff."

Lia and Jules and Keko found pieces of dry wood and sticks lying around under the trees and built a fire. Uncle Jack sat back in a chair with his guitar and began playing a tune from back in his day, while Rapp took a harmonica from his bag and set up next to his uncle, keeping time with his foot. Soon, everyone was humming along and singing a few words of the chorus.

Snappy happy, happy snappy . . .

They worked their different tasks together as well-oiled cogs—unique parts running smoothly toward a collective goal. All individual impulses were set aside, and guitar and harmonica music, and vibrations spilling from their lungs, wound through their hands and through their hearts, binding them and giving them purpose.

Even Emma, who had never heard music like this before, knew the universal melody and hummed with all her might. After all, the goal was to get her home.

Dusk settled in, and soon it would be pitch black, no city brightness to beam light up into the night sky. The music and camaraderie had soothed Emma, and everyone had taken notice. Snappy happy, they decided to kick back, sing songs, and eat their fire-cooked camp food.

They would wait until daybreak to hike up to Emma's house.

CHAPTER SEVENTEEN

———

Sonnet
1895

Wafts of cooking berries and baking bread lured me by an invisible cord from Emma's bedroom down the back staircase to the sunny kitchen. Cook set a small jar of blackberry jam into a basket and slid a paper-wrapped loaf of her sourdough bread in beside the jar. Each basket came labeled with a miner's name and cabin number. There were fifteen baskets. If each basket took fifteen minutes to deliver, I would be out of the house, independent and free, for over four hours. Giddy at the thought, I stuck my finger into a lidless jar and sucked the warm goodness off.

"Now, Maxwell will take you 'round, Miss Emma. Do not dally. Your mother wants you back for your dress fittings." Cook smiled at me and brushed a straggly red hair off my face.

"If I'm supposed to be leaving in a few days, how will all those dresses be finished?"

"The ones that are complete will go with you. The others will be sent in a trunk, I suppose. That is for someone else to worry about, not you, my dear."

Jan Von Schleh

I smelled her perfume before I heard her. "There you are, Emma. Missus Love and her assistant, Goldie, will be here at three o'clock. It is imperative that you are back by then."

I slowly faced her. "Finished so that you can send me away—dear Mother?"

Thorn looked at me like I had spit on her. "Why—your impertinence—"

"It's honesty, not impertinence. The truth is you want me out of here. Gone." The words were out of my mouth before I could stop myself.

She raised her hand and tightened it around my elbow. "I do not know who you think you are to speak to me in such a manner. But I can tell you one thing, young lady. You are not the lady of the house. I am. I am your father's wife. Not you. And you will respect me as such." Her face had turned red and splotchy.

Of course, she was John's wife. Of course, I *wasn't* John's wife. Her long octopus fingers choked off the blood in my arm and her wet eyes scared me. I had sunk to her level and instantly regretted it. "Let go. Please."

Thorn dug her nails into my flesh for a second longer as she leaned in toward my ear. "Your countenance will no longer haunt me."

Someone cleared their throat.

She gazed around me to Cook, momentarily startled, as if she had forgotten she was in the kitchen. She blinked a few times, refocusing, and dropped my arm, clicking her shoes across the wood floor and out the room.

Cook, frozen, held two jars of jam in the air. Her brown eyes filled with her own tears. She whispered, "About time you took a stand. I'm glad you said it. Someone needed to. I will truly be sorry to see you leave, my girl. You have always been a sweet light in this house. And I know the little ones will be overcome with grief." A sob filled her throat. "Especially Jacob, our sensitive little man." She sniveled, tears flinging from her eyes. She set the jam down and sniffed. "She's a selfish one to send you away like this—"

Now my eyes brimmed with tears. Her usual face, as round and welcoming as a friendly Halloween pumpkin, was mottled with sadness. "You are the kindest person in this house, Cook. I'm glad they'll have you. You'll just have to learn how to push them in the swing."

"Indeed. If I can manage to walk to the swing and back with these gouty legs." She sighed and looked around at her kitchen, getting her bearings again. "Now, here is a picnic basket for you and Maxwell to share. You'll have your own jam sandwiches with a pear apiece and a bottle of lemonade."

Maxwell rapped on the screen door and trotted in, surveying the baskets of jam and bread. "I've brought a crate to carry the baskets to the . . ." He looked from me to Cook and back again. "To the carriage."

I helped him fill the crate. "I'll walk with you, Maxwell."

I stroked the horses' velvety noses. He gave me time to recover. "I provoked Emma's mother. I shouldn't have. She just made me so angry." I rubbed my arm. "And then I felt bad and then Cook felt bad for me and then I felt even worse for her. Cook trusts that I'm the person I say I am, and she deserves to know the truth. I wish I could tell her. I wish I could hug her."

"But what would the truth do but upset her?" He held the

red carriage door open for me. "Your predicament is to act shrewdly, keep your secret among your friends, and do *not* forsake our plan."

"If I was wise like you, I probably wouldn't be in this trouble to begin with."

"Oh, I've certainly been in trouble before, especially when I was not so wise."

"I find that hard to believe. You're like an adult stuck in a kid's body."

Maxwell crinkled his face and laughed. "When grandfather's father quit the tribe and left his family, the only possessions remaining from his time with the Salish were his books, a gold watch, and his young son, Simeon. Years later, Grandfather put those ancient books to good use and had me memorize them as school lessons. And because of his demanding instruction and all the trouble it caused, I can now spout the prose and poetry of Shakespeare and the philosophy of Aristotle. So, you see, wisdom comes of trouble, and only with time do you see it."

"Well, I hope I find my wisdom soon," I said. "And your spouting Shakespeare doesn't surprise me a bit. Since you're so smart, be my dictionary. What does *countenance* mean? She said when I leave she won't be haunted by my countenance."

"The way someone appears. Their face."

"Just the sight of Emma drives her crazy. Her own kid."

Maxwell flicked his eyes up at the house. "And she most probably is eavesdropping."

He pushed his red-and-gold cap up and ran over the list. "We take the first thirteen baskets and deliver them together. I'll then drop you at the cabin. You retrieve the clothing while I go deliver the last ones. Be ready for the carriage at half past two when I come back for you. Thirty minutes is all you will have."

The carriage crunched through the gravel and cut off in the same direction we had taken down to the big river the day of the picnic—the day I'd had to put up with Olive and Pearl in order to be blessed with meeting Maxwell.

The jumble of new cabins, and the humanity that lit them, were light-years from what existed in ghost town Monte Cristo, where only a few ramshackle survivors had somehow withstood more than a century of harsh mountain weather and engulfing forest. But on this sunny summer day, the area teemed with people. The mountain was alive and full and welcoming.

Maxwell and I knocked on the first cabin door. No one answered. He joggled the door open and stepped into the tiny space, leaving the basket of jam and bread on the table. We distributed the rest of the baskets the same way. Some doors were locked and some were open. I hoped the stray dogs and cats didn't get the ones we left behind on windowsills.

We stopped in a field for our picnic along the way. Maxwell asked me about my family, my life, my world. I was the professor and he was my student, and as the sun beat down on us, and bees buzzed around the wildflowers, I lectured my curious new brother, who was impatient to pick every last factoid out of my brain.

Wound up in my happy memories of home, my audience of one was enthralled by my stories. He questioned, he probed. He inhaled information along with the mountain air. I could have laid around that meadow, gabbing with him the entire day.

⌒

WE had no blackberry jam for the inhabitant of the four-teenth cabin, but I did save my pear for him. Tor flung open his door and jogged to the carriage. He helped me out, nod-ding at Maxwell, who turned the carriage around and left to take care of the last two deliveries.

Tor held my hand, his eyes never leaving my face, and walked me through his door. He took me in his arms and held me to him. I pushed my body up close, as close as I could in my layers of clothes, next to his thumping heart. I breathed him in . . . sunshine and horses and the fir-scented wind off the mountain. He kissed me. And this time he knew who I was.

I unwound myself from his arms and moved to the middle of the room, setting the pear on his little table. A blue-and-white enamel pot sat on top of a small pot-bellied stove. I could smell the cold coffee grounds inside it, and his ragged breathing was all around me. I stared at two red wool blan-kets folded neatly on the end of a narrow bed. . . .

"I can't fight against it," Tor finally said.

"I know, I know," I whispered. I glanced back at him. Those eyes of his deserved a long paragraph, a page, an entire story. They devoured every inch of me. Hyperaware of being alone with him, everything I had been trying hard not to dream of was here, and I didn't trust myself. My body made me afraid of what might happen if he ripped me from the pot-bellied stove and up against him again.

I turned back to the blankets. The wool was as thick as winter socks, and the loops were uneven and nubby. Slate-colored threads, barely visible, were scattered throughout the red. I had never seen a blanket as clearly. "It's so confusing. Maxwell and Simeon said there are no mistakes. So why are we here together in Monte Cristo?"

"Perhaps it has nothing to do with us. Or perhaps it is beyond understanding, and we will never know."

He waited until I looked at him again. His fists scrunched and then opened at his sides, hanging. He swallowed hard, as if he had something big caught in his throat. "Sonnet, if Emma does not return . . ."

"I have to go back to my life, Tor."

"If you stay and she does not come back . . ."

"Emma will come back. She has to."

"Please, listen to me. If you stay here and she stays there. Reassure me . . ."

I smiled. "My family would be horrified to think I would marry so young. It isn't done where I come from. Girls, if they get married at all, don't get married until they're older. Girls get to have a life, too. I want to go to college, Tor. I want to have a life."

"How old must you be to take me as a husband? I'll wait. My parents would have been pleased if I married someone like you."

I laughed. "How about twenty-five? Ten years from now."

He crossed the room and took my hands in his, laughing, too. "Ten years will never do. How about when you are nineteen? Four years from now. I'll be an old man of twenty-two by then."

"Is this some kind of barter? Okay. If Emma doesn't come

back and I stay, I'll marry you. I just can't promise when. How's that?"

"It is sun rising on a dark and desperate life."

"What does that mean?"

The light had gone out of his eyes. "Aloneness is dark. Dark and desolate."

His parents *would have* been pleased if he married someone like me. "Where's your family . . .?"

"They were taken from me in a house fire when I was but fourteen. My mother and father and two young sisters." He unbuttoned his shirt, bringing it down over his shoulders. Shiny white scars twisted over his chest and neck and ran down his back.

"I tried to save them . . . but being just a boy, the fire was too hot. I hadn't the strength." He rolled up his sleeves and held out the backs of his hands and arms. The hair grew in patches here and there where the fire had leapt across his skin. "I left my country after that and came to America. I really do understand how alone feels."

I ran my palm across the smooth welts on his chest and found it hard to breathe. He had watched his family die. It was unbearable.

Kerry's lonely trip across the ocean to find work, Maxwell's sad roiling river that took his parents away, and now Tor's fire of death burrowed ribbons of sorrow into my heart. My problems were nothing in comparison to theirs. He stroked my wet cheeks, at tears I didn't know were there.

"What were their names?" I whispered.

"My mother was Elin. My father, Peder, and my sisters, Inge and Ensi." The corners of his mouth turned up. He wanted me to know it was okay. "I so rarely utter their names out loud. Thank you, Sonnet, for asking. This way they stay alive in my heart."

I remembered my picnic with Maxwell earlier, and talking about my family. I knew exactly what he meant.

I closed my eyes and thought of tiny, female versions of Tor. Inge and Ensi. They must have been beautiful. I didn't ask their ages. I couldn't take it. Instead, I held his scarred hands in both of mine and put them to my heart. More than anything I had ever wanted, I wished to make up for his pain.

"You aren't without family. I have something to tell you. Something strange and wonderful. You'll like it, and if your parents were alive they'd like it too. I know your descendant, your family. His name is Rapp Loken—*Loken* just like you, Tor. He's almost a copy of you except his hair is darker. It's an amazing coincidence. That's why I thought I knew you at the hotel. Remember how I stared?"

He nodded. "Is he your sweetheart?"

"No." I smiled at the old-fashioned term. "I met him the night before I traveled here. My twin brother, Evan, and I had a birthday party at my aunt's and uncle's place. He heard the noise as he walked by the house and just showed up—his uncle lives down the street and he's staying with him for the summer. Anyway, my brother liked Rapp so much, and was so tired of always being the only boy, he invited him and his uncle on our picnic the next day. Rapp's face was the last thing I saw before the closet door shut. But I've actually spent more time with you than I have with him."

Light came back to his eyes. The earth started rotating again. "Rapp. A good Swedish name for a boy who looks like me. For a boy who carries my family name. Thank you for telling me this."

"See? You'll have a wife someday and kids. You won't be alone."

He looked beyond me out the window. His face radiated heat. For her.

"You love her." I reached up and touched a lock of curly hair, smoothing it straight between my fingers. I let go and it bounced back into place.

"Yes, I love her. And you are so like her." He smoothed my face with the side of his rough finger, as we listened to clattering hooves and the creak of carriage wheels.

He moved away from me and put his arm out the window, waving at Maxwell.

"I have what you came for and I must get back to the barn project." Tor handed me a leather bag. "The smallest clothes I could find are in there along with the hammer and nails."

"It'll be good to put on a pair of jeans again and keep them on, even if they are too big. Girls don't wear big dresses like this where I come from. Just short stretchy dresses with bare legs."

"The things you tell me about your world I find hard to imagine."

"If you manage to live long enough, you'll see some of it for yourself someday."

Our eyes met and held each other's with the miracle of our circumstances. Tor pulled me to him again and we kissed as if he was mine and I was his. As if it was okay.

He took my hand and walked me to the carriage.

Thirty minutes.

I had laughed and I had cried. I had turned down a marriage proposal and then accepted another on my terms. My new friend's childhood agonies had entered me fully and completely, granted in by my own permission.

Thirty minutes. The time it took to walk through Tor's door as one person and leave as someone else.

The soft leather seat formed around me like a warm body snugged up tight. I let the carriage rock me back and forth against it as the scenes out the window rolled past without my seeing them. Dull and super-alive were all mixed up inside me, and mysteries and secrets peeked from the mountaintop just beyond my reach. I ran my hands up my arms and felt Tor's fire dance across my skin. I put my hands to my face and breathed in hard, pulling him deep inside me.

"LET me draw this on over your head, Miss Emma. I used your blue linen dress as a pattern because that one seemed to fit you best. You have filled out over the summer, my dear, but children your age do, now, do they not?"

We were in Emma's bedroom in front of the large oval mirror. The seamstress and her assistant had laid out a pile of dresses in different stages of completeness and a variety of fabrics. I held a sumptuous, half-finished, red velvet dress out in front of me. I put it to my face and inhaled the new material smell, dragging the smoothness across my cheeks. "Pretty fancy, Missus Love. This one is obviously not for the classroom."

She nodded at the blue cotton dresses and navy aprons.

"Those two there will be for the classroom, miss. The velvet, silk, satin, and Belgian linen are for out and about. The better to catch the eye of a potential husband. Baltimore will be a fancy place with lots of young men spying for a rich, young lady like you. You must take better care of yourself and remember you will be in a big, important city, not a small mountain town. Your hair must be coiffed in the latest style, and you must remember to apply rouge."

Goldie giggled. I sent her a wink. "No husband for me. Not for many years—"

"Missus Love!"

Thorn stood hard in the doorway. My hand flew against my throat and covered the ring hanging above the unbuttoned dress. I dropped my attention to Missus Love's grayish streaked bun and let my hair fall over my neck and shoulders as she knelt at my waist, plucking pins out of a little cushion wrapped around her wrist.

"I could hear the two of you prattling on from downstairs. There is a job to be done and we are pressed for time. What is it that you do not understand about this dire situation, Missus Love? Emma is leaving on Sunday and her wardrobe must be ready."

"Madam Sweetwine. I have been sewing and talking at the same time for over thirty years—" Missus Love continued to pin material around my sleeve. "And my dresses are the finest. Why, I even have customers as far away as Sedro Woolley. Are you disparaging my work?"

"No, of course not, I—"

"Good. Then please let me get on with the job you have tasked me with. These will get done as the others have always been, in more than an acceptable manner and on time. You know my work."

Thorn went quiet except for the tap of her shoe. I braced for a sudden slap across Missus Love's face.

"I will take you at your word," Thorn finally said, backing away from the seamstress and leaving the room.

Goldie waited a minute and then shut the door.

"You're sure brave," I said.

"I have worked with every kind of woman. Some are good and some are bad. I'm the same way with them all. I have to stand up for myself on occasion or get mowed down by the uppity ones. I have been a war widow since I was nineteen years old. I take care of myself."

"Good for you. You're ahead of your time. You are the most modern woman I know in Monte Cristo. A real career person. Earning your own way, making your own life. You inspire me."

"A seamstress and an inspirer. Did you hear that, Goldie? Me! A modern woman who earns her way? Take note, my dear Goldie."

Acting more than pleased, with a smile that stretched her cheeks into round shiny lumps, Missus Love, with Goldie by her side, fluttered around me for the next two hours, folding, draping, pinning, hemming, and fluffing.

"Now, then, I am done, young lady. I'll return on Saturday afternoon with the finished garments in time to get them all packed into your trunks. Thank you for being such an uncomplaining mannequin."

Missus Love and Goldie swept up the pile of material, patterns, half-made dresses, and a canvas sewing kit as big as a suitcase, and hauled it all out the bedroom door. They thumped and bumped down the stairs and out to the porch.

I put on a simple muslin garden dress with a large front pocket. Keeping my feet bare, I cracked the door open and listened. The silence I had counted on. The occupants of the house were busy dressing in their formal wear for dinner.

I knelt on the floor and towed the leather bag out from under the bed. I dropped the hammer and nails, and the two envelopes I had prepared earlier, into the dress pocket.

I snuck downstairs and over to the piano. Glancing around, I bent underneath it and inserted one of the envelopes between a wooden slat and a beam. I heard murmuring coming from the kitchen. Cook and Bess were talking.

The dining room was my next target. Bess hadn't turned on the gas chandelier yet. I still had a few minutes.

The top drawer in the sideboard was heavy and filled to the brim with candles, just as I knew it would be. I reached in. Heavy footsteps approached from the kitchen. I slid it shut and dove underneath the table.

Cook was whistling a mindless tune, the smell of roasting potatoes and ham following her from the kitchen. I watched her feet as she found a serving platter. Her footsteps echoed back down the hallway and into the kitchen.

Stealing back to the drawer, I piled candles on the floor. The lightened drawer was easy now to dump next to the wax mound. I took the hammer, two nails, and the second envelope from my pocket and stuck my arms into the empty space. I quickly nailed each end of the envelope to the inside frame.

I balanced the drawer back on its runners and threw the

candles in. Footsteps approached again from the kitchen. I rammed it closed and dropped the hammer into my pocket just as Cook rounded the corner.

"Have you everything you need, miss? I thought I heard banging."

"Everything's fine."

She gaped down at my bare feet and bulging dress. "Can I help you with something?"

"I . . . I just wondered what kind of cake you baked for dessert tonight. Is it . . . chocolate again?"

"No cake tonight, miss. But I did make apple cobbler."

"Even better! Thanks, Cook."

She widened her eyes at me in confusion. But I knew her well enough. She would never tell.

I ran upstairs. Kerry and I would be the only ones to know.

Shutting Emma's door, I reached between the feather mattresses, feeling around for my leather and silver bracelet. Pushing the bracelet, hammer, and leftover nails deep into the leather bag, I brought out Tor's red-and-black flannel shirt. Balling it up, I used it as a pillow as I lay down on my side across the rose-patterned rug next to the bed. I exhaled a sigh of relief and wiggled my nose into the shirt, breathing him in again . . . feeling the gentleness of him on my cheek, and held his leather bag close like a sweet little baby in my arms.

CHAPTER EIGHTEEN

Emma
2015

The morning sun lifted the mist that had gathered around their heads toward the towering treetops, as Team Switch, with Keko and Uncle Jack in tow, hiked up the steep hill, pushing through heavy branches and zigzagging over the forest carpet and around mossy logs.

At the old front porch, they stopped and gazed up at the mansion. Lonely shafts of dappled sunlight lit the weathered siding here and there, and way up on top under the rafters, bits of flaking yellow paint called to Emma across the years.

The crow was back, just as they were, flapping its sleek, blue-black wings and gazing down at them from the curve of the roof. It cocked its head and listened to their chatter.

"Your house was quite a spectacular lady," said Keko, her words loud in the hushed air.

Emma nodded. "Indeed. She was. I always imagined the house as feminine, too." She turned to the fraying gables where they raised and dipped over the once-grand home and stared at the boarded-up windows as if she expected to see someone there. "When I was younger, I called her Sylvia, because we lived in a sylvan forest," she whispered. "Is it childish to name a house? Along with my dolls, she was one of my only friends."

"Of course, it's not childish." Keko put her arm around Emma's shoulders and gave her a hug. "It's endearing, just like you."

Emma quivered out of her daydream and trod alone up the porch stairs, avoiding splinters and holes and blackberry thorns. She grasped the hand-and-ball knocker in one hand and the doorknob in the other. She thrust against the door with her shoulder. Emma stepped inside and turned to the others with a grand sweep of her arm. "Please, honored friends, welcome to my humble home."

They passed her in the doorway, hugging and kissing her one by one. The ruin would give a sane person nightmares, and Emma had called upon bravery to confront the horrific remains of a past dead life. She hoped she made them all proud.

They followed each other and gathered in the middle of the dark, cold parlor, the silent piano standing witness to their hushed strategizing.

"Are you okay, Emma?" asked Uncle Jack, with a quick pat on her back.

Emma took a deep breath and nodded. "I am." She was still getting used to so many hearts caring about her. She could do anything as long as she had these people by her side.

"So . . . we start searching for clues or a sign or something," said Lia.

"If you don't mind, I'll just wander on my own." Keko pointed to her head. "I want to focus, so please don't interrupt and keep the noise to a minimum. That'll help me."

"Whatever you want, Keko. I think I'll poke around outside," said Uncle Jack. "I hope to find some outbuildings hidden around or maybe something under the house. You never know." Evan followed him out the door.

"Let's go back up to the closet where I found the photo, Emma. You can tell me whose room it was—you know, give us some context." Rapp brought a flashlight out from his messenger bag and switched it on. "This time I can light up the space and see better. I'm pretty sure there's more."

"Don't just leave us standing here. Jules and I want to come, too," said Niki.

They hurried after Rapp to the second floor, around a corner, and up four stairs to a landing with a single door.

"So peculiar," said Emma. "Why would a family photo be hidden in my mother's bedchamber?"

Six tall rectangular windows ran across a curved wall. Niki rubbed off window grime with the side of her hand and peered outside. "This room faces out the front of the house. The covered porch is just below."

"Can someone hold the flashlight?" Rapp had dropped to his knees in the back of the closet. He handed it to Lia and pointed at where the ceiling sloped on an angle to the floor. "Right there. The photo I found the other day had been sticking out, making it easy to find. But there might have been more behind it."

He shimmied on his belly to the farthest point under the slanted roofline and turned over on his back. He reached up and put his hand between two boards and jiggled old paper out from between them. "Thought so." He crawled out of the closet backwards with the treasure clamped between his teeth.

Niki took the papers from Rapp's mouth as he emerged from the closet.

"We're just lucky this stuff wasn't eaten up," said Lia. "See, staying positive gives positive results."

"And so easy, as if it was all left just for us," said Jules. "Like you knew where to look, Rapp."

"Well, that would be weird," he said, rubbing some of the black off his knees. "Maybe I'm psychic, too. Someone is sending me a sign." He waggled his dirty fingers in Jules's face and made a *woo-woo* sound.

Jules batted his hands away as if they were annoying flies. "Well, maybe someone *is* sending us a signal. And it might just be Sonnet."

"Maybe it's *me*." Emma looked at Rapp without a smile. "Maybe it's not so hard to understand. Perhaps I am back hiding clues now for you in a place Mother would never think to scrutinize. Her own bedroom."

Rapp looked like he was ready to waggle his fingers in front of Emma next.

"Stop!" said Niki, rattling the papers. "This place is making us all crazy. We can trip each other out another time. Let's just concentrate on what we have here."

They gathered close. Lia held the flashlight.

"It's another photo." Niki held the faded card out before them. The edges were nibbled away like the other, but the image in the center was plain to see.

Shot in the same location as the other, the Monte Cristo Ice Caves Fair banner hung across painted peaks. Two young boys sat on a tufted bench clutching a toy soldier in each of their laps. But instead of facing into the camera, their heads were turned and blurred. They focused on a female to their left being hustled out of the camera's range by what looked like an arm across her neck.

"Let me see." Emma took the photo. "My brothers. This face is blurred but she is wearing the same dress as in the other photo. The one I was not going to wear to the fair." She blinked. "Sonnet."

"Oh, my god." Jules's reached out, her turn. "Someone is dragging her away from the camera. You can see she's struggling."

"Someone didn't want her in the photo." Rapp took the other image out of his bag and held them out together. "Shine the light here, Lia. The sleeve." Rapp compared them. "It's the same dress as your mother's, Emma."

"Yes." Emma stared at her mother's arm. She could only imagine the danger Sonnet was in.

"There's something else." Niki picked up crackling yellow papers that had dropped to the floor. "It's too dark in here to see."

"Let's get out of here. This place is giving me the creeps," said Jules.

"And making us crazy," said Rapp.

"And possibly psycho." Lia made a face at Rapp as he laughed at her.

"I would like to see my room first, if I may." Emma ran down the short flight of stairs to the second-floor hallway.

"This is the nursery where my brothers sleep. Guest room. Guest room." She tapped at the doors as she walked. "This is my bedroom."

Keko sat on Emma's bedroom floor, frowning. She reached out to Rapp. "Here, help me up." She slapped dust off the back of her jeans. "This is where Sonnet is staying."

"My room. You were sitting where the bed goes," said Emma.

Keko nodded. "Yes. I need to get out of here."

They trundled down the stairs and out to the porch where Keko gulped for air. "I have never had such a clear reading of someone. I'll need to take a break and come back later. I'm completely overwhelmed."

Evan came running through the trees. "We found a barn collapsed on what might be an old carriage. Follow me!"

He led them up and through a forested hill to a mound of wood where Uncle Jack hauled weathered boards from the heap and tossed them to the side. Slivers of dark blue paint and black metal glinted from underneath.

"It appears to be Father's carriage," said Emma. "It was usually stored in the lower barn. This barn"—she paused— "was being constructed." She pinched the end of a long-corroded nail from where it lay on the ground next to the splintered lumber and raised it out in front of her, twirling it in the drab light.

Keko's gaze rested on Emma. "Wait, Jack." She ran her hands across a board. She scrutinized Rapp, roaming over his face and down his body. "Jack, do you have ancestors from these parts?"

"Not that I know of. Why?"

She stared at Rapp again and then swung her gaze hard at Emma. "What is it? Tell us."

Emma raised her head from the nail, with no choice now but to tell the truth. "He was building this barn when I . . . went away. He . . . he is my betrothed. It's our secret, our pact."

She gripped the nail tight in her fist until it hurt. "He appears similar to you, Rapp. Indeed, so similar, it's as if he were your elder brother. His name is Tor. Tor Loken."

"Tor *Loken*? There's someone in Monte Cristo who looks just like me and has my last name? You knew all along and never said anything?"

"I'm sorry. I wanted to, but . . ."

"Our Loken heritage is from Sweden," Uncle Jack interrupted. "Is that where he's from, Emma?"

"Yes, from Sweden."

"This is the beau? The suitor?" said Lia. "Why didn't you tell me he looked just like Rapp? This coincidence could be some sort of— I don't know—a clue or reason this crazy thing happened."

Emma looked at them all and wished she could begin anew. Why had she not told these good people? They had every right to be angry. They had given her everything, and she had given them nothing of herself in return.

"And aren't you like fifteen years old? *Betrothed?* Doesn't that mean engaged in old-speak?" Niki crossed her arms.

"Yes, but it will be a three-year engagement. Tor and I swore ourselves to secrecy. I should have told you, but I was frightened. If my mother were to discover this secret . . ." Emma shuddered. "He has no one to recommend him. A carpenter who works with his hands. *Tor, the immigrant* and

Emma, the entitled, are two names that should never be spoken together. Society would cast me out and my family would be shamed."

Lia looked sick. "How . . ."

"We plan to leave together for Seattle when I finish school. Just disappear. I'll be old enough by then to not have the law after Tor. If I went away, truly, I doubt my mother would mind."

"So, Sonnet's dealing with a guy who thinks he's engaged to her and who happens to be a long-lost Loken relative who looks just like Rapp," said Niki. "*And,* dealing with a crazy mother who seems to be abusing her. What she must be going through right now! Show them, Rapp."

He handed the newly found photo to Evan. "She's being attacked by Emma's mom."

"And, these . . ." Niki held out the yellowed papers. "It's hard to make out. The writing is so swirly and faded. It's some sort of correspondence from . . ." She bent the papers toward the light. "It says 'The Oldfield's School for Ladies, Baltimore, Maryland.' And here . . . 'Emma Sweetwine, age fifteen. Registered: September 3, 1895.'"

"Oh, my god! They're sending Sonnet to Baltimore." Jules shivered and threw her arms around herself. "What will we do if that happens?"

Silent and helpless, Team Switch looked around at each other.

"What we'll do is we won't give up hope," said Evan, finally. "We can't."

Emma's heart ached for her friends, and she felt even worse for Sonnet who was now subject to the abuse that would have been hers to endure. She peered over Niki's shoulder and read the ominous words for herself. As if she were the white-ruffled lamp in Lia's room, her switch was pressed and the light in her head turned on.

"Of course, my mother is sending me to boarding school. What a perfect plan to rid herself of the unwanted daughter. But if I were there, I would run away before I was forced on a train to Baltimore. And Sonnet must, too."

She unclenched her hand. The rusty nail sat like a relic from the Roman Empire in her palm. It stained her skin with flakes of red ore, as if they were specks of ancient, dried blood. She knew the last time the nail had been touched by a person, that person had been Tor.

Out of every dreadful thing she had witnessed in this long-dead place, the one-hundred-and-twenty-year-old nail bothered her the most. She glanced over the pile of boards where Rapp still stood. He had not moved his eyes from her face.

CHAPTER NINETEEN

—

Sonnet
1895

The scissors were cold against my forehead, and the thread stretched my skin and stung as Doctor Withers tugged it out. He set the pile of crusty strands aside and patted my hand, still hanging over me, closer than he needed to be. "There now. You are much better. You gave your dear mother and me a scare the other day."

Dear mother.

His sweaty body was still wrapped up in a heavy wool suit as if it was winter, and he still smelled like tobacco and cheese. He ran his hand down my side and across my belly as if it was a doctor thing to do. I struggled out from underneath him as he pressed his scratchy body against me. I waited in the far corner next to the fireplace, holding my breath and pretending to study the bricks.

He took his sweet time packing everything up, a dangerous obstacle between me and the bedroom door. I reached over and wrestled the window open. I would squawk for help, kick and push him over against the doll, and bolt for the hallway if I felt him sneaking up behind me.

Bess walked in with three men and three empty trunks and set me free. "Your mother wants me to start packing, miss. I shall finish up tomorrow when the rest of the clothes are delivered. Skedaddle now. You are just in the way here. We'll keep the door closed so the boys can't see. Run along."

I rushed past Doctor Withers, giving him the same hellish look I had given the Gold Nugget Hotel doorman, and ran from the room. He slid out behind me with the men. Creep.

I banged down the back stairs to an empty kitchen, where I knew I wouldn't be followed. On the counter sat the last two pieces of blackberry pie. I grabbed the pie tin and a glass of milk and walked out to the front porch. Down at the barn, Jacob was running and pushing Miles on the swing, their long blond hair flowing out behind them. When they saw me, they waved and called, "Come push us, Emma."

My two precious boys in this house of horrors wanted me to play. I scarfed up the pie and milk on my way to the swing and then took over for Jacob, pushing Miles as high as I could. He rocked and screamed, his joy piercing the late morning sky.

It was Jacob's turn. He clambered up on the swing. I pushed and pushed, sending his little body flying toward the heavens. He ripped across the wind, as ecstatic as any little boy would be, and that joy thrilled me back, as delicious as the blackberry pie I had just devoured.

"Good morning, Miss Emma. Good morning, Master Jacob, Master Miles."

I towed the swing to a stop. Jacob, Miles, and I lined up in front of the young man. "Good morning, Mister Loken." My tongue flicked imagined pie crumbs off my lips.

He unfroze his eyes from my mouth and smiled down at the boys. "I'm meeting your father here today. He wants to see the work progressing. Do you approve of the new barn?"

They nodded their heads. "Yes, sir," said Jacob.

Tor swung his head over his shoulder and then back at me. "Will I see you tonight at the fair?"

I shrugged. "They don't tell me anything. My status in that house is basically like a big, dumb doll."

"Just in case, I'll look for you."

Sunshine filtered through golden hair hanging out from under his hat. A dusting of sawdust sat on his cheek and caught in his curls. In this parallel universe of time my body hummed with a yearning so intense it stunned me. I reached for his hand and pulled him close. He touched a wayward strand of my hair, sweeping it from my face. Our heads came closer. We smiled at each other. . . .

Banging drummed across the clear air. Above the porch, a shadow moved inside the turret where someone was using their fists to pound on one of the windows.

"Mother," whispered Jacob. He and Miles edged up close to my sides and took each of my hands.

"I must go." Tor tipped his hat and loped away from us, back up the hill.

The boys and I stood next to the limp swing and waited.

"EMMA! I want you over here. Now!" Thorn seethed at us from the porch with Kerry dodging around behind her in the shadows of the doorway.

I sauntered over with the boys, leaving the pie tin and empty milk glass behind in the dirt. "Yes? We're playing . . ."

"You disrespectful . . . take Jacob and Miles, Kerry . . ." She never took her eyes off mine. Her yellow hair puffed and quaked, and beads of sweat were closing in on her poodle-dog bangs. "You—come in the house. You dare exhibit your wanton behavior in front of my sons."

"Mother—"

"No, Jacob. Your sister is in trouble now. It is no one's fault but her own."

On the roller coaster again, I tore around a dusky corner heading straight toward Tor's darkness and desolation. Jacob and Miles whimpered. I stood without moving, their little hands stuck to mine, my eyes still on hers. She came down the stairs and grabbed at my arm. I yanked it from her. I felt what little bit of wisdom I had draining away.

"Sending me to Baltimore isn't good enough for you? You need to whip me, too? You're nothing but a big bully. Taking out your frustrations on a defenseless girl."

"Why, the insolence, the willfulness. You imagine I am too stupid to know what's going on between you and that—that low-born immigrant. I can see you from the window, Emma, and in front of everyone. You are a slut. Just as your mother was."

My mother—was?

"Please, please you mustn't use those words, Mother!" Jacob sobbed. His tiny nails dug into my fingers. Miles wailed and clutched my dress, tripping as he moved behind me. Kerry ran down the stairs and tried to wedge her little body between us. Thorn twisted her arm and hurled her away.

She had her hands on my shoulders, squeezing, pushing, shaking.

"You wonder what's wrong with Jacob—" I couldn't help myself. I slid into a white-hot place and screeched into her face. Over a week's worth of pent-up anger and frustration tripped from my mouth. "Your craven treatment of Emma is what's wrong with Jacob. He suffers because of it. You think he doesn't notice? You think it doesn't affect him? If you were nice to her, he'd be fine—he just wants you to love Emma. Just love her. But you can't see beyond your hate."

"High and mighty, talking as if you were Queen Victoria. Jacob is *my* boy, not yours. They are *mine*. They will never be yours." Trumpeting like an enraged elephant, Thorn backed away and then lunged. Her arm swept up and came at me with lightning speed. Kerry grabbed at it but it was too late. Thorn's fierce slap across my face rang out over the tops of the boys' screams. Taking Jacob and Miles with me, I skid over the gravel and flew face-first into a rose bush. I crashed down through its fat stem and branches into the neatly raked dirt tucked around it.

I unearthed my head from the thorns and rolled onto my side, rubbing dirt from my eyes. Bess and Cook stood in the doorway, their mouths hanging open. The men working on the barn had started to run down the hill. In the uproar, none of us heard the black-and-blue rig racing up the road.

John was raging, his feet barely touching the ground as he shot from the carriage, Maxwell on his heels. He waived his arms around forcing the workers away as he ran to us. "I have everything under control! Go back. Continue your jobs." He jerked his head to Bess and Cook. "Back in the house with you two. Cook, prepare the mid-day meal for the boys. Maxwell, take the carriage to the barn."

He dragged me up and knelt in the dirt, taking his sobbing sons into his arms. "There, there." He stroked their shiny hair and kissed their wet cheeks. "Kerry, take the boys up to the nursery and get them ready to eat. Clean them and change their clothes. Bandage any cuts."

He glared at his wife. "Go to the study, Rose. There has been enough of an outdoor spectacle today."

I watched them all go. Like ants, they scattered, off to do their jobs. Attempting to turn madness into sanity.

John called back to me as he entered the house. "You too, Emma. You are old enough now to hear this. Come."

The entryway mirror reflected an ugly red welt in the shape of a hand stretching from my mouth across my cheek to my ear. A thorn stabbed into my lip. I ripped it out. Fat drops of blood fell to my dirty white shoes. Scratches scarred my chin and cheeks and dirt smeared my ripped linen outfit. The bow sagged from a hank of fallen hair. I pulled it out. Like a wild, repulsive animal, my mop of copper hair hung in my filthy, bloody face.

John waited for me and shut the study door. Thorn glided to him, her hips swaying back and forth under her dress. She laid her dainty hand on his lapel. He swiped it off and pushed her from him. "Sit down, Rose."

John beheld the battle's damage stretching from my head to my feet. He traversed the war wounds across my face. I saw little fissures cracking his heart. "Has this happened before, Emma?"

"She deserves—"

"Quiet!" he roared. He held up his hand. "For once, Rose, let the girl speak."

"She hates me," I said. "She won't leave me alone."

"Your own niece, Rose! Your niece and my daughter," said John.

Niece? What? I fell backwards into a chair.

Rose attacked. "My sister was no better than a prostitute—and now her daughter is, too. I will not *stand* for it, John. Not under my roof!"

"A prostitute? Your sister was a girl of fifteen."

"Oh, my sister knew what she was doing—trying to catch herself a rich husband."

"And what about you, Rose?"

Her head shot back as if she'd been hit. "I am upstanding. Godly. I deserve a man of society, of means. I desire our family to be of you and our sons and myself. No reminders of past sin. Nothing unclean. Can that be wrong?"

"Unclean? Emma is family, an innocent human being, not a reminder of sin. You, Rose, are divested of all sympathy, human decency, and understanding."

Thorn jutted out her chin. Like a dog with a bone, she wouldn't let go. "She is a bastard, John. A child born of immorality."

John exhaled. He hung his head. His powerful hands lay on his knees in tight balls. He whispered into his lap, "Our child is not a bastard. Our child was born of love." He raised his head to me. His eyes were wet. "She was just fifteen when you were born. Your mother, Emma. Your beautiful, sweet, good mother was the daughter of the maid who worked in my parents' home. The daughter of our Irish maid." He turned to his wife. "Your younger sister, Rose. The daughter of a maid. Just like you."

"You promised to never mention this!" Blue-snaked veins undulated in her neck.

"And you promised to love Genevieve's child if I married you—" He thundered back.

The grandfather clock, as steady as the rising sun, as solid as the earth we humans called home, marked its beats as the Sweetwine husband and wife faced each other in double fury. It gonged once—lunchtime. I could smell tomato soup, probably sitting in its beautiful china tureen on the dining room sideboard, waiting for its diners, unnoticed, just like me.

The drama was played out, the actors exhausted.

John's handsome face sagged. "Now. There has been enough scandal. When word gets out, as it surely will, the whole town will be wagging their tongues. To counteract this, we will, as a family, go to the fair tonight. And again tomorrow. We will all get along. You will not ruin my reputation over domestic matters. Do you understand me, Rose?"

Instead of tears of defeat dribbling down her face, she gathered herself together and pursed her lips. She narrowed her eyes at me.

"Rose! Do you understand me?"

She nodded.

"Good. Send some of your powder to Emma's room and have Kerry fix up her face with it before we leave for the fair later today. Emma will be gone on Sunday—your wish that I have gone along with. I expect you to control yourself until then."

He looked at me finally like a father should look at his child. "I should have involved myself in this . . . this debacle a long time ago. I blame myself, my dear girl. I bowed away from family matters when my gaze should have held steady. I have avoided a very real problem in this—" He wobbled his head. "This grand house of ours. I am sorry, Emma. You go now. I shall have your lunch sent up on a tray."

It was like I had left my body sitting on the chair, and was a pair of eyes floating around under the ceiling, looking down at the show. I was bothered way more than I should have been. After all, these weren't my parents, and this wasn't my life.

I flopped back down into my body and jetted away from the room and the craziness, feeling Thorn's eyes on the back of my neck. I knew for her—for Emma's aunt—this wasn't over.

IN silence, the Sweetwine family boarded the black-and-blue carriage and headed to town to take in the opening of the Ice Caves Fair. Jacob sat across from me on his mother's lap and stared. The powder had taken the edge off Thorn's handprint and scratches, but the pain across Jacob's little five-year-old face as he looked at me spoke volumes. The brutality inflicted by his mother on his sister was plain for him to see.

Jacob had a bruise and a cut on his cheekbone and skinned knees. And Miles, sidled up against me, had cuts on both hands and scratches across his forehead and legs. Collateral damage. Fight night at the Sweetwine house.

I took Miles into my lap and turned to the window, hugging him and kissing the top of his sweet, blond head. I couldn't stand to look at her.

AS the senior townsperson, and along with the Mayor of Monte Cristo, John had been tapped to make one of the opening speeches before the throngs of expectant revelers. As he climbed to the wooden stage, I slowly backed away from the family and slipped into the crowd.

I felt Tor come up from behind. He took my hand and swept his gaze across my face, wincing. "I saw the entire thing. I was running down the hill when Mister Sweetwine came home." He ran his finger down my cheek. "You are still the most beautiful girl here, even with her marks on your face. What's this?" He touched the scab on my lip.

"A thorn bite." I kissed his finger and edged close to his side. "A thorn from her rosebush. Her proxy."

"I would kill her if I could."

"As long as I have you with me right now, I'm happy, Tor." I rubbed my fingers over his and felt calluses. "You and I wouldn't make sense to anyone else, would we?"

"No, we scarcely make sense to ourselves."

I kissed his hand and dropped it. It wasn't worth the risk. "After we went into the house there was another fight between those two about long-buried secrets. Emma's mother is really her aunt and it turns out Emma's *real* mother is dead. They were the Irish maid's children in John's childhood home and Genevieve had Emma when she was just fifteen. It must have been a scandal! John called

Genevieve beautiful and sweet and good, and the way he said it, it was as if he still loved her. Like he had never gotten over her."

"Beautiful and sweet and good, like you and Emma." He started to laugh. "Madam Sweetwine . . . an Irish immigrant's spawn. A paddy. That pompous woman. She's still competing with a dead sister for her husband's love and taking out her misery on a blameless girl. You remind her every day she was not his first."

"Gen-e-vieve," I breathed. "Even the name sounds like romance."

"And Mister Sweetwine knows he was a lucky man to have loved like that. Even if but once. I feel for him."

"Me, too."

A dirt path led to the main tent where John could be heard finishing up his speech—the wooden megaphone did an impressive job transferring his booming voice over the fairground. Stalls were set up on either side of us. Vendors hawked food and trinkets, games for prizes. Soon fairgoers would be here lining up for the fun. Tor stopped and bought cotton candy. I took a couple of sweet bites and let the strings of pink, fragranced sugar melt in my mouth. I handed it back and sighed. It was time to go, and I was in enough trouble. "I better get back before they miss me."

A sudden jolt of electricity ran down my spine and seared across my skin, knocking my breath away. I could smell flowers. *Jasmine?* Across the path stood a woman in a long ruby gown. Red-and-white-striped curtains covering the stall behind her fluttered in the breeze and stood as a backdrop to her coffee-colored beauty. Above her head hung a red board painted in black letters: FORTUNE-TELLER – FUTURE TOLD BY LEROUX. Her brown eyes bore into mine.

I wandered over, drawn to her.

"You have to go on back to your family now." Her words played in a gentle rhythm. "You come see me tomorrow when you have more time."

"You stare at me like you know me," I said. "I could feel you from across the way."

She reached over with a cool hand and moved the hair away from my forehead, scanning across my scar and the powder-covered handprint staining my cheek. The tip of her finger touched the scab on my lip. "Come see me tomorrow. Get along, now. It would be no good if you stayed. Haven't you had enough trouble already today?"

"I've had enough trouble for a lifetime." I couldn't *get along*. I couldn't move. She was like an oasis of shady palm trees in the middle of a hot desert, a raft of the smoothest wood suddenly appearing on choppy water. I could no more twist my eyes away than I could slit my own wrists. "You read people's futures *and* their pasts?"

"Special people."

Another jolt of electricity and an overwhelming feeling of excitement lit me up. "Okay, then! See you tomorrow, Leroux."

I squeezed Tor's hand and let it fall. "Gotta go!" I turned and ran, as well as I could in the cumbersome dress, to the big tent where John and Thorn were probably already missing me.

CHAPTER TWENTY

—

Emma

2015

"Just a sec." Evan set his phone down on a rotten tree stump and pressed on it. "Thanks for calling, Professor Kapoor. We're in Monte Cristo, hiking up to the house for a second day of searching for clues. Everyone's listening. You're on speakerphone."

"Emma's still with you?"

"Yeah, she's here. She's listening."

"I've been doing some research and I wanted to inform you of some vital information. Information I trust—I hope—will be helpful in your decision. You ready?"

"Go ahead."

"I've spoken to other experts in the field, and we all agree that Sonnet and Emma can't meet. I told you this the other day. They trade places or they both stay put. There's more, though. It has to do with corrupted time distention and gravitational impart waves, but I'll break it down into layman's terms. In order for Emma and Sonnet to pass each other in transport and land in the correct time arc, they must have identical circumstances implemented at the right moment, just as before. In other words, you somehow must mimic exactly the conditions of last time, and they must be done at exactly the optimum moment on both ends. The time-flaps— the different timelines bumping up against each other—must open and close in sync. I truly don't know how you will coordinate this. We believe the first time occurred by happenstance. In other words—you were lucky."

"What do you mean about making our decision, Professor Kapoor?" asked Jules "There's a decision to make?"

"I won't sugarcoat it. This will be a dangerous journey. Best case scenario, you somehow pull it off. The second-best case scenario, Sonnet and Emma stay where they are. I believe this is the safest bet."

"What's worst case scenario?" Evan stared at the phone.

The professor's voice grew soft. "We believe that the worst case will find them landing in the wrong time continuum. Or even worse, maybe one leaves and the other doesn't make it out, putting them together in the same time."

"Wow, that's a lot to wrap our heads around. Okay, Professor. Thanks. We'll get back with you if we have any more questions." Evan pressed his phone to off. An owl hooted in the silence, sitting somewhere above in a cedar tree. Team Switch looked around at each other, digesting the news.

"Maybe Sylvia is ready to give up her secrets," Rapp said. "We'll just rip into her. As they say, 'When the going gets tough, the tough get going.'"

"Yeah. Let's go tear her apart. There's gotta be something there. Sonnet has left us something. I can feel it." Lia swept at branches, ready to plow through only to suddenly spin around. "The piano!" She turned and started running.

They fell on the baby grand like locusts. Sticky cobwebs clung to their skin and rodent droppings flattened under their feet. Clouds of dust rose up in spirals as they moved above, below, and over the sides of the rotting wood. They raised the cover and felt down around the piano wire. Rapp crawled underneath and turned his flashlight on, pointing it at the underside. Lia crawled in and lay next to him, running the tips of her fingers up in between the slats.

Rapp focused the light. "I see something. There, Lia." The flashlight fell on a tiny yellowed strip of paper. Lia grasped an edge. It broke off in her hand and turned to dust.

"It's stuck." Lia wiggled her hand in as far as it would go and felt around. "I think it's all nibbled up."

Jules crawled in. "Let me try from this side." The edge she touched turned to powder between her fingers, too. "We need a knife or something. Every time we tug, tiny chunks break off. If we could just catch it."

"We should just rip this bad boy apart. A knife's not gonna do it," said Rapp, pulling at a board.

"Wait," said Evan, running from the room and calling back over his shoulder. "I saw an old, rusted saw under the house yesterday. I'll be right back."

Emma wandered with Lia out onto the porch to find a spot of sunshine. The crow sat sentinel on a knob of railing, watching them with black, darting eyes. It kept track of their plodding labors throughout the ruin it thought of as its own. It was getting used to them by now, approaching ever closer and closer.

"You're awfully quiet, Emma."

"The professor's words troubled me. I listened carefully. What I understood is the journey back to my time is perilous and even with trying, I might not return. I felt the professor's choice was for me to stay here and for Sonnet to stay there in order to minimize harm."

Lia sighed. The professor's words had struck dread into all of them. On the other side of looming danger dangled Sonnet.

Emma broke off a brown strand of blackberry bush. "What shall I do?"

"What do you want to do?"

"I love my new life here. I have never had such a good time, not in my entire fifteen years. But, I want to go back to Tor or die trying. I'm ready to give all this up."

"You're not scared?"

"Of course, I am." Emma rolled a hard, dusty blackberry around her palm. It took hot sunshine to love a blackberry to fruition. "If Sonnet and I are unable to switch places—if I stay here and she stays there—will she love the ones I love? Will she be me and live my life?"

"You mean love Tor? Is that what you would *want*?"

"As hard as it is to imagine that, the thought of him being alone is worse to me than the thought of my own death," Emma said. She turned to the crow. It blinked twice. As if it understood.

"This someday marriage to Tor is way more than just a convenience to get you out of your house and away from your awful mother, isn't it?" asked Lia.

"I love him." She threw the blackberry over the railing.

"Does it seem odd I would want them together? Sonnet is the closest thing to being me."

"No. What it sounds like is that you really love the ones you love. Enough to let them be loved by someone else if you can't be there. But let's just stay upbeat that this will work out. That you and Sonnet do switch places and everything turns out okay. We'll be paralyzed if we sink into negativity."

Emma hugged Lia tightly, a gesture of affection she had taken to with passion. "You always say the right thing. I'll miss this wonderful existence—this thrilling world made as much for girls as for boys. I have had the time of my life here. And I have never had a true friend before. I am lucky to have Tor, this I know, but Sonnet is lucky to have a friend and cousin like you."

And, besides, this was Sonnet's life, not hers.

Unless she stayed—

Evan ran by, waving around a rusty piece of metal. "Hey, you saps. I found the saw."

"Let's go watch," said Lia.

Evan crawled under the piano and raised the saw above his body. His first cut back and forth rained wood bits down on his face. "Ugh." He sat up on his elbow and swung his head, shaking off fragments.

"We can push the piano over, Evan." Emma said.

"Huh?"

"On its side. It will make it easier to work on."

"It might disintegrate." Evan crawled back out.

Rapp said, "Who cares, right Emma?"

"Not I."

They lined up across the curved side.

Niki said, "On the count of three. One . . . two . . . three."

With an almost human moan, the beast turned over and crashed to the floor, sending a foul mixture of dirt and splinters of wood flying into the air. A dull, off-key crescendo vibrated through the house. Its front leg snapped. It rocked and creaked and groaned and finally settled.

"Mother's piano rests at long last," said Emma into the swirling cloud.

Evan stepped forward with the saw. "This will make it easier. Someone hold the board in place so it doesn't just fall off."

With the cuts made, Rapp rocked the section from its resting place and held it upright in his hand. Pieces of paper lay scattered across the wood. He set it down on the floor.

Lia got down on her knees with Niki next to her. "Rapp, shine the light here." She prodded. "This little piece in the middle. There's an *O* and an *M*. And a space and then *SO*."

Niki said, "It could be *F-R-O-M-S-O-N-N-E-T*."

"Yes! What else could it be? And it could have been an envelope with a letter inside. See the layers?" Jules leaned across Niki and made an attempt to pick up a piece only to have it crumble. "It's unreadable."

"I won't give up. We have the rest of the day to dig around this big house. If she left one note to us, she left others," said Lia.

Rapp's phone rang. "We'll be right down." He stuffed it back in his pocket. "Uncle Jack and Keko fixed lunch. Let's go eat and come back later."

"I'm all for that," said Evan, brushing his palm back and forth across his bristly, dirt-drenched hair. "Fortify for our afternoon work."

TEAM Switch, with Uncle Jack and Keko in tow, returned after lunch. Keko found a rusted tin soldier with a paint-chipped blue uniform caught in the back of a fireplace grate in the nursery. Except for wear, it looked exactly like the ones clutched in the little hands of Jacob and Miles in the second photograph.

CHAPTER TWENTY-ONE

Sonnet
1895

Saturday and bath day. I sat back in the tub and let the warm water lap over my shoulders. The row of half-empty trunks would be filled to overflowing later today. Missus Love would deliver the newly made dresses, and Bess would fold them in tissue paper and add them to the already-wrapped mounds. The clothes, shoes, and accessories Emma had either outgrown or were considered too deplorable for her fancy new Baltimore life hung on hangers or sat in piles on the bottom of the wardrobe.

I sighed, my thoughts rummaging around in the corners of the Tor complication. There was nothing to do about it—and at the same time, no getting over it.

Little feet scampered down the hallway. Jacob and Miles chased each other and played, their high-pitched voices seeping through the crack under the door. I wrenched myself out of my daydream and dipped my head back into the cooling bathwater, swooshing my hair around. After soaping up, I grabbed two pitchers of clean water and poured them over me. It would soon be time to go see Leroux. The reflection in the mirror still showed a handprint and scratches across my face. I would have to remember to dust powder on them.

I had one precious hour before the carriage left for the fair. I dressed and hurried out to my secret place in the meadow to write my last letter.

JOHN held the door open and gave a hand to his silent family as we filed, one by one, into the carriage. Jacob and Miles, in their best linen sailor suits and black button shoes, sat on either side of me, their blond hair glowing, their curls still partially wet. It had been bath day for them, too.

Maxwell had orders to drop the family off at the boardwalk and return to the house to pick up Kerry, Cook, Bess, and the hired hands. John had given the staff the entire day off together. A first of its kind, according to Kerry. A peace offering over the war they had all witnessed yesterday. Even Maxwell had five precious hours to himself before he rendezvoused with the family at the boardwalk to take us back up the hill to home.

John stepped from the carriage and lifted his youngest son into his arms. "Come children, there are games to be played." He strode off with Miles on his hip and Jacob at his heels. I followed close behind.

"John, the family photographs." Thorn called after them, demanding his attention. "I want to arrive early before the riff-raff gather. And the children will get soiled if you take them to play . . ."

He continued along the path and yelled back, "After the fun, Rose. I'm taking the children to enjoy a game. As you well know, they more than deserve a good time at the fair today. If you want to meet us at the photographer's booth, please do. Or come. Either way."

John turned his face into the mountain wind, his elegant, high-topped shoes already gathering dust, and wound down through the entertainment stalls to find a ball-throwing game. He put a penny down on a counter and opened his palm to the red ball. "I shall instruct you as to how it is done, boys, and then you will each have a turn." He squinted at the hoop. With a convoluted, whirling backhand he pitched the ball forward and missed.

The man behind the counter gave him another ball. "You get three chances, sir. Different prizes depending on how many of the three go in. I move the target back each time."

He missed again. I held my breath. He wobbled out his arm, swung, and threw his third ball. This one hit the rim, teetered for a second and plopped through the wooden circle. Jacob and Miles cheered. The man handed John a tin soldier, its uniform painted bright blue with white-and-red accents.

John laid another penny down and set his oldest son on the counter. Jacob threw and missed all three times. John replaced Jacob with Miles with the same result. Their little arms didn't have the strength to reach the hoop and their faces drooped with disappointment.

"My turn," I said, to the Sweetwine family.

They stared as if I had just set myself on fire.

"Dear . . ." John shook his head.

"Put a penny down for me, please." Behind me, Thorn's

angry tongue click and the boys' joyful whoops were the opposite realities in my Monte Cristo constellation of existence.

John heard, too. He laid a penny on the counter.

I sized up the target while people gathered to watch the girl. I backed up a few feet, wound my arm behind my head, and threw the ball. It sailed straight through the target with a satisfying *swoosh*. The boys screamed. John gawked. Thorn seethed.

The man moved the hoop further away. I reared back and threw. My second ball soared directly through the center. Bullseye! The crowd laughed and clapped and more people elbowed in behind me.

The man moved it back again. I took three deep breaths, wound and threw. Another direct hit. Miles, Jacob, and the mob went wild.

The man swept his arm at the grand prizes and pointed to the biggest doll. "How 'bout this pretty baby doll?"

"Thanks, but I'll take another tin soldier."

"You can have a bigger, better prize, young lady. You certainly warrant it."

"Just the soldier is fine."

I handed it to Miles and took the other off the counter where John had set it. I held it out to Jacob.

"Thank you, Emma."

"Right, then. Good work!" John twirled the end of his mustache at me and winked.

The toe of Thorn's pink suede shoe tapped pillows of dust into the air. She held her pink parasol out against the sun. "John . . ."

"Yes, then, come along. I believe the photographer's booth

is over that way." He jostled Miles up under one arm and Jacob under the other. They squealed and hung on to their new toys, reveling in their father's attention.

I trailed behind as we jostled through the promenading people, scanning across stalls for red-and-white curtains. Where was she? There were so many people today, I had lost my bearings. Tightness circled my throat and made it hard to swallow.

Faith does not make things easy, Sonnet. Faith makes things possible.

I unclenched my fists and rolled my tight shoulders and neck. I swallowed the panic back down and listened to Simeon speak to me.

So lost in my thoughts, I ran into Thorn's pink lace-covered parasol pointing back at me like a sharp sword. A wood sign with black letters dangled above our heads. PHOTOGRAPHS— FIFTEEN CENTS APIECE.

"We shall have two images, please. One of the entire family and one of just the children. My name is Mister John Sweetwine."

"That will be thirty cents. I know who you are, sir." The man held back a canvas flap and we entered a crude photo studio. A small wooden platform held different props. "Which background, Mister Sweetwine?"

John surveyed the three choices. "The countryside. With the mountains in the rear. Just like Monte Cristo."

The assistant rolled the background into place and draped a white swag across the top of the mountain. Black lettering across its silky surface announced, MONTE CRISTO ICE CAVES FAIR, AUGUST 21–23, 1895.

In the center of the platform, men arranged two high-backed chairs. A faux marble pillar stood off to the side of one chair, and a bouquet of flowers in a clear vase sat on top of it. John plunked down and put Miles on his lap. Thorn sat on the other chair with Jacob next to her. As the surplus Sweetwine, the only one without blue eyes and blond hair, the assistant motioned me to stand apart—cozied up to the pillar. He folded my hands on top of each other beside the vase.

"Hold still, now." The photographer put his head under a black cloth and yanked a metal chain on the side of a wooden box. I jumped at the loud explosion and flash. A cloud of black smoke and the smell of rotten eggs spilled through the air.

"Fine, just fine." John uprooted Miles from his lap. He waved his hands around his head, whooshing the smoke away. "I shall take a break outside while the children have their photograph taken."

"The Ice Caves Fair Saloon is around the corner, sir. Gentlemen take their breaks there." The photographer winked at John.

John's eyes skittered across to Thorn and away to the canvas door flap. "You will find me at the saloon then, with the other men." He handed the man three dimes and left before she could protest.

The chairs were replaced by a small blue bench. "Stand at the same spot, miss, and the young 'uns here." He patted the bench. Miles and Jacob scrambled up with their shiny new tin soldiers. The photographer walked around behind his camera and tossed the black hood over his head.

Thorn glowered from the side of the platform. I whisked my hair back at her. She darted over. "No, I will not have you in this one." She grappled at my neck, dragging me away from the camera as the lace collar caught in her fingers. I heard a rip and felt buttons tumble down my chest just as there was another flash and explosion.

The cameraman peered out from under his hood with a frown, flapping at the air with his handkerchief. "You moved."

Thorn spotted the ring hanging below my throat. She was too fast. Her hand was a white blur rushing at my neck. She jerked. A long drip of white and yellow and black fell into her palm. Her fingers snapped over it, making a fist. "What have I told you about fripperies on girls?"

"Give it back."

"We are finished here. Come, boys." She caught her sons' hands, hauled them off the bench, and marched to the flap, throwing it open and dragging Jacob and Miles out before anyone had a chance to help her. I started after her and re-membered my open dress.

The photographer ran and handed me a shawl—one of the props. I wrapped it around my shoulders and hugged it across my chest. "Thanks. I'll try to get it back to you." I nod-ded in the direction of Thorn's exit. "She's crazy."

"I can see that."

He hurled the canvas flap open to a sea of hats and bon-nets and parasols. They bobbed and swayed together like corks on water with the occasional dirty leather miner's hat popping up between. Thorn and the boys had disappeared. My ring. Was gone.

STEPPING out into the sunshine, I skimmed over the chaotic scene. A face came at me, sweating rivers under a black hat. In a second, he would be close enough for me to catch a whiff of cheese and spot slimy drips rolling onto his wool coat. The hands of a small girl and boy wedged into his. I tilted away from the sun, rushing from Doctor Withers as fast as I could. I made myself small, pushing and shoving through the crowd.

I was moving in raggedy circles. My feet hurt and my body was sweaty. My cheeks felt sunburned. I stopped under a tree, out of breath and lost.

"Charming girl, has your father misplaced you?"

Another voice slurred something into my ear. Lurching miners caught me from either side, breathing alcohol and tobacco fumes into my face. I knocked away a dirty hand that was slinking up around my waist and wacked at a short man whose smirking face pushed an inch away from mine.

"Really?" I tried backing away, but the tree stopped me. I was trapped.

"Aww, now. I just want a little kiss." The tall one lunged. I socked his filthy hand off my neck and bunched up my fist, slugging his stomach. The other one wrenched my arm. I leaned down and bit him. He screamed and fell backward. The shawl had fallen to the ground, my open neckline like candy to their leering, bloodshot eyes.

"Leave the young lady alone, Hodge! You too, Duffy." Another miner had come along and snatched my shawl off the ground. He caught my arm and led me from danger. "You can hit! But, you should not be walking alone, miss. Not a good idea today. Too many eager men drifting about."

"Eager is an understatement." I fixed the shawl back around my shoulders and took in my savior. His face was gentle and his hands were clean. "Thank you. I'm trying to find a certain stall. Can you help me? The fortune-teller? Her curtains are red and white striped."

He chuckled. "You're too young to need your fortune told."

"I have an appointment. I'm in serious trouble."

Up the path, Hodge and Duffy had stopped passing the glass bottle around. They stabbed at each other's chests. Their words escalated in volume.

The miner looked away from them, back to my welted and scabbed face. His eyes touched on my torn collar. "All right, then. I'll escort you. I saw it that-a-way." He held my arm, tunneling an opening through the masses.

I kept my head down and covered my hair with the shawl. "I had no idea Monte Cristo had so many people."

"Besides the hoity-toity townsfolk, the men have all come out of their mines. Working underground and digging in hard rock with just a flicker of light for months on end turns some men wild. Like our Hodge and Duffy."

"Am I some hoity-toity townsfolk?"

"Yes, you surely are, miss. A pleasant one, though."

He walked me up and around and finally to the red-and-white curtains. Voices murmured inside. A small sign tied to a pole next to the tent flap read: WITH CUSTOMER, PLEASE WAIT.

"Do you want me to stay with you?"

"No, thanks. I'm safe here. I really appreciate you taking care of me. What's your name?"

"Jimmy Barrows, miss."

"Jimmy, if someone asks if you saw me, please say no."

"Our secret, then. I sure hope you find what you're searching for." He tipped his dirty hat and left me under Leroux's sign.

I sat down in a rickety wooden chair, flapped dirt off my hem, and tried to straighten the front of my dress. I leaned my head back in the sun, my sore feet hot in Emma's long stockings and shoes. The air sizzled—perfect weather for shorts and flip-flops. Even if I had a thousand years, I would never get used to the clothes. I sighed and tried to push my blistering misery away, swatting at a fat fly with rainbow-colored wings buzzing around my nose. "I hope I see you in amber someday, you stupid bug."

"Hello, please come in." Leroux stood above me, just in time. The thought of my grandmother's ring on Thorn's hand had sent me sinking into a black pit of despair.

A well-dressed lady with peacock feathers in her hair emerged from the darkened tent and blinked into the bright sunshine. She snapped open a flowered parasol before walking away.

"I don't have any money, Leroux. But that man with me last night will come and pay you. I promise."

"I understand." She held the flap open and motioned me to a round table. Her eyes traveled across the hand imprint she had seen yesterday. She sat down opposite me and took in my torn dress. "Another bad day, my dear?"

"Yes, horrible. I can tell you about my problem—"

"Shush." She put a slender finger to my lips. "No talking now. Let me get to know you in my own way."

She moved a brass clock to a small desk in the back and

set it down next to three brown-and-white photos in tarnished silver frames. She sat down again, held my hands, and closed her eyes. Her breathing slowed.

Except for the murmuring of people walking past the tent, the ticking clock and our steady breath were the only sounds. Her eyeballs rolled around under their lids. Perspiration dotted her forehead. Her lips quivered and her hands trembled.

Her eyes flew open. "I knew you were special! You are a time traveler!"

I nodded. Like Simeon, someone else could see me.

"You are from the future. Many years into the future."

"One hundred and twenty years."

"You want to know how to go home."

"They're sending me to school in Baltimore tomorrow. I can't go. I have to stay in Monte Cristo. I'm sure my way back is here."

She ran her hand down my cheek. "She struck you. She tore your dress. Someone who calls herself your mother."

"Yes."

"What is your name, child?"

"Sonnet McKay."

"Sonnet. Little poem. What a lovely name."

I wanted to climb into her lap.

She got up and glided around the room. She stopped and held one of the photos, lifting the spotted image out in front of her. "Before she died, my momma told me she met a time traveler once. In the waning days of President Lincoln's war, a man from the future found her. He somehow heard about my momma and came all the way from New Orleans to the plantation and our poor little cabin. Just an itty girl I was then. She probably sent me outside while they spoke. Wouldn't have wanted to trouble my dreams with their fearsome talk. I have wondered about her dying words and waited for a visitor of my own, as she promised I would have someday. It has finally happened. It appears your world has bumped up against ours, Sonnet, and we have somehow come together in this high mountain town."

I watched her still, slim back draped in the ruby dress, talking to her momma's photo and getting used to the idea of me.

She turned, smiling and believing. "You have good instincts, my girl. You cannot go to Baltimore. The way back to your time is here in Monte Cristo."

"Can you see my future, Leroux? Do I go home?"

"The same way you came, you shall return."

"The closet?"

Leroux's hands reached for mine again. "I see a closet, yes . . . for both of you. Somehow the same closet. Someone else searches for a way back. Your destinies are intertwined. She is struggling, too."

"Emma? Someone like me?"

"Someone like you. Someone very much like you. They are here in Monte Cristo, Sonnet, right now, hunting for a way to get you home."

Of course, they were. And Emma was with them. I closed my eyes and imagined my family right here. Right here with me. I swallowed down the love that had caught in my throat and held on tight to Leroux's words. "When?"

"You will know it when the time comes. Have faith, child. Everything you need to know is already inside you."

I smiled and hugged her. "It *must* be true. Simeon said the same thing—"

The flap burst open. A small figure stood in front of us and gasped for breath.

"Kerry! How did you know I was here?"

"Tor said I might find you at the fortune-teller. They are scouring the fair for you, Sonnet. Mister Sweetwine has gone for the sheriff. We must accelerate our plan." She tossed me the leather bag. "Change now. I'll be up the road to the right. Follow me but stay thirty paces behind. I will lead you to Tor and the horses waiting beyond the fairground."

"Kerry, wait. On the envelopes, write, 'Emma's closet, same as before.' And Kerry . . . Thorn stole my ring."

She nodded and ducked back through the flap.

I dropped the shawl and stepped out of my clothes. I towed on the flannel shirt and baggy jeans, tightening the belt around my waist. Leroux helped me stuff my hair into the hat. I slung the leather bag over my shoulder with the corduroy jacket still inside.

Leroux gathered the clothes from the floor and threw them into a chest. "Your man friend owes me nothing. I now have a fine new dress."

"A dress that needs major fixing. And the shawl belongs to the photographer here at the fair. Take it to him if you can and tell him you found it in the dirt."

I clung to her and kissed her cheek. Jasmine lingered on her skin and in her hair, and I knew that scent would remind me of her until the day I died. "Thank you, Leroux."

Her smile was a beautiful promise. "You are stronger than

you know, Sonnet. It has been an honor meeting you. God-speed, my dear girl, my little poem."

Leroux held the red-and-white flap. I ducked out, blinking at the sudden sharp light. With the hat low on my head, I followed thirty steps behind Kerry, away from the Ice Caves Fair and up the narrow path to Tor.

CHAPTER TWENTY-TWO

Emma
2015

$\mathscr{E}$mma, loving every minute of their gypsy existence, watched from the riverbank as her friends splashed around in the river while the early evening sun still burned at them through the trees.

Niki and Evan called to her, "C'mon, Emma. Get in the water."

She had never had so much attention. It filled her up, stuffed her full. She knew now that love doesn't just seep away. There was enough to go around for everyone. What you gave returned tenfold. A lesson her mother had never learned.

Waving her hand, she promised she would come soon, wanting another minute by herself to gaze into the pure green water. She saw, instead of river rocks, a moving picture, like a modern movie playing in her head.

The Ice Caves Fair would be this very weekend. Ladies and gentlemen and their children would sit right here at the river's edge in their Sunday-best clothes, picnicking and cooling themselves in the shade. After a time, they would make their way down the hill to town and join the teeming crowd. The entire Monte Cristo population, and inhabitants from the surrounding areas, would wander here and there, open parasols shading the ladies from the hot summer sun. There would be food and games and interesting people who brought their talents and set up in tents, counting on the public to pay for their services.

Tor and Emma had planned to secretly meet and steal some time for themselves. For a second and in a panic, Emma almost forgot what Tor looked like and searched the water for Rapp. She spotted him jumping off a partially submerged boulder, suspended in the air and holding his long arms around his folded legs. He roared, "Cannonball!" before he landed with a deep plunge next to Evan's waving arms and laughing face.

Emma, not for the first time, thought about Rapp and his bloodline reaching all the way back to Tor. She and Rapp had not spoken on the subject since the afternoon she had been found out. Everything had returned to normal between them. But she knew they both thought about it. And here she was again—wondering. Before she could get too deep into those thoughts, she pushed them away. As if she'd banged a wardrobe door shut, Emma doused any further contemplation of Rapp.

She would not jinx time or her place in it. She would not dwell on the decayed envelope inside the piano that had turned to powder at their touch, or about missing the Ice Caves Fair. She would not think about climbing into a long metal tube in a few days and flying through the sky to Africa if their mission ended in failure. She would not think about living Sonnet's life forever.

Or imagine Sonnet, with Tor, living hers.

Jules sat down beside her. "Hey."

"Hey, what's up?" Emma said, and they put their foreheads together and giggled. One of Team Switch's favorite pastimes was to get Emma to say contemporary words and phrases in her proper way while they laughed and teased her.

Jules said, "You're just sitting here like a sad lump. Is everything okay?"

"Everything is okay. Why are *you* not in the river with everyone?"

"I'm working up to it. I hate getting my hair wet without a hair dryer close by. Truthfully, I'm not much of a camper."

Jules would be beautiful with a rat's nest for hair. Her unblemished face glowed like the finest porcelain doll, and her delicate features were faultless. So very different from her own freckled face. "Except for your eyes, you and Evan hardly look like brother and sister."

"I mostly look like my mom. Sonnet and Evan look like Dad and Aunt Kate, as if they were their little mini-me's. Well, you know. You've been around Aunt Kate. It's weird."

"Does that bother you, Jules? That you are different?"

"I don't mind being different. I do get annoyed sometimes over the hubbub around Sonnet and Evan being twins, though." She laughed. "If you were all here together as triplets, it would probably send me over the edge."

Emma sighed. It would have been wonderful to be triplets with Sonnet and Evan, and be a member of this most perfect family. But Emma knew better than to express that secret longing to Jules. "Sorry."

"It's okay," said Jules. "When it comes right down to it, I like being unique. I know I belong . . . and that's what matters."

Emma had never quite fit inside her own family circle. But like a member of a clan or a tribe, she knew she belonged to this collection of people.

Tan arms reaching up from the river motioned in the distance. "Hey, Jules. Get over here." Niki, the mother ship, was calling to her barnacle.

"Chop, chop," said Emma to Jules, winking.

Jules laughed. "Yes, well, chop, chop, it's time to go ruin my hair." She shook her yellow mane and picked her way over the narrow shoreline toward the splashing.

Lia swam to Emma's dangling feet, floating loose in the cool water, and tickled them. "It's absolutely too nice in here, Emma. You're missing all the fun."

Emma stood, unmindful now of her bare body in Sonnet's swimming clothes, and followed Jules over the smooth river rocks to the boulder where Rapp had plunged down next to Evan. She had found the courage to leap straight out of the *Buck Swan* into Lake Washington. She could certainly do this.

She waited for Jules to jump, and then she jumped, too, shouting "Cannonball!" as she flew into the river and her tribe's waiting arms.

SAYING he was going to distract them from their disappointment in not finding any meaningful clues yet, Uncle Jack climbed up on the van's roof and rifled around in the big box, finally finding the items he was searching for. He brandished a fishing pole around in front of them as if it were some sort of grand treasure. "I'm going to show you all how it's done and then you can each have a turn. We're going to catch trout for dinner."

He waded to waist-high water, holding the rod with its imitation insect attached to the hook, and cast the line out in front of him. His long, unbound hair and browned skin made him a picture of the native people that fished along these rivers in Emma's time.

Keko set the tin soldier down on a tree stump and waded out toward Uncle Jack over slippery rocks, still wearing her tennis shoes. Team Switch lined up along the bank. They were counting on at least a few trout to go with the tinfoil-wrapped potatoes baking in the nearby campfire coals.

Keko unclenched her fist and sprinkled tiny pieces of bread around on top of the burbling water. They slowly absorbed water and sank, lured downstream toward the translucent fishing line reaching into the river.

A school of fish swam by Keko's and Uncle Jack's submerged legs, the setting sun lighting speckles on their silvery, shimmery scales. Within minutes the line tugged and the pole bent backwards, making a large "U."

Uncle Jack shouted, "A gift from the great spirits . . . bring the net!"

Emma turned her wet back on the struggling fish that jumped and towed the rod taut right in front of her. She would not watch the thing die—but she would eagerly eat it. She had always turned up her nose at seafood at her parents' table, but not here. Her stomach growled in anticipation. She had never been as hungry as she found herself in this place. Eating fire-grilled speckled trout was just one of the many ways she had been altered. Except for Tor and her brothers, it would be hard to go back to her old life. She felt uneasy and torn.

She was being wrenched in both directions by nobody other than herself.

"YOU'VE been quiet all night, Keko," said Rapp, standing tall next to the fire pit. He pushed three marshmallows onto his long stick and poked them out over hot coals that had rolled out to the sides of the bonfire. "Like you're worried. Is something wrong?"

A tide of darkness had descended, and dancing fireflies joined them around the campfire as the fish and baked potatoes they had just devoured became a distant memory. Content with her own burnt marshmallow, Emma plucked it off her stick while blowing on it at the same time, and flattened it with a piece of chocolate between two graham crackers. As far as she was concerned, this made-up creation was possibly the best thing she had ever eaten. But instead of roasting another marshmallow, she set her stick down, waiting for Keko's reply.

Up to this point their conversation had stayed deliberately positive. "Upbeat" was how Lia had put it. "We have to stay upbeat!"

Keko faced the blaze, sitting on a log where she had been slowly swaying to Uncle Jack's guitar song. The orange-and-magenta painted streaks running through her long black hair glowed like a pretty clown's wig, and licks of fire reflected in the brown almonds of her eyes. "I may as well confess. I haven't been in touch with Sonnet's actual presence since the day I first sat on the floor in Emma's bedroom. I feel nothing but strife emanating from the vibes now."

"What does that mean? Should we be worried?" said Jules, looking worried.

Keko said, "I don't know what's wrong, Jules. I just—can't explain it."

"But you're the expert. What's your best guess, Keko?" Uncle Jack put down his guitar. "Let's just get this out in the open and talk about it, or none of us will sleep tonight."

Keko sat for a minute gathering her thoughts. "There seems to be something antagonistic going on that's more or less sucking all the vitality away from Sonnet. I'm having a hard time finding her through all the sludge of hostility."

Niki said, "This is really stressful. This whole stupid thing."

"But she's still there, right?" Lia's voice quivered and her eyes filled with tears.

Evan whipped his stick from the fire and gazed at his six perfectly browned marshmallows. "Okay, Keko. What do we do?"

"First, Lia, I do believe she's still there. Second, Evan, we have to just keep going. Putting one foot in front of the other and scouring the house for clues. Third, Jules and Niki, yes, this is stressful and, no, I don't want you to worry. You all must stay strong for me. I need your tough, focused energy around me to keep me in a place where I can pick up on Sonnet again. Okay?"

The fire threw sparks into the air as the black night encircled them in silence. Like little magical beings come to visit from a faraway planet, the swarm of fireflies put on a show, twinkling around in the light.

Rapp turned to Uncle Jack. "Do you know a cheerleading song?"

"A *what?*"

"You know, that music, or chanting, or whatever they call it, so people can cheer on their team."

"Ah, yes." He winked at Rapp and seized his guitar where it leaned up against his chair. "You mean like the 'Queen Anne Grizzlies Fight Song?'"

"Exactly," said Evan. "Come on Jules. We need to cheer for Keko. Get up and teach us your moves. And anyway, this will be something Emma can take home with her. Thanks to you, she'll be the first ever cheerleader in the entire world."

Jules laughed and shouted, "Come on!" and towed everyone to their feet. They followed her around the fire, kicking their legs in the air, spinning their bodies and gesturing their arms as Uncle Jack half-yelled and half-sang the "Grizzlies Fight Song" and hammered on the guitar's wooden back in time with his bellowing. Rapp picked up the words and yelled along.

Evan, jumping around behind Keko, caught her around the waist and twirled her up in the air. "You feeling it, Keko? You feeling our energy?"

Team Switch chanted along with Evan. "You feeling it, Keko? You feeling it?"

"Yes, yes! I'm feeling it!" Keko's flying hair turned into a blur of colors and she laughed so hard she cried. And in the star-bedecked Monte Cristo night, with just the fire and the fireflies lighting her lithe body, Jules taught everyone her moves. And those moves and that cheer and their love for each other gave them all the hope and courage they needed to keep fighting.

CHAPTER TWENTY-THREE

—

Sonnet
1895

Tor sprawled against a tree trunk, his long legs stretched out, brown working boots crossed at his ankles. His hat slid down his forehead and covered his eyes against the sun as if he were napping. Two horses grazed nearby on the long, swaying grass. Kerry breezed past him and aimed an old Irish song at his reclining body.

"Come over the hill, my bonnie Irish lad.
Come over the hill to your darling
You choose the rose, love, and I'll make the vow
And I'll be your true love forever . . ."

Tor rolled off the ground, took the leather bag out of my arms, and gave me the smaller horse's reins. I swung up onto its back and he handed me the bag again. The leather crunched under me in a familiar greeting as I settled down into the saddle. I gave a silent word of thanks to my mom, who had torn me, years ago, from my books and forced me, kicking and screaming, into horseback riding lessons. Simeon and Maxwell were right. There were no mistakes.

Tor ripped a large green canvas bag out of the grass and threw it on his red horse, before slinging himself on, too. The small open field disappeared under our horses' galloping hooves. We raced each other toward the dark forest rising beyond us. As we slowed and entered dappled shade, it felt like an air conditioner had been flipped on, cooling me and slowing the violent beating of my heart. We rode single file up a hill, thick with trees and underbrush, and across a rocky outcropping. The mountain trail grew steeper as we made our way. Rounding a bend, I saw a large sign in the distance hanging over small wooden buildings pressed up to the side of a sheer cliff. A sign rocked in the wind: MYSTERY MINE. We were here.

We trotted the horses beyond the largest building and into a small enclosure behind a barn. Tor brought the bags into the bunkhouse and set them on the floor, banging the screen door shut behind us. The men working the Mystery Mine wouldn't return until late Sunday. They were all at the fair.

Dust motes swirled around, funnels from the sunshine streaming through dirty windows. The wind blowing in from the open door stirred a strong smell of sweaty men and a faint smell of animals. I pulled the hat off my head and shook out my hair.

Tor put his arms around me and hugged me tight. "I can't stay long. My cabin will be one of the first places they search after Madam Sweetwine saw us in conversation the other day."

"I know. Don't worry. I'll be fine. It's a relief to be out of that awful house and gone from her."

"Let me show you some equipment and supplies." He dropped the canvas bag on the table and twisted a small basket of food from its depths. "This can go in the icehouse. We'll go find it in a minute." He tugged out his two red blankets. "Use these. Stay away from the men's bedrolls or you will wake up with fleas."

He set a kerosene lamp and matches on the table and showed me how to light it and turn the wick's flame up and down with a screw in the side.

"Stay in the bunkhouse or in the barn. If you have to go out after nightfall, take this with you." He set a gun on the table. "It's loaded. There are coyotes and cougars about at night. Even bears will come 'round if they smell food. And don't build a fire, Sonnet. I'm not sure how far the men will range up the mountain searching for you."

A small bundle inside a pillowcase came next. I dumped my jeans, shirt, and tennis shoes onto the table. Kerry had remembered a buttonhook. "These cloth shoes I'm wearing won't last another ride. The stirrups rubbed the seams open on the sides."

Tor watched as I took off the high button shoes and long stockings and laced up the high-tops over my bare feet. I cuffed his jeans a couple times so they didn't drag on the ground.

"I like you in men's clothing. I like your red boots."

Boots. I smiled.

"The sun is going to set," he said, taking my hand. "Come with me to find the icehouse."

The screen door slammed behind us as we stepped off the

porch. "I'm surprised there's no barking dog protecting the mine," I said.

"Oh, there was. I rode up earlier today and cut him loose. He shot into the forest like a furry cannonball, as if tasting freedom for the first time. When he gets hungry enough for real food in a few days, he'll return."

We found what we were looking for under the kitchen. I took bread, chicken, and apples. Kerry had wrapped a piece of chocolate cake in paper for me. I added it to my little pile of food. Everything else went back in the icehouse. Tor located a well and pumped water into a jug. Our feet dragging, we walked back to the bunkhouse still holding hands.

The lantern cast a warm glow between us. I could smell his sunshine skin.

"I hate leaving you."

"Don't worry. Really, Tor. I'm going to go to the barn and see if I can find a brush for that nice horse that got me here. It'll be therapeutic for both of us."

"Her name is Noel. I won her in a game of blackjack on Christmas Eve. Card playing is what we unattached men do around here in winter." He ran his hand through my loose hair and swept it across my cheek. "One of us will come see you tomorrow and take you up to Simeon's, depending . . ."

I nodded and moved away from him. I took the last envelope from the bottom of the leather bag. "If something happens and I don't see you again, I have a letter for you to give Emma. I think it's important that it come from you." He glanced at where I had written *Emma Sweetwine* across the front and *Sonnet McKay* in the upper left-hand corner. He stuffed it in his pocket.

Next, I took my leather and silver bracelet and adjusted the clever knot to make it bigger. I held his arm and rolled the leather circle up over his fingers and around his wrist, tightening it to fit him. It lay on patches of golden hair and smooth white scars. "Emma will know this is from me. But it'll be okay. After she reads my letter, she won't mind if you wear it. She can wear it, too. It's from a little village in South Africa, close to where I live."

I rubbed my finger across it, stamping the picture of it sitting on his wrist into my heart. "Thanks for everything you've done for me."

He touched the bracelet. He touched the scab on my lip. I took his hand and kissed it. He took me in his arms. We pressed into each other in the dusty light, and I didn't know if he saw Emma or Sonnet, and I didn't care. Whoever I was to him, for that moment on top of a mountain, in a rustic bunkhouse for gold miners, Tor and I were the only ones who existed.

He kissed me hard one last time, running his hands slowly down my back, keeping the feel of me on his palms. We stared at each other for a long moment, and then he stepped away, dipping his arms from me, and ran a scarred and callused hand across my face, wiping away tears. "I will never forget you, Sonnet. I promise."

His jaw clenched and he swallowed hard as a solitary tear ran down his cheek. Something sharp stabbed at my heart. He heaved himself away and walked out the door. I followed him and watched from the porch as he walked his horse out of the enclosure and swung onto his saddle. Without a backward glance, he rode off through the mining area and rounded the bend, disappearing from view.

My knees snapped closed, the bones in my legs turning to rubber. I slid down the doorjamb to the floor as knives sliced through my body and hot, wet, streaming tears singed down my face. My body ached with a searing pain—as if someone had died. The bend in the road would stay empty. Tor wouldn't return.

My head fell back against the bunkhouse siding, so heavy I couldn't hold it up.

Creaking, swaying trees were my only companions, whistling their desolate sound off the gunmetal cliff behind the building where I huddled. The lush perfume of roses sailed on the wind. My head lolled sideways toward the scent. Off the far end of the porch grew a lonely rosebush blooming delicate yellow buds tinged in pink. I hadn't noticed it, hadn't seen it until the moment I needed it.

Blinking away my last straggling tears, I stared at the surprising find, accepting finally it wasn't a mirage. I scooted over and ran my fingers across a velvety petal.

Against all odds, a hardscrabble miner had loved and nurtured a single rosebush on this inhospitable, rocky mountain. Someone like Jimmy Barrows, who had the goodness of heart to think of others besides himself. It was a beautiful gift for anyone who found themselves on this lonely porch.

"Thank you, whoever you are," I whispered, and plucked a pretty bud, holding it to my nose. I turned my face to the setting sun. The singing sighs of the wind in the trees bounced off the stone and echoed down through the valley.

Something black soared into the halo of the sun's brightness. As big as a raccoon, the bald eagle cruised in a slow, wide-winged circle around the tops of the trees. Its orangey-yellow beak curved into a sharp point from a white-feathered head, and orange talons stretched as it reached forward to grab and hold a branch heavy with pinecones. The eagle flew alone, determined in its journey, majestic in its solitude.

I watched until it disappeared inside the tree and then nestled the rosebud down into my pocket. I walked to the kitchen and found a broom. I hiked out to the bend and spent the next forty minutes walking backward, sweeping the broom back and forth over the dirt and rocks. When I was sure I had erased every last hoof print, I found Noel waiting patiently in the enclosure.

"Pretty little Christmas girl. Do you want me to pay attention to you?" I heaved away her saddle, pulled off the reins and bit, and gave her an apple. Nudging her in front of water and hay, I found grooming tools on a shelf in the barn and brushed her until her tan coat shone. I settled her into the barn for the night.

The lamp in the bunkhouse cast bobbing shadows around the room as it flickered behind the glass, glinting light off the cold, shiny gun that lay on the table where Tor had left it. The dark night closed in around me, so still my growling stomach was the only sound. I ate Cook's fried chicken and buttered bread and gnawed on an apple. I wadded up the mess and threw it outside behind the kitchen in the garbage pile.

I lugged the supplies out of the bunkhouse and dropped everything next to Noel. With the lantern still lit, I took the red blankets and made up a bed on a perfect bed-sized bale of straw. I climbed in, still wearing Tor's clothes and my tennis shoes, and ate a few bites of cake, wrapping up the rest for my breakfast.

My tear-puffed eyes stung and rubbed sand across the insides of my lids. Letting them close, I let Tor in, and watched his solitary tear weep for me. It formed a puddle in his eye, pooling over the green marble swirls of moss and fern and pine. It molded into a translucent drop on his lashes and trembled there, falling after a moment to his cheek and inching down over the sunburned face where sawdust sometimes lay. I watched as it rolled and caught on his lip before continuing its journey to his chin, mixing with the golden stubble, flattening into a spot of wetness, no longer a trickle of salty river.

I held the picture for a moment longer and then let it slide away. It landed . . . a video gently placed in a box. I closed the lid and locked it. I would take it out again someday. When I was stronger.

Noel's snuffles and snorts soothed me and thoughts of my best friend, my best cousin, Lia, and the letters I had hidden for her gave me hope.

I let go of the day.

WITH a gasp, I sat up. My sleepy heart caught in my throat. Men's deep voices called to each other from beyond the barn.

CHAPTER TWENTY-FOUR

—

Emma
2015

With a gasp, Emma sat up. Her sleepy heart caught in her throat, her dream still visible on the tip of her mind. She took hold of it before it floated away. "Lia!"

"What?" Lia turned over and rubbed her eyes.

Jules called from deep in her sleeping bag. "What's wrong, Emma?"

"Lia has the answer. Lia holds the key to unlocking the secret."

"We need to listen to Emma. She is feeling something strong, something true. Something is being communicated to her." Keko sat up. "I have been so focused everywhere else, Lia, I haven't paid attention to you."

Lia shook her head. "What could it be?"

Niki yawned. "Huh? Who's communicating with Emma?"

"It was Sonnet," said Emma.

The tent grew quiet.

"There's another letter."

"I believe you, Emma. You and Lia and I will go to the

house when the sun comes up. If it's in the stars, we'll have our answer." Keko settled back down in her sleeping bag. "We'll have plenty of time tomorrow."

EMMA and Lia nudged at the front door as Keko pointed Rapp's flashlight around the dark-as-night entryway. "Let's go, Lia," said Keko. "You take me through what happened that day."

Lia led them to where the piano once stood. "Okay. We came into the house through the front door. Everyone ran straight upstairs and started goofing around, scaring each other, acting silly. I realized Sonnet wasn't with us so I came back downstairs to find her. She was standing here—" Lia tapped her foot on the floor. "—and acting dazed. For a second, I thought she might even be talking to herself."

They moved up close to the pile of piano debris. Keko ran the flashlight over the mess. "I felt Sonnet's presence all over the pieces of paper you found. You were right to focus there."

"I just don't know what else there could be. The piano was easy. She knew I would realize it was the only stick of furniture in the house."

Keko handed the flashlight to Emma and put her hands on her hips. "There's more."

Lia pressed her lips shut for a moment, glancing at the ceiling. "So, we were talking. We heard the others all screaming and running around upstairs. I convinced Sonnet to go up there. She didn't really want to."

"So, you left this room and went upstairs."

"Yeah. We stood at the bottom of the stairs for a few

minutes and then went up. We were gonna find and scare them."

"Let's retrace your steps."

Keko and Lia made their way back through the empty room to the staircase as Emma illuminated the way.

"We climbed the stairs like we're doing now and started down the hallway. We heard footsteps coming so we ran. But we ran the wrong way and stumbled into Rapp. I think he had just come running down from there." Lia pointed to the small staircase leading up to the third floor.

"The maid's quarters," said Emma.

"That's exactly what Sonnet said. 'There must be another floor. Maybe the maid's quarters.' She liked to watch those British tearjerkers with her mom and knew all about old houses and where the maids lived."

Lia turned around and started back down the hallway. "Rapp took Sonnet's hand and said, 'Let's hide' and chucked us into that room. Emma's room. He came in behind us and shut the door. Rapp told us it was his favorite room in the house, so far, like he'd already been in there. Then he walked to the window and I left. I knew Sonnet kinda liked Rapp so I wanted to leave them alone."

"That's all?" Keko frowned.

"She was acting jumpy. Like she couldn't catch her breath. I thought maybe it was her allergies. She'd been sneezing from all the dust."

Keko moved to where the bed once stood and shut her eyes. "What else? We're missing something. Go back to that day, Lia. Slow down. What are we missing?"

"Let me start over." Lia shut her eyes while Keko held her

arms. "We moved away from the piano. Okay, I remember now. Sonnet walked, not to the staircase, but to a hallway behind us. We went into another room. Sonnet rubbed dirt off the tile on the fireplace and said something like, 'Wow, peacocks!' while I went to the built-in cabinet."

Keko said, "Lia, the dining room? You're in the dining room, right?"

"Yeah. We went in there just before we went upstairs. I found a candle in a drawer and showed it to her. I was talking all crazy about ghosts and not wanting to take the candle out of the house. And then Sonnet said, 'A candle and a piano—left behind. Like a message from the dead.'" Lia swallowed, her eyes growing large. "That's what Sonnet said to me. 'Like a message from the dead,' and then I said, 'Like a hologram beamed in from heaven.'"

Keko's hands tightened around Lia's arms and shook them. "There's something from Sonnet! In the cabinet."

"That's it!" Lia spun out of Keko's grasp and ran from the room, yelling as she went. "We searched all the drawers yesterday. But we didn't bother to look behind them. I'm such an idiot! She wouldn't put it *inside*—it would have been found eventually by someone."

Lia ran to a drawer. "This is it. The one with the candle. Hold the flashlight on it." She rocked it up and down until it opened and handed the stick of wax behind her to Emma.

"Watch out." Lia dropped the drawer to the floor. It landed with a bang.

"There!" Emma pointed the light at the right-hand framing. "See it?"

"Yes. It's in one piece, nailed into the frame on both

ends." Keko touched it. "I sense Sonnet at work here." She jiggled the first nail until it fell out. "I don't want to have the paper fall with the other nail to the floor."

"I'll hold while you pull the nail." Lia put her arm inside and pinned the paper against wood.

"Got it. Okay, I'll hold it . . . you take the edge, Lia, and bring it forward."

Emma focused the beam of light. *From Sonnet* was written across a yellowed envelope. Someone had scrawled, *Emma's closet, just like before,* sideways across the end in different script.

Lia held it to her heart and shrieked. "I'm so happy! Let's take it down to the campsite and read Sonnet's message with everyone. We've been through so much together. It's only fair."

Before they could make it out of the house, the rest of Team Switch, along with Uncle Jack, barged through the battered front door to meet them.

If you're reading this letter, it means you remembered, Lia. A message from the dead! I've pulled off being Emma with the so-called family. The nanny, Tor Loken (yes, he must be related to Rapp), the carriage driver, and his grandfather are the only ones who know the truth. They are helping me, and if it wasn't for them, I would be crazy right now. I found out the parents are sending me to school in Baltimore with no intention of ever bringing me back. I met with the grandfather (he "has the sight"), and he agrees that I must stay here. If I haven't found a way back by Sunday, I'm running away. What I know so far is this:

There will be an identical storm

Emma and I can't be in the same place

This has all happened for an unknown reason

I'm trying to stay hopeful, but in case I don't see you again, I want you to know how much I love you all. A day doesn't go by that I don't think of you. All of you. I didn't appreciate what a great family I had until I got here and was forced to live Emma's life. It's not all bad, though. Her brothers are the most wonderful little creatures. Besides the people who are helping me, they are the highlight of my life. And Emma is lucky to have Tor. He's the best guy ever.

Love,

Sonnet

"She must have left the house." Jules pointed to the envelope. "That's someone else's writing on the corner."

"Kerry's handwriting," said Emma.

Rapp read the letter and cryptic message on the envelope again. "A storm. And Emma's closet. Just like before."

Niki tapped on her phone. "The weather tomorrow in the Cascade Mountains is supposed to be sun with a hundred percent chance of a quick rain squall coming in from the mountain ridge above us. At noon."

Lia said, "That was the exact weather prediction on the day of our Monte Cristo picnic. The day Sonnet left and Emma came."

"Does this mean we are switching tomorrow and I'm going home?" Emma asked. "To the best guy Sonnet has ever met?"

"Yippee! It's all coming together," yelled Jules, twirling in the air.

"So, what do you want to do on your potentially last day here, Emma?" asked Evan. "Stick around? Drive somewhere in the van? We could show you some more of our world. We have twenty-four hours."

Emma thought for a moment. All she really wanted was to spend this last day with her friends right here at the campsite. "I would like to float together in the river. Eat s'mores around the fire and listen to Uncle Jack and Rapp play beautiful music. Relish these last moments with you all and seal them tight inside me so they are not forgotten. And then go home tomorrow to Tor and the life I was born into."

She glanced over at Lia, the best friend she had ever had, and found it impossible to say more.

THE park ranger showed them no mercy. He tore twisted vines and spiraling ferns away from the sign and pointed. "Right here: NO CAMPING. NO FIRES. DAY HIKES AND PICNICS ONLY."

"We weren't aware of the rules, Officer. The sign was completely covered. It's not really our fault, you see," said Uncle Jack.

"And because of that I won't write you out a citation. But you have to pack up your gear. The tent comes down, now. You can stay for the rest of the day, but your group is required to be offsite by sundown. Those are the rules. Storms come out of nowhere around here and bring flashfloods from rising rivers. It's going to rain tomorrow and you don't want to be caught in a dangerous situation."

Jules smiled at him, sliding her eyes to his badge and back to his pitiless face. Her words dripped sugar and her fingers stroked through her hair. "Can't we please have just one more night, Ranger Karl?"

"Ma'am, you and your friends need to be gone by sunset. I'll be back to check, and if you're still here, whoever owns the van will receive a citation, and I will escort you down the mountain myself."

"Where's the closest hotel?" Keko asked.

"Head past Granite Falls. You'll find decent lodging in Snohomish. Try the Countryside Inn." He pulled the brim of his hat straight at Jules. "Have a good day." He flicked the corners of his mouth up at her, before sliding back into his big, shiny truck, slamming the door shut, and driving away.

"Well, Ranger Karl liked *you*, Jules," said Lia.

"Is that even allowed?" Rapp crossed his arms and stared at the receding vehicle as it was swallowed up by greenery.

"Liked her, yeah, just not enough to break the rules." Niki kicked at the dirt. "So, now what?"

Evan smacked his lips. "Snohomish? I wouldn't mind going back to the Flower Patch Diner for some bread pudding."

That was Evan, thought Emma. Even during a crisis, his mind could not stray far from his stomach.

CHAPTER TWENTY-FIVE

—

Sonnet
1895

$\int$ tumbled out of my straw bed and crawled on hands and knees across the hay-covered floor. My heart banged and clanged and my fear-choked breathing was tortured, strangled. Men's voices called back and forth, but I was too far away to understand what they were saying.

I pressed my face to a narrow space between the barn siding. Light danced in the distance. Four lanterns. Three men sat like silvery specters on horses, their faces turned from the moon and hidden in shadows. A single lantern bobbed lower to the ground. One of the men had climbed off his horse and was now rambling around where I had swept the broom across rocks after Tor left.

Another rider dismounted and the two men headed in my direction. I turned and swept my eyes over the barn's dark interior. *What was the layout as I had searched for grooming tools earlier in the evening?*

No layout, nothing. Just a big empty barn. Except for

burying myself under hay, there was no place to hide. And if they came in they would spy Noel and my things and find me anyway.

I peered back out. One of the men had bypassed the path to the barn. His lantern moved close to the bunkhouse. The screen door squeaked open and banged shut. The lantern light dipped around inside. I caught their words, shouted to each other, clear in the night air.

"See anything in there, Barry?"

"Nope, nothing. No girl here. No sign of anyone."

Noel snorted. I froze. My heart started again with a painful jolt. I crawled back over to her in the dark and caressed her muzzle. She blew and nudged at my shoulder as I leaned over and felt around in the canvas bag for an apple. I held it in front of her. She ran her lips across my palm and chomped.

I waited for the barn door to burst open, ready to call it quits. After a few minutes of agony, I listened to the men crunch across rocks away from us.

After what seemed like an eternity, the light evaporated. The sound of hooves faded.

And night-silence closed in on me again.

I collapsed into the hay. On hands and knees, again, I inched my wobbly body back to the red blankets and bale of straw. My shaking eventually stopped, and my heart calmed down, but I didn't sleep. Daylight would come soon. I would have to leave the Mystery Mine later today before the miners returned.

Hard-driving hooves beat toward me, slapping another shock to my heart. Just one horse this time. I scuttled to the side of the barn and pressed my face against the boards again.

Streaking across the rising sun and heading straight toward the Mystery Mine galloped a beautiful, brown-spotted Appaloosa. A blue-and-black-checked cap sat low on the face of the rider.

I tripped over myself, running to open the enclosure gate.

Maxwell, as if guided by a divine being, rode straight to me. He leapt out of the saddle and jogged, leading the horse into the barn. I rammed the door shut behind him and flew into his arms. "You're here, Maxwell! Four men were stalking me early this morning."

"That I know. I tailed them. I've watched over you all night."

"Tor—"

"He's suspected in your disappearance and held captive at his cabin by the town barber, one of three men deputized yesterday." He smiled. "Monte Cristo is in an uproar."

"How did you get away?"

"Mister Sweetwine asked me to take one of the horses and go looking for you. Maybe he thought I could find you with my 'magic powers.' I feel sorry for him. He is truly out of his mind."

Maxwell lugged the saddle off Starlight and let me water and brush her while he went out back to rescue the food basket from under the kitchen. He refilled the pitcher and brought everything back to the barn.

We ate the rest of the chicken and bread and chocolate cake. The last two apples went to Noel and Starlight. I reached into the bottom of the basket. "Cook's snickerdoodle cookies! Kerry sure loves me." I held one to my nose and inhaled cinnamon and sugar before I bit off a chunk.

"Indeed. Kerry does love you."

"I'll miss her. I'll miss you, too. The thought of not seeing you again—" I stopped myself.

He bent his head to his cookie and broke the snickerdoodle in two. He put half in his mouth and chewed.

"I feel like it's getting close, Maxwell."

"It will soon be time for you to fly away from us. You have called on your destiny. We have just helped you find your wings. None of us want you to leave, but leave you must."

Eagle wings. I would grow them soon.

My full stomach and Maxwell's company brought me peace, and the horses' soft nickering to each other sang to me like a lullaby. I laid my head back on the leather bag and ran my eyes over Maxwell's wise face, as kind and decent as his grandfather's. "I feel safe. I'm so glad you're here with me. Thanks for watching over me all night."

"You are my friend, my family, my sister. I would do anything for you." He settled down next to me, held my hand and curled up, tugging his cap low on his face. "It smells like rain." He sighed, and our breathing steadied with sleep.

A clap of thunder woke me. I heard random raindrops quicken and lazy drizzle turn to fat drops. The hair on my arms stood up as I ran to the barn door and hauled it open. The sheer cliff beyond the Mystery Mine was dazzling in its slick, sun-speckled wetness. Above the cliff, black clouds pushed away white ones and skated toward the sun.

Without knowing exactly what I had been waiting for, I

knew it had finally arrived. "My storm's coming, Maxwell!"

I turned back to him as he bounded out of the hay and strode toward me. He didn't glance outside at the rain. His eyes were on my face. "It's time to go home."

"STAY on my rear," said Maxwell. "I'm taking us the back way on an old overgrown Indian trail that no one has knowledge of around here except Grandfather and me. We'll loop around and enter the Sweetwine property from the back. The route is steeper and harder to traverse, but it's faster, and we can avoid the town and the sheriff and his newly minted deputies."

Maxwell tossed the canvas bag on Starlight. I buttoned up Tor's corduroy coat and swung up onto Noel's back. I waited while he ran back to close and latch the gate. He jumped up on Starlight and trotted away with me following. The Mystery Mine disappeared behind us as we rounded the bend.

Partway along the same path Tor and I had traveled yesterday, Maxwell guided Starlight into a dense, dark grove. We slowed and maneuvered our horses downhill and around trees with trunks as big across as the old trampoline that had sat in Lia's backyard until she and Niki no longer jumped on it. Undergrowth swung at my legs as drops of rain dripped off branches and fell on Tor's leather hat sitting low on my head. Besides the long green tree branches thwacking against us, the only sound huffed from Noel and Starlight as their hooves gently moved across the carpet of pine needles.

I glanced down at my damp high-tops peeking out of the stirrups.

Maxwell brought Starlight to a sudden halt. I jerked Noel to a stop behind them and watched as Maxwell slowly moved his coat aside and pulled a gun out of his belt, cocking it. Out of the corner of my eye I saw a flash of movement and heard a deep snarl.

A mother cougar with two small cubs at her rear crouched low off Starlight's left flank. Her intense gold eyes watched Maxwell as her twitching muscles tightened, ready to spring. She panted and showed us her long, sharp teeth.

Starlight whinnied and started to move backward, causing Noel to snort and back up. The cougar swiveled around at her cubs, giving Maxwell the chance he needed to bring his gun around and shoot, his aim purposely off to the side of the magnificent animals. Startled out of her striking pose by the gun's deafening boom, the mother leapt into the air and yelped at her cubs. She turned and bounded away, her babies on her rear. With a noisy suck, I filled my lungs.

Maxwell moved Starlight sideways a couple of feet up against a boulder and turned in his saddle. "Thank you for not screaming."

I brought Noel alongside Starlight and laughed at him. "I'm not a screaming kind of girl."

"I hope no one heard the gunshot. We shall sit a moment. And I want to find a place for Tor's bag. There can be no connection back to him." He gazed around the damp quiet and shoved the gun back under his jacket and into his belt.

He pitched the bag off Starlight's back and jumped down, rifling through it. "Is there anything in here you want?"

"No. You keep the rest of the snickerdoodles. Kerry will know what to do with my clothes. Everything else is Tor's."

He put Tor's gun in his saddlebag, and threw the green bag under the overhang of the boulder. "Perfect color. It will blend with nature and stay dry until I can get it."

He swung back onto Starlight. "We are only about fifteen minutes away, but most of the ride now is steep. Noel will make it just fine. Keep the reins loose and your eyes ahead of you. We tie into the trail leading to grandfather's cabin five minutes ahead. Instead of going up the mountain, we go down."

"I remember it from the other night, although it seems like an eternity away to me now."

A sudden crash of far-off thunder was followed by a quick flash of lighting, zinging over our heads.

I pushed up Tor's hat. "I feel like the storm's following us."

Maxwell tipped his head to the darkening sky barely visible through the tree branches. "I believe you are right."

We made our way down the mountain on the steep, sheer path that ran along the side of the cliff to the lower woods. We guided our horses through the river and came up behind the new barn project. Beyond sat the many-colored Sweetwine mansion. A rainbow shot from wet trees and bowed across the sky, holding the house inside its vivid arc.

"Wait, Maxwell. I don't know what will happen when we get down there. I want to thank you now for everything you've done for me. I'm so grateful to you and your grandfather for seeing me—seeing Sonnet—believing in me. I couldn't have done this without you."

His chocolate eyes swam.

"You should get out of Monte Cristo. It'll soon be deserted. A ghost town."

He nodded. "This mountain is where I'll be. At least while Grandfather walks the earth. After that . . ." He shrugged, his eyes roaming over the tops of the steep cliffs surrounding Monte Cristo. "I'll see more of the world."

I followed his gaze. "The clouds blowing in are chasing away the rainbow and hiding the trees."

"As if those trees and the clouds that sit atop them connect heaven and earth. And we are mere mortals—no bigger, no more important, than fragments of consciousness and flesh sandwiched between."

"Monte Cristo. A place between heaven and earth." I watched as a sudden gust of wind blew around the dark hair hanging down from under his blue-and-black cap. "You don't need to quote Shakespeare or Aristotle, Maxwell. You're already a poet and a philosopher. You've just put everything into perspective with your two simple sentences." I missed him already.

Random raindrops turned to rain. He twisted in his saddle. "Are you ready, sister?"

"I'm ready."

We galloped side by side through the long meadow grass with the wind and rain in our faces. I rode to the front porch and jumped off, throwing Maxwell Noel's reins. "I might need you. Emma's bedroom is upstairs, the last one on the left."

"I know where it is. I'll come up the service staircase from the kitchen."

I ran up the stairs and burst through the door, striding into the parlor toward crackling logs and firelight. John stood in front of a blazing fireplace. I took off my wet hat and shook out my hair.

"Emma? Is that you?" He walked to me and held me out in

front of him, bewildered as he scanned down my clothes. "And are those trousers?"

Thorn came hurtling in from another room and stabbed at my arm. "You have missed the train. All the money spent—"

"No!" I jerked away from her icy fingers. "Never touch me again. Do you understand? Never!"

John scooped me away from her. "Leave her alone, Rose."

"Where is it?" I scanned her hands and saw only a wedding band. Thunder boomed and lightning cracked. I ran to the window and turned my head to the sky. Black clouds had pushed away all the white ones. I didn't have time.

I raced to the staircase where Kerry waited for me. I grabbed her wrist. We sprinted up the stairs and down the hall to Emma's room. Maxwell closed the door behind us and wrangled the brass bed in front of it.

"But your ring, Sonnet!" said Kerry. "You must have it with you."

"Find it. Take it to one of the gold dealers in town. Sell it. Those are real diamond chips and white gold. It's got to be worth a train ticket. Get away from here. You can't work for her anymore."

"Where will I go? The only people I know are in Monte Cristo—"

"My McKay ancestors settled on Queen Anne Hill . . ." I tried to remember Grandpa's tales about his family. "In the 1880s. They would be in Seattle now, Kerry. Find them. Ask them to help you find work."

"Let me in, Emma," John yelled, his voice tight. "I just want to talk to you." He banged on the door. "I want you to know I have reconsidered Baltimore."

Maxwell climbed up on the bed to hold it steady. "Hurry!" he mouthed.

John was pounding now. "Please, Emma!"

The lace on the windows jumped as the wind howled and rain hit the glass. Thunder banged and lightning zipped through the room. I ran to the closet door and caught the porcelain knob. The air in front of me glistened and gleamed. "It's time!"

Turning around, I smiled at my friends . . . my brother and sister . . . and my heart ached with love. It felt like we had been together in Monte Cristo forever.

I imagined feathers. Talons. A ferocious curved beak—

A violent gust of wind banged the window open behind Kerry and blew her white cap off, tumbling her red hair around her shoulders. With that gust, the closet door slammed shut, taking me with it into its dark depths.

Howling wind roared across my body, twisting Tor's red-and-black flannel shirt around my waist. My hair swirled and danced in the air.

My arms drifted up from my sides and one by one I held them out, pressing the palms of my hands against the glassy, wet sides of the closet.

A sudden piercing light illuminated an image.

Knees to knees.

Arms out.

Hands pressed against the slippery closet walls.

Our fingers inched toward each other's—

With a sucking sound, the girl tilted backwards and rocketed out of my sight.

I fell to the ground with a thud and rolled into a tight ball, spinning in a circle across a splintery floor.

I covered my ears.

Pressing.

Pushing.

A sudden silence and darkness . . .

I lay in a heap and panted and trembled . . .

. . . and listened as John yelled and pounded his fists on the door.

CHAPTER TWENTY-SIX

———

Emma
2015

*A*s usual, Emma awakened first. She fumbled at the blankets in a moment of confusion and then relaxed, sensing the warm, small bump of Lia under the covers. They were at the Countryside Inn, scattered around in what was once a large Victorian home. Keko snored from a couch in an adjoining nook, and Niki and Jules were rooming across the hall. As the inn was full up with other customers, Evan, Rapp, and Uncle Jack had slept in the van.

They had decided it was too risky to stay at the campsite after Ranger Karl bid them goodbye yesterday. After using words Emma had never heard before as they watched the back-end of the ranger's car disappear down the narrow, green-choked road, Uncle Jack finally calmed himself and said something to the effect of, "Well then, we'll just take our business elsewhere"—and as if a mule had kicked Team Switch into action, they dismantled the tent, accounted for their piles of belongings, and doused the smoldering campfire with handfuls of soil. Off they went down the mountain to find Evan's bread pudding and a place to spend the night.

Emma slipped out of bed and sifted through her sack of clothes. She spread everything out on the floor in front of her. She would reflect carefully about her choices today. If luck had it, they would be her going-home apparel. After a minute, she chose Sonnet's black yoga pants, a turquoise-and-white striped top, and turquoise high-topped Converse tennis shoes. Lia had said that Sonnet was wearing her other pair, red ones, when she disappeared two weeks ago. Perhaps Sonnet would also choose to have them on today and the co-incidence—a balance of sorts—of wearing the same shoes would bring them good luck in their opposite journeys home.

She started for the bathroom to take a shower and wash her hair one last time with the heavenly coconut shampoo while Lia and Keko still slept. Emma had let a few inches grow between herself and Lia yesterday, and today she would allow a few more. It would be too painful to tear herself away all at once.

OMINOUS clouds, stringy with black edges, blew across the morning sun and darkened the Inn's bacon-and-coffee-scented dining room as Team Switch, Uncle Jack, and Keko sat in a snug group around an old wooden table. Emma couldn't help but smile at the mound of waffles and straw-berries and whipped cream placed before her by the tattooed and pierced waitress. She would never say anything impolite, but this pile of sweetness pleased her more than the smoky fire-scrambled eggs and burnt toast she had eaten the last several mornings.

Keeping time with the rest of them, Emma jammed bites of waffles into her mouth. Instead of feeling embarrassed, as she would have when she first came to this new world, eating fast was just her habit now. Any dining decorum had disappeared after the first several meals standing at Aunt Kate's kitchen counter with Lia. And anyway, they were in a hurry. It was time to get back up the mountain and confront the identical storm that had brought her to this place.

A faraway crash of thunder boomed at them through the narrow windows. She flinched and glanced at the round wall clock above the coffee machine.

"Let's finish up and hit the road. It'll take us awhile to get back to Monte Cristo." Uncle Jack took a plastic card out of his wallet and set it into a small black tray.

Evan set the last of the Team Switch money in the tray and flipped the card back at Uncle Jack. "You've done so much. This is on us."

Rapp said, "Are you ready for this, Emma?"

"I'm ready."

She ate one last bite of strawberry and pushed her plate away. Her stomach roiled, and butterflies fluttered against her heart.

THE van jolted to the side of the road and came to a firm stop before sliding back and sideways. The slow spattering of rain had turned into fat raindrops and quickly covered the front glass before being scoured off by the swishing blades. Needle-covered tree branches scratched like cats' claws at the box on the van's roof. A large tree had fallen across the road, and heavy foliage scraped up against the left side of the van, preventing those doors from opening.

"Damn!" Rapp tugged a baseball cap on his head. He tossed his messenger bag over his shoulder, jumped from the car into the storm, and hauled them all out of the side of the van into the mud. They scrambled over the downed tree and slid up the mucky road through the rain.

"Wait!" Uncle Jack had tangled his legs in vines and toppled over. "I've hurt my ankle."

Keko knelt next to him. "I'll help Jack back to the van. You guys go, now. It's almost twelve. I'll try to catch up."

Evan rubbed the wetness off his face and raindrops out of his hair. "Are we on the right track? Everything seems different today."

Niki pointed. "I think our camping spot is just up there. If we can find that, we can find our way."

They found the camp and found their way, struggling through dense wet forest and racing the menacing storm up the slippery hill, helping each other to Emma's house.

Evan pushed open the front door and they ran in, enveloped in the house's stormy gloom.

Rapp switched on his flashlight, the narrow beam straining to show them the way. Reaching out to the banister, they bolted upwards, stepping on each other's feet, rain and mud from their shoes making the stairs slick.

They ran holding hands down the corridor, rushing to Emma's room.

Thunder boomed and lightning flashed. Rain pelted the old windows. They stood in a circle hugging Emma, tears and rain on their faces. Emma held Lia close and whispered. "It is the hardest to let go of you."

She stepped away and gestured to Rapp's bag. "Please?"

Emma dropped to her knees and found the tin soldier and photographs. "They're all I have of home." Emma held the soldier out to Niki.

She kissed her finger, running it across the photograph and her brother's little faces. "Keep it safe," she said, handing it back to Rapp. She took the rusty nail out of her pocket and pressed it into his hand. He embraced her.

The wind howled and rain hit the glass like small stones hurled from the sky. "Hurry!" cried Lia, through her sobs.

Emma ran across the room and turned the porcelain knob. The air inside the closet glistened and gleamed. "It's time!"

Turning around, she smiled at her friends, her companions of the heart, her fellow soldiers in her battle with time. Her heart ached with love.

She held on tight to the memory of two orca whales sailing above a salty wave.

A fierce gust of wind banged the window open and blew Rapp's dark hair forward, tumbling his cap to the floor. With that gust, the closet door slammed shut, taking her with it into its dark depths.

Howling wind roared across her body, twisting the striped shirt around her waist. Her hair swirled and danced in the air.

Her arms drifted up from her sides and one by one she held them out, pressing the palms of her hands against the glassy, wet sides of the closet.

A sudden piercing light illuminated an image.

Knees to knees.

Arms out.

Hands pressed against the slippery closet walls.

Their fingers inched toward each other's—

With a sucking sound and a flap of a black-and-red shirt, the girl tilted backwards and up and away, hurtling out of Emma's sight.

She fell to the ground with a thud and rolled into a tight ball, spinning in a circle across a wooden floor.

She covered her ears.

And squeezed her head.

A sudden silence and darkness . . .

She lay in a heap and panted and trembled . . .

. . . and listened as someone yelled and pounded his fists on the door.

CHAPTER TWENTY-SEVEN

Sonnet
2015

The pounding stopped. The door squeaked open. I dropped my chin to my chest as hands reached in, dragging me out of the closet. I quivered against the wall.

"Sonnet?"

In front of me stood my brother, my wonderful, funny, much-loved brother. "Evan! Was that you beating on the door?"

He knelt and put his arms around me. "Yup, that was us." Behind him stood my grinning sister and cousins. And Rapp.

Evan shouted his incorrigible laughter and towed me up so that I could stand. Jules and Lia held my hands as everyone pressed close.

I leaned my head back on Evan's shoulder. "I've been gone—"

"We know," said Jules. "We've been trying to get you back. We found your letters."

Evan said, "We've all been so crazed—"

"Emma has been here with us." said Niki. "She was you."

"And I was her."

"We have so much to tell you," said Lia.

Rapp stood behind Niki and watched me with Tor's eyes. My gaze skid away. "Is that a tin soldier, Niki?"

"Keko, our friend, found it way in the back of a fireplace grate."

"We found this, too." Rapp held out an old photo. In the image, Jacob and Miles sat on a bench clutching tin soldiers. Noticing something almost out of camera range, they had turned their blurry heads, watching Thorn's hand raking my neck.

"That happened just yesterday. My brothers, Jacob and Miles. They were terrified. And then she took their hands and dragged them off the bench and away from me. I never saw them again." I lifted my head from Evan's shoulder and put my hands over my face. I felt myself falling.

Rapp stepped forward and caught me. As he spun me away and through the house, my brother, sister, and cousins raced behind us across the mansion's old wooden floors. And then there was something else.

Tight in the grace of Rapp's arms, I could hear the echo of my own footsteps, running down this hallway in love and in hate.

Two weeks ago, before I had even traveled, I'd felt myself in 1895, living in that year already, sensing Tor already. That day. I was remembering my own memories before I had even made them. Because this house had kept me a part of the mystery—the *life*—it had cradled forever within its walls. This house had known me.

⌣

THE crow on the roof cried out as Lia slammed the old door shut behind us. Rapp set me down on slippery pine needles and held me tight to his side, just as the sun poked out between tumbling, blowy clouds. In a tight band, we moved away from the closet, away from the house and down the hill, away from the dark, silent forest of Monte Cristo.

CHAPTER TWENTY-EIGHT

Emma
1895

*E*mma dropped her chin to her chest and shut her eyes as two sets of hands reached in, helping her out of the closet. She could smell fresh mountain air and lemon oil. She could smell the sweet cedar aroma of the new lumber used to build the Sweetwine house three years ago. She was home.

"Miss Emma?"

She raised her head and squinted. In front of her stood Kerry and the family carriage driver. They lifted her up and smiled down at the turquoise shoes on her feet as if they were greeting an old friend.

Her room had changed. Wooden trunks sat together under the windows, new garments filling them to the brim. Her brass bed blocked the doorway.

"Emma!" Her father walloped his fists on the door. "Answer me!"

"I need to tell you many things before you see him," Kerry whispered close to her ear.

She longed to crawl into her big, beautiful bed, but there

were a few things that remained undone. With all her strength, she called out. "Yes, I am now changing my clothes. I will be down momentarily, Father. Please take your leave of my door. I will come to the study to speak to you there."

"I will be waiting, Emma."

Maxwell and Kerry heaved the bed back to its original position. Before Maxwell could leave, Emma took his arm. "Whatever your hand has been in this day, and indeed these two weeks, thank you, Maxwell."

"It's good to have you back, miss. Many things have changed since your disappearance. Mostly for the best, I wager, as long as you remain strong."

He tipped his black-and-blue-checked cap and slipped out the door, treading softly toward the kitchen staircase.

"Tell me what I need to know, Kerry."

So, Kerry spoke to her about the last weeks, of all the shocks and truths and reckonings, while she wound around, removing Sonnet's wet clothing from Emma's shaking body and helping her into a dress. She brushed out Emma's hair, still wet with rain, and went to tie it with a bow.

With a gentle movement, Emma took the brush from Kerry's hands. "No, please, leave it down as is today."

And with the understanding now of her parentage, a kind of peace cuddled down around Emma's shoulders, as if an angel had draped her in a cloak of tenderness and had sung her the sweet melody of a forgotten mother's love.

EMMA settled onto the couch. The rain had stopped, and the sun peeked through dark clouds that were lumbering away from Monte Cristo to another place beyond the mountain town. Her brothers laughed and played in some remote part of the house, and Cook whistled and brought the midday meal down the hallway to the dining room on her large silver tray. Emma could smell dill and warm rye bread. Nothing had changed, yet everything had changed.

Emma's mother—*no, her aunt!*—struggled in through the study door as her father tried to shut it.

"My daughter and I will speak alone, Rose. This matter is between Emma and me now. I will not allow you to insert yourself."

"Emma is my—"

"Is your what, Rose? Tell me. What is she to you?" Her father spoke softly, with care, while Rose stood her ground in the doorway, her hands braced on the wood against her husband's weight. She was like a terrible storm that touches down and causes great havoc, just to blow from the muddle moments later, caring not about the damage left behind. Emma wondered if Rose beheld her dead sister as they stared at each other and if that vision was what caused Rose to finally coil away.

"Please, dear. Leave us." Emma's father was gentle with her, his voice full of pity. It was the pity that did it. Instead of angry passion, her father treated her as one would treat a wayward pet dog or a small, stubborn child. And when his passion fled, Rose no longer held the power. Her delicate beauty and flirty nature could no longer sway.

Rose dropped her arms and pressed them hard against her silk dress.

This sad person, trying to force her way into the library

and eternally stand in the way of a relationship between her and her father, was finally out of Emma's head. Rose could hurt her no more.

Her father closed the door. Instead of retreating behind his desk, he brought a smaller chair and placed it in front of her. He sat down and held her hands.

"I'm sorry I worried you, Father."

"What is done is done. I am glad now that you have returned."

"I can't stay here, but I do not want to go away as far as Baltimore."

"We sent for numerous brochures. The institutions vary in location and, in fact, there is one from Seattle. Would that please you? I will give them to you to read. Your education will be for you to choose now, Emma. I will follow your judgment in this matter."

"Thank you. Will you be okay?"

"*Okay?*"

She smiled. "I meant, will you be fine?" She would make mistakes like this. "I hope you do not suffer because of me. With her."

He pinched the end of his moustache and sighed. "Rose and I will come to an agreement satisfactory to all. She is a good mother to my sons, and I have all the confidence she will continue to show them the affection a child deserves. But she was never a good mother to you, Emma. I want to sincerely apologize for that again. I hope you believe me when I say I am truly sorry. There will be changes, you will see."

"This means everything to me."

The clock chimed once. It was time to join the family around the dining room table.

"You will come dine with us, then?'

"No, Father. I wish to retire to my room now."

Purple stains shadowed his eyes, and lines feathered his forehead and mouth. His usual ramrod back slumped. He seemed as weary as Emma. She leaned forward and put her arms around his neck, comforted by the familiar smell of lime shaving cream. She brushed her lips across his cheek and felt him stiffen. It was not their way. But perhaps she could slowly change their way and bring the love she had been privileged to learn about into this cold house.

Alone, without hands or help from friends, Emma climbed the staircase and walked the long corridor to her room for the second time that day. She pushed her bedroom door shut, threw off her clothes, and climbed into bed.

Tor. Emma would wear a disguise and walk all the way to his cabin tomorrow if that was what it took to be with him.

CHAPTER TWENTY-NINE

———

Sonnet
2015

*L*ia put her head around the bedroom door. "Finally. We've been waiting like crazy for you to come back to us."

I sat up and stretched. I'd woken to find myself in Lia's bedroom, lying in the bed we shared every summer when my family came home to Seattle for our yearly vacation. I had started teasing her when we were both thirteen that it was about time for the white canopy to go. We weren't little princesses anymore. Maybe turning fifteen in another month would finally inspire her. But she had so far resisted.

Lia sat down on the edge of the bed and held out a peanut butter and jam sandwich and a glass of milk. "Just for you."

"How did you know I'd be starving?" I held the plate to my nose and sniffed blackberries.

"Because you've been asleep for over twenty-four hours. Evan wanted to come in here and wake you this morning. I had to fight him off. Even Rapp has been moping around, waiting for you to come alive."

"Where is everybody?"

"We told Mom and Dad you were sick. Everyone has been leaving you alone, just doing their own thing. We didn't want it to seem suspicious. They never knew what happened, Sonnet. We just substituted Emma for you. If my parents had found out, they would have called your parents, and then your parents would have gotten on a plane and come back, and everything would have gotten so complicated. Like it wasn't already. We just had to figure it out ourselves with the help of Rapp's Uncle Jack and Uncle Jack's psychic friend and a time travel-believing professor."

"Good thinking." The words stuck together in my peanut butter mouth as I thought of the help I had gotten on the other end. I knew I would speak about it all someday. Just not this day.

"We've been dying to talk to you," Lia said.

"Yeah, I want to know what happened."

"It was so insane. Nobody knew what was going on at first."

"That's the way it was for us, too."

"Us?"

"Me and my friends there. One of them was Kerry the nanny. She was my *you*."

Lia plucked at the duvet cover. "Emma slept in here instead of you. You'd think it would have been weird, but it really wasn't. It was like you were still here."

I drank down the rest of the milk, never taking my eyes off her face.

"This whole thing is pretty outrageous, isn't it?" said Lia, finally.

"Yeah." I set the glass down. "I need to take a shower. You have no idea how much I've been wanting that."

Aunt Kate opened the door. "Sonnet . . . you're finally awake. How are you feeling?"

"Better."

"Well, you were sick and sleeping two weeks ago, too. And then you were sad. Should I worry about you?"

Lia, standing behind Aunt Kate, mouthed the word *Emma*.

"I'm all good now. I promise, I'm back to being me."

She checked out my black-and-red shirt and big jeans leg sticking out of the covers and frowned. "Why are you sleeping with those clothes on?"

"Just cold. I'm gonna go jump in the shower."

"Good. You really look like you need one. We're leaving for Grandpa's in less than an hour. Here, hand me the plate and glass. I'll see you two downstairs."

Lia waited for the door to close. "Dinner at Grandpa's for your last night. You guys are leaving tomorrow."

I got out of bed and stretched and yawned. "Back just in time. I feel great. We can talk more when I get out of the shower."

"Sure. Whose clothes are those, anyway?"

"Tor's. I wore them for my escape."

"Well, *that's* gotta be a story."

"Most definitely."

"Emma told us about Tor. Such a coincidence about him and Rapp. I guess they even look alike. You should have seen her face when she saw him. Like seeing a ghost. I thought she was going to fall over."

"I can only imagine. I know I acted pretty strange when I first saw Tor. I'll be right back."

I swung my hair to the side and put my face close to the bathroom mirror, running my finger along the purple line. The fourteen tiny marks along the sides of the scar where the thread had been were almost gone. Doctor Withers had done a good job. I had to give him that.

The handprint across my cheek had disappeared and the scab on my lip was smaller now, but I would always have the scar on my forehead.

Tor's jeans and shirt lay in a heap on the floor where I dropped them. I took the browned and crinkled rosebud from the jeans' pocket and set it aside. I would press the Mystery Mine rose between the pages of a book and keep it as a memory. I slid Tor's belt out of the loops and ran it through my hands, touching the tattered hole where he had worn the plain metal buckle. I lifted it to my nose and breathed in the leather smell. The smell of him. I set it back on the pile.

"I promise I will appreciate having a shower until the day I die," I said to the heavenly stream of just-the-right-temperature water as it ran down my back and shoulders. Instead of rubbing a foul bar of soap on my head, I squeezed silky coconut shampoo into my hair.

Ahhh. Divine.

Except for the scar on my forehead and the jeans, shirt, belt, and rosebud lying on the floor next to the tub, the last remnants of my 1895 life ran down my body and swirled around the drain, leaving me to start living my 2015 life once again.

⌒

"HEY, kids." Grandpa grabbed at the five of us and kissed the tops of our heads as we walked by him into the house. Another summer and Evan would probably be leaning over him, kissing the top of his head.

The last one through the door, I burrowed my face into Grandpa's blue sweatshirt and circled my arms around his waist. He smelled like his usual peppermint mixed with lasagna tonight—his specialty since Grandma died. The sharp smell of garlic bread wafted through the old Victorian house he had lived in practically his whole life. Doing the exact opposite, his son, my father, had lived all over the world as a diplomat, never settling anywhere for very long. It occurred to me for the first time that those two things might somehow be related—reverse lives, balancing each other out, sharing in the knowledge. "Grandpa, I love you so, so much."

"You haven't left yet, my sweet Sonnet. Let's not get sad until tomorrow, or you'll have me crying in my wine tonight."

"Hey, what's this? Everybody's down? Is it a full moon or something?" Uncle Vince came up the stairs and headed to the kitchen carrying a cooler full of pop.

"Come on," said Niki. "Let's go out to the yard and play bocce ball."

We made a circle on the grass. In the distance, a ferry slowly plowed through Elliot Bay, making its way toward downtown Seattle from Bainbridge Island.

Jules said, "So tell us what happened, Sonnet."

"I don't even know where to start."

"Just start talking," said Niki.

"Well, I was dragged out of the closet on the other side of time. I was hurt pretty badly. Stuff had fallen on my head and knocked me out." I showed them the scar. "A nasty doctor came and gave me some bitter medicine that basically paralyzed me. Then he put seven stitches in my head. They threw me in bed for two days, and I stayed delirious with the medicine they kept forcing down me. I didn't realize I was in 1895 until the afternoon I could finally get out of bed. And then I freaked out."

"Emma told us about her life. Her father and two little brothers. Her hidden engagement to Tor. Her horrible mother. It sounded like she was super mean," said Niki.

"Yeah," said Evan. "In the photo, she was practically jerking your head off."

"She's insane with bitterness," I said. "It turns out Emma's mom is actually her aunt, her dead mom's older sister. And her dad is still in love with her dead mom. And Rose, that's the aunt's name, can't handle having a reminder of her husband's love for her sister around the house. So, she beats up on Emma. If she was here, she'd probably get treatment for—I don't know—anxiety or something. There, the bad thoughts are just left to bounce around in her head."

Lia said, "What a mess. Her *aunt*? I don't think Emma knew that . . ."

"No, but she'll find out soon enough. Kerry knows and so does Tor. They'll tell her."

"Sonnet, you keep talking about it like it's happening now. Those people are all dead and gone. It's past tense, not present tense," said Niki.

I bent a strand of grass between my fingers, snapping it. "Honestly, I'm having trouble wrapping my head around that fact, Niki. For me it was just yesterday."

"Aunt Kate is calling us in for dinner," said Evan. "Let's go."

After everyone left, Lia stayed behind and scooted up next to me. "What's going on? You seem . . . I don't know. Older. Changed. Full of secrets."

"I don't mean to be secretive. So much happened. The last two weeks have seriously felt like two years. I'm just not ready to talk about it yet."

"Is it Tor?"

I put my arms around my knees and laid my head on them. "I guess I can't hide anything from you."

"Did something happen?"

What had it been? What could I say? "We saw each other when we could. We kissed. I don't know—it wasn't so much what we did—it was how we felt about each other." The ache was rising to my heart. I let it wash over me. That familiar pain.

"He didn't accept that I wasn't Emma at first. And then after he got over the shock and accepted it, he asked if I would be his if Emma didn't come back. We were so attracted to each other, and we knew it was wrong, but it was so complicated, Lia, so confusing. He had only her and he really, really loved her. That was hard for me. For both of us because he cared about me, too. We were never just still with anything for certain. Like the tide. Smooth for a minute and then churning . . ."

"Did you love him?"

Past tense. The ache squeezed and squeezed at my heart.

River water had crashed against boulders the night Tor and I rode to the top of Simeon's mountain, where the moon and the stars kissed the earth. Where I had cuddled my body back into the curve of his warm chest, wrapped in his arms, his beautiful, damaged arms, adored and wanted.

Yes. I had loved him.

Lia put her arm around my shoulders. "I don't want you to feel bad. Emma would understand your pull to each other. We think you might have been living a past life. You really were Emma while you were there. And if you were Emma, Tor really was your boyfriend. And maybe even your husband and the father of your children someday. None of it could be helped. Emma understood that. She wanted you to be with him if she couldn't make it back, Sonnet. She told me. That's how much she loved him and how much she thought of you."

I nodded at my best friend through my tears and turned back to Elliot Bay, a blanket of undulating diamonds spread out beyond us. I felt the thrill of pressing up close to Rapp and his messenger bag that first day, the mystery of the mansion still in front of us. I felt the agony of watching Tor round the Mystery Mine bend and ride his red horse away from me. Understanding spilled down on top of my shoulders and dripped slowly to my heart. My crazy, excruciating love for both Rapp and Tor—all of it, every bit of it—had been written in the stars.

Lia sat close, sopping up my sadness. After a while she nudged me. "I'm gonna get some of Grandpa's lasagna. Do you want me to bring some out to you?"

"I'll come in. Give me another minute."

"Always and forever. As many as you want."

I took her arm before she could leave. "I saw her, Lia. I saw my turquoise-and-white T-shirt. She was there and then she was gone. It was like seeing me and, at the same time, seeing someone I—I loved."

Lia gave me a hug. "Everything's gonna be okay, now. You're back where you belong and so is she."

I sat alone on the grass for a while longer and watched the sun sink behind the Olympic Mountains.

In the empty kitchen, I got myself a plate of lasagna and walked down the hall to the open window in the living room, bypassing the noise and fun in the dining room where Grandpa had them singing and Evan had them laughing. A salty breeze rippled through my hair, and the chirp of crickets kept time with Grandpa's song.

The earth was rotating as it had done from the beginning of time, turning day into night. The sun had disappeared but its force behind the mountains lit the cobalt sky with neon swaths of pink and purple, orange and red.

I caught my breath. There it was—the truth of us—splashed across the heavens, and I knew. Love doesn't just vanish. It lives in the beauty that circles the world, spinning its net across the universe, lighting the sun and the moon and the stars. It was there for whoever had the courage to lift her head and wipe away her tears and look.

I unbound my heart and let my love for him fly away to join the colors of the sky.

"Good bye, Tor," I whispered to the magnificence. "It's time for me to let Emma have you back . . ."

CHAPTER THIRTY

———

Emma
1895

The exquisite mountain air gusting in through the open window woke Emma from a deep, sweet slumber. Across the room in a shaft of sunshine sat Kerry, head bowed over a book, red curls escaping from her cap. Emma had almost forgotten how much strength there was in that small body. She knew not much about this small Irish nanny who had been a constant in her life for almost four years. She felt sorry she had never taken the time or interest in her. Or the interest in any of the Sweetwine hired help. She had been too enmeshed in her own troubles and had been bred not to notice or care much about the people who worked their hearts out for them.

"Good morning, Kerry!"

Kerry raised her head up from the book. "Good morning, Miss Emma. You have slept for a day and a night and now into day again. I hope you are rested."

"I feel wonderful."

"I'll ring for a lunch tray."

"Yes, please—I'm famished."

"Miss, I was wondering . . . if I might be so bold as to speak to you . . . a favor as it were . . ."

"Ask me, Kerry. And please do not be fearful to speak to me about whatever worries you. I must tell you, I come back to this place a changed girl. I have seen another way to live."

"Sonnet thought you might be changed. Now I have seen it for myself." Kerry beamed. "Tor, Maxwell, and I have a plan for this day. We hope you can join us."

How was it that such a simple one-syllable word—Tor—could cause her body such physical anguish and the utter collapse of any thinking area of her mind. "Does he know I have returned?"

"Indeed. I have sat with you on and off since yesterday to deliver a message from him, relayed through Maxwell to me."

"You and Maxwell both know about Tor and me?"

"We know everything. The three of us became quite close in our joint endeavor to see Sonnet off and you back home. Your secret is safe with us."

What a relief. Two people already in this old world were accepting of Tor's love for her. "Please tell me how I can be of help. Tell me Tor's message."

"He wishes to meet you today and this will free me up to accomplish my own errands. We have devised a plan to make this happen."

She might see him this day. Her heart grew large, surely too big for her chest. "Please tell me."

"Maxwell will escort me to town to pick up the photographs taken at the fair. He is then taking me to a gold appraiser he has knowledge of. Someone who can keep a confidence. I have found the ring your aunt stole from Sonnet. She thought she had found a proper place to keep it hidden, but I know her too well. She has no idea it is gone from its hiding place. I am leaving, miss, and Sonnet gave me the ring to fund my train ticket away from here. I can't stay in this house any longer."

During their short conversation, Kerry had casually called Sonnet by her given name four times, as if the year was 2015 and it was the most natural thing to do. Yes, Kerry and Sonnet had been friends. "How does this involve Tor and me?"

Kerry smiled. "You ask to come with us. But instead of going into town, we take you to Tor."

"Will *she* allow me to leave with you?"

"Oh, I think she will," said Kerry. "There is trepidation in her eyes now when your name is mentioned. Thanks to Sonnet, I think you will find more freedom in this house for yourself."

Emma flew out of bed and swung the oak wardrobe doors open. She jiggled a board loose on its wooden flooring and from the hiding space took a small purple sack tied with gold ribbon. "Take this. Order doubles of the photographs. There are two. Although one is blurry, you must order it. Keep the rest of the coins for yourself. You will need them for your trip from Monte Cristo. And Kerry, there is a registration receipt somewhere in the house for the Oldfield's School for Ladies. If you could find that for me, I would be forever in your debt."

"Of course, and I thank you for the coins." Kerry untied the ribbon and took a small paper-wrapped object from deep in her pocket. Before she could drop it in the bag, Emma held out her hand. "May I?"

The paper held a broken gold chain and cross, and a rectangle of onyx that in turn held three tiny diamonds sitting on a thin platinum band. It looked like a little domino. Emma slid it onto her finger and turned it to the light. The sun caught the diamonds and reflected a rainbow pattern that shifted from the wallpaper onto the high ceiling. "Sonnet's ring," she whispered. She moved her hand and the kaleidoscope of colors moved with it, radiant stars and their halos of light, twinkling across her room.

"Kerry, was she wearing a black-and-red shirt when she left?"

"Indeed, she was, miss. It was a borrowed shirt from Tor. She was in disguise, dressed as a boy, for her escape. Why?"

"It must have been a dream." She *had* seen Sonnet. A fleeting glimpse. In Tor's shirt. After a moment, she drew the ring off her finger and kissed it, silently wishing it a blessing on its way to someone else's hand. It would more than pay for passage to Seattle and several months lodging in a ladies' boarding house while Kerry looked for a new position. She would be set in her new life.

"I almost forgot. These are from your father." Kerry put her hand back in her pocket and held out several small brochures.

Emma quickly found the one from Seattle.

TOR walked her through the cabin door and took her into the hot, golden circle of his arms.

Emma had never been this alone with him, had never been inside his little dwelling. It held the sweet smell of new lumber and sunshine, the scent of leather and horses, and, to her, this plain, tiny home was a thousand times grander than her father's opulent mansion. She breathed him in, unsteady, her body moving on its own, thoughts suddenly fleeing. She stood on her toes because her body told her to, and raised her head to his. He kissed her and ran his hands to the small of her back, forcing her hips against his own.

Their kisses were gentle at first, and then became an inferno that burned her under her clothes, as if the sun were in the room with them, shining on bare skin. His hands on her were fire, blistering licks of flame, and he moaned, a song of passion that caused her own whimpered sighs.

And the cold stone of doubt that Emma had been carrying in her heart crumbled into a million pieces and blew away, fairy dust to their secret world. She knew now the fragility of love, the preciousness of it, the suffering in having it torn away. She loved Tor beyond anyone's questioning, anyone's judgment. Love was their treasure, their gift to each other, and she would never again hide it in darkness.

"Emma . . ." With a frown, Tor shifted away, glancing at a leather and silver bracelet on his wrist.

He began to say something about Sonnet, started to explain the last weeks. Emma pulled him back to her and laid her head against his chest. His heart rocked and thumped, a wild animal, as it lay above her own. "No," she whispered, finding it difficult to form words. "Nothing from the past. Not now."

Tor raised her face to his and smiled, running kisses

from her forehead down her nose to her lips and kept her tight in his embrace. "Tell me about our future, then."

Emma's body settled down and the stabs of passion quieted, leaving her to turn her mind back to the day. "Father will let me choose where I go to school now. I have seen a brochure, a lovely place in Seattle. A unique institution for girls recently opened in the mansion of a prominent man of business and society. A Mister George F. Fischer. His grand house is so immense, the teachers conduct classes in his ballrooms, and students live in his many bedrooms. And he and his wife are associated with the Chautauqua Assembly on Vashon Island. I have been to Vashon, Tor. There will be summer campfires and clambakes, concerts and art . . ."

Her words vanquished his smile. She had rushed and shown too much excitement. Nothing changed in his bearing. But it was as if his insides sagged.

"You will leave Monte Cristo then. After all."

"I can't stay in that house with her, you must know that. I want a good education. I have seen another way to live. Not only boys can be educated well."

"So, I have heard." He moved away and stared past her out the little window.

"What life do we have here with her spying on us, Tor? You must leave, too, find work in Seattle. There is a big city to build. There are scores of every kind of people who will come and make their lives there. They will want houses built. They will want stores and churches and schools. Instead of moving away from this mountain in three summers, we move now. You follow me after you have finished Father's new barn and before the snow falls. We will more easily meet and be together in a place where we are not known, where people like us can be seen without worry. You shall build us a home when you have time between projects. And when I have graduated from The Fischer School, we marry, as agreed to by our sworn secret."

The window stood open to the mountain breeze. The curtains puffed in and out, and a vast stand of trees loomed beyond them. She watched him as he viewed their form with still eyes as if the trees were not there, seeing instead an outline of a life taking shape, as clear and sharp as a modern movie. She waited for him to come back to her.

"It's as if the one I knew no longer stands before me, Emma. You have become fearless. And you must know there is nothing in Monte Cristo for me but you."

He no longer sagged.

"Is that a yes?"

His murmurs and hands and mouth arched her back and made the air too dense to breathe. He whispered for her love—and she willingly gave it to him. And with her assent, he took her heart and made it his own. Tears welled in his green eyes and ran down his sunburned cheeks, mixing with the golden stubble on his chin. They rocked each other.

And Emma knew love.

WITH the thud of horses' hooves and the squeak of metal wheels, their time had come to an end. Maxwell was back to fetch her. Tor helped her in across from Kerry. Finally wrenching her thoughts and her body away from her beloved, and with a pang, Emma saw the same broad smile on

Kerry's face as Evan had always had on his. The selling of the ring must have gone well. Her fellow conspirator was delirious in her happiness.

Tor passed her the envelope he had taken from a bureau on the way out the cabin door. He rapped lightly on the carriage to let Maxwell know his passengers were ready. Emma righted the surprising letter in her hands. *Emma Sweetwine* stared back in bold black letters across the front. In the same hand, *Sonnet McKay* had been written in smaller letters in the upper left-hand corner.

CHAPTER THIRTY-ONE

Sonnet
2015

*L*ia held my hair out in front of my face and slowly cut bangs across my eyebrows to better hide the Monte Cristo scar from my mother's soon-to-be nosy gaze. I fluffed them up. We stood back and admired her work in the mirror.

"Have you ever noticed how we all have the same eyes, Sonnet? All five of us kids. Different hair, skin color, and bodies, but the same hazel eyes."

"Yeah, just like Dad and Aunt Kate," I said. "And now that you mention it, like Grandpa, too."

"Seriously strong eye genes."

I stared at her. "Come with me to Grandpa's. We can ride over really quick. I'll take Niki's old bike."

"You said goodbye to him last night. And anyway, Rapp's with Evan, waiting for you. He wants to see you before you guys leave. He thinks you're ignoring him."

I could hear Rapp and Evan dribbling a basketball around on the patio under the deck, laughing their heads off.

Two weeks. Best friends.

"Did he get with Jules while I was gone, Lia?"

"Not even a bit."

"Really?"

"I swear. He wasn't interested, *at all*. And neither was she."

"How about with Emma?"

"No! Absolutely no sparks between those two, either. Everybody was just friends, Sonnet. What do you think he is? An overheated Casanova?"

"Just asking. I'll talk to Rapp later. I promise."

The neglected pink-and-purple bikes hung on hooks in the back of the garage. Now that they were teenagers, Niki and Lia weren't riding them anymore. We yanked them off the wall and rode through the Queen Anne neighborhood, the shade cool now as we passed under century-old oak and maple trees. Fall hovered in the air, which meant school would start soon. My Seattle vacation would officially end later tonight when Uncle Vince and Aunt Kate drove us to the airport.

"What are you girls doing here? What a nice surprise." Grandpa was picking dead blossoms from the red and pink rhododendron bushes that lined his yard. His end-of-summer ritual.

"I wanted to talk to you about my ring before I leave, Grandpa. You know . . . the history and stuff."

He shoved his baseball cap up off his forehead. "Well, I don't know too much about it, Sonnet. It came down through the family from my grandmother. She may have brought it from Ireland. I'm not sure about that, though."

"What was her name?"

"Kathleen Mary Margaret Hanley McKay. A mouthful. Let's go in the house and get some lemonade. We can go through the old family Bible and see if there's something in there. Families used to keep track of things by keeping important papers in the Bible. And our family tree is in there, too."

He set a carton of lemonade on his desk and rummaged around his study. "When Grandma was still alive, the house stayed neat and tidy. I'm not as capable in that department."

He stood on his toes in front of the bookcase and ran his hands across the top shelf. "Here we go. What's this? I haven't seen this old box in probably forty years." He brought down a big leather book and an old metal box and set them on the coffee table. Lia and I sat down on the loveseat on either side of him and watched as he blew dust off the tattered black leather cover and flipped it open. Crispy, yellowed papers tumbled out. He set them aside.

"Here you are, girls. See across the bottom of the tree? Niki and you, Lia, run up this line to your mother, Kate. Jules, Evan, and Sonnet run up to their dad, Terrence. And then both run up this road to me." He traced the lines with his finger. "See how it works?"

"Grandpa, you were born in 1945, Mom in 1971, and Uncle Terry in 1970." Lia studied the dates. "And your dad, Patrick, was born in 1910. So, he was thirty-five when he had you."

Lia moved her finger through the names. "Kathleen Mary Margaret Hanley married Arthur McKay in 1897. They had four kids. Casey, Edward, Sonnet, and Patrick. Your dad was the baby."

"Our Sonnet here was named after my Aunt Sonnet," said Grandpa with a quick rub to my back. "My grandparents built this house and raised them all right here."

Lia touched the children's names. "Their kids all died, except your dad, Grandpa. All of them died in 1918, the same year."

"The Spanish Flu came through Seattle and killed hundreds and hundreds, including those three." He shook his head. "I don't think Grandma Kerry ever really got over it."

My head jerked up from the page. "Grandma *Kerry*? I thought you said her name was Kathleen Mary Margaret?"

"She went by Kerry. She took it as a nickname for the little ones—she worked as a nanny until she married. Quite a woman, a little bitty thing. She left her family to come to America alone when she was just thirteen."

"Twelve," I whispered. "Not thirteen." I felt the couch shift. I clenched my teeth, fighting tears, and ran my finger over Kerry's name. *Born 1879 – Died 1975.* My friend lived to be ninety-six years old.

Just as I had hoped she would, Kerry had eventually left Monte Cristo and found the McKay family on Queen Anne Hill. She married their son Arthur and called her baby girl Sonnet—named after me, not the other way around. Her two oldest boys died at sixteen and nineteen years old. And Sonnet died when she was fourteen. *Fourteen.*

The children's birthdates swam on the page in front of me.

My sweet Kerry. I didn't think I could bear it.

A tear rolled down my cheek and spattered on top of Aunt Sonnet's name. I got up from the couch and walked down the hallway to the bathroom where I stood at the sink, catching my breath and splashing cold water on my face. I heard Grandpa walk past the door and down the hallway toward the kitchen.

Lia eventually cracked the door open and wedged herself in. "That's your *Kerry*? The nanny? She's our ancestor?"

I nodded and sniffed and rubbed a towel across my eyes.

"Grandpa left the room and I started digging around inside the old box and found this." She handed me a stained envelope with *Sonnet McKay, born 2000* written across the front in old-fashioned writing. "And here's your ring. I found it in the box, too. But how can that be?"

My ring glimmered up at me from the palm of my hand. Nothing made sense and everything made sense. I wiggled it on my finger and kissed it, welcoming it back. "It's just a beautiful mystery like my entire life lately. How can any of this be? Let's go outside, Lia. I'll read it out there. Will you go tell Grandpa?"

I sat down on the newly mowed lawn. The old-fashioned writing curved in elegance across the paper, so different from the blocky letters that everyone used now. I turned the envelope over in my hands and lifted it to my nose. It smelled musty. It opened easily—the old glue had evaporated leaving behind shiny brown marks on the edges of the flap. The date on it was August 11, 1974. My birthday, twenty-six years before I was born, and a year before she died.

"Read it to me, Lia. Please?" I handed the letter to her as she sat down next to me. I lay back on the grass and watched puffy clouds skate across the baby-blue sky.

Dearest Sonnet,

If you are reading this letter, you have found the Bible and have seen the family tree. I remember how you cried for me when I told you my story of leaving Ireland when I was just a wee girl. You had such a big heart and are most likely sad about my darlings taken to heaven so young. Don't be. I want you to know I have had a truly good and happy life.

I kept the ring, Sonnet. It was all I had left of you. Instead, I sold my cross and the gold chain you wore around your neck. Along with some coins from Emma, it was enough to buy me passage to Seattle and a new life. You sent me to the McKay home on Queen Anne Hill. And that is exactly where I was meant to be.

You told us of your life and your family that night we rode up the mountain to old Simeon. And he had a message for you. He said you had come to us in Monte Cristo for a purpose. We now know, do we not, the reason was to bring me the ring and send me to Seattle, to the arms and the love of my Arthur. Our youngest, Patrick, lived through the flu epidemic and eventually had Brad, your grandfather. I have lived long enough now to meet my great-grandchildren: Terry, who will one day be your father, and little Kate, who will be your aunt. And you will come to Monte Cristo when you are fifteen and I am sixteen and be the great catalyst of my life. And the catalyst for our entire family.

I have kept you in my heart for nigh on eighty years, but I will not live long enough to see you again, my dear girl. For you, it has been just a moment, but for me a lifetime. Even with the tragedies, I would not wish for anything more. Thank you for that, Sonnet. Thank you for my life.

Your great-great-grandmother and devoted friend,
Kerry McKay

Lia put the letter back in the envelope and set it down next to me. She stretched out, her head next to mine. "Wow. Just wow. Who gets to have fun with their great-great-grandmother when they're both the same age? It's really just too much to even contemplate, and you lived it. Just three days ago, you were living it."

"I know. I'm the luckiest girl in the world. She kept Patrick alive so I could be born one day. And even after all those years, she was still thinking of me. She never forgot me."

"She's the one with the strong eye genes? That was the tip?"

"She had our eyes. How did I not see that when I was with her?"

"I assume you were pretty busy freaking out about how to get back here. Not a lot of time to check out people's eyes."

Just Tor's. I folded the envelope with care and put it in my pocket. "Let's get back. Rapp's waiting."

Grandpa handed me a packet wound up in rubber bands as we got on our bikes. "It's just some old photographs of the family. You seemed interested. I thought you might want them. Is everything all right?"

"Everything is perfect. And thanks, I'll take good care of them." I set the package in the bike's white basket. I'd wait to go through them when I got back home in a couple of days. I couldn't take any more family emotion today.

"Glad to see you're wearing your birthday ring. I wasn't sure you liked it at first."

I held my hand out to him. The tiny diamonds sparkled in the sun. "It's the most beautiful ring in the world, Grandpa. I adore it. It will always remind me of where I come from when I forget to remember."

He threw his head back and hooted. "Well, that's wonderful. I think."

At that moment, I had never loved anyone as much as I loved him. And after my birthday-brattiness, he still loved me, too. My grandfather—and Kerry's grandson.

I really was the luckiest girl in the world.

∽

RAPP and Evan met us at the door, hot and sweaty, with half-eaten sandwiches in their hands.

"Where were you?" Evan asked.

"We just biked up to Grandpa's. I wanted to say goodbye one last time."

"Can I talk to you, Sonnet?" said Rapp. "Alone?"

We walked out onto the deck and leaned up against the wooden railing. The yellow birthday balloons were gone and the birthday cakes long ago eaten. Rapp set his messenger bag down on the decking and broke his crust into three pieces, flinging the last bites into the yard for the birds. Nothing to come between us today.

"I've been wanting to apologize." He clapped the crumbs off his hands. "I'm so sorry about wanting you to hide in the closet that day. If it hadn't been for me, none of this would have happened. It was such a mistake."

I remembered how I felt standing with him in the mansion's dark bedroom. Shy and stupid and scared. That moment seemed like a lifetime ago. "Someone very wise told me there are no mistakes. His name was Maxwell and he lived in Monte Cristo a very long time ago. You couldn't have stopped it, Rapp. It was all meant to be. It was . . . destiny. All of it. Even meeting you."

"You knew my ancestor, Tor. What was he like?"

"He looked just like you. Different hair. But you have his same body. Eyes. Everything."

"No, what was he like as a person? As a human being? Emma told us what he looked like."

What was he like?

Aunt Kate's yellow roses flung their beauty at us from the sunny part of the yard. A few days ago, I had been at the Mystery Mine and stumbled onto a lonely rosebush. The miracle of roses, the sight of an eagle, and Tor's belief in me had given me the strength to save myself.

"Tor was smart . . . and he was also resourceful and . . ." I paused, thinking. How could I paint a human heart for someone else to see? "He had this compassion, this empathy for others, that allowed him to listen, really listen and to let his own feelings just . . . show. His mom and dad, and two little sisters, Inge and Ensi, all died in a terrible fire when he was fourteen. He tried to save them and was horribly burned. After that, he left for America by himself. He suffered and was alone in the world—it's why he loved Emma so much. But, Rapp, he was so much more than his pain. He didn't let it define him. He woke up every day in his little one-room cabin that held a few pieces of humble, handmade furniture and nothing else, and made the most of the tough life he'd been given. The amazing thing was that he was happy. Really happy. You know?"

Rapp nodded. "I think so. Yeah."

"He played blackjack and was good at it, good enough to win a pretty Christmas horse named Noel. He ran a crew of men, and most of them were older than him, but he had their respect because he was such a hard worker and was so kind. He even had the respect of the richest man in town, which is saying something for back then."

"In the letter you hid for us, you said he was the best guy ever. You liked him a lot."

"I couldn't have found my way back without him."

A lacy, flame-red tipped leaf from the Japanese maple tree next to the deck fluttered down and landed on the railing next to his hand. "All I could think about when you were gone, was, *I just wish I could have kissed her.*"

"That's what you thought?" I tried not to look as shocked as I felt.

He flicked the leaf. We watched it spin around and around to the grass, below. "It felt so right standing next to you when we found the house. So peaceful, as if it was just you and me and no one else standing in that forest. And then later in Emma's bedroom . . ." He turned to me with eyes as intense as the tight knot inside me. "But you were so aloof. A million miles away. And now you're back and I'm jealous of a ghost."

He had liked me that first day as much as I'd liked him. He had wanted to kiss me. "I have something for you. Wait here."

I ran upstairs and found a stack of clean clothes on top of my suitcase. The best aunt in the world had done my laundry. I picked out Tor's jeans and black-and-red-checked shirt and reached for the belt. I pulled my hand away and stared at the curl of leather.

No, the belt wasn't mine anymore. What was mine from Tor, I held inside me. My pressed rosebud and the battle scar on my forehead were all I needed. I added the belt to the bundle and hugged it close. I ran back downstairs and held it out to Rapp.

"That ghost? He would want you to have his stuff. He was pretty excited about the idea of you."

He held them out, pleased. "Vintage. All right. Thanks."

He took off his T-shirt and put on Tor's shirt, a perfect fit, leaving it unbuttoned. An old, rusty nail, bent and coiled around a leather cord, hung from his neck. He buckled the belt low around his hips, and threw the jeans over his shoulder.

He still smelled like paradise. "So, will you stay in Seattle with your uncle?"

"I might be staying with Uncle Jack. Still trying to convince my mom and step-dad. I'd rather live here with my uncle than live at their new house with them. I hate that it has to affect my life just because they decided to buy into a winery and move to the other side of the mountains. I'll be way over in the tiny town of Cle Elum, and my friends will be in Seattle." He sighed and shook his head. "But we're all cool now. We made up. So, TBD. If nothing else, I'll be here again next summer. Will you?"

"I'll be here."

The trees in the back yard swayed and rustled as we stood close together, and the almost-fall sun sat softly on my shoulders. I was glad to be standing alone with him—glad we got to finally talk about things that needed to be said. I wanted to know him. Everything about him. I wanted him to know me.

Reaching up, I tucked a lock of his hair behind his ear. Letting myself go, I leaned into my heart and took the plunge—something I was getting pretty good at by now. I put my arms around his neck and stood on my toes. I kissed him. His lips were warm and soft and vaguely familiar, and his hands were hot through the material on my back. He wrapped his long arms around me and crushed me to him, rammed up against Tor's jeans still lying across his shoulder, as if the three of us shared in the moment.

He kissed me as if he was hungry for me. As if he'd been waiting forever and was amazed he finally had me in his arms. It was as good as I had imagined it would be. As good as it had been with Tor, but better. Because this time it was the right thing to do.

With a happy sigh, I stepped back. "I guess I better go concentrate on my suitcase. Always a challenge when it's time to pack."

He caught my hand and pulled me against him for one long, last, incredible kiss. He nuzzled my neck and whispered in my ear. "Now that I finally have you, I don't want to let you go. You might decide to slip out on me again."

"As if that was my choice." I laughed and snuggled my head under his chin and knew I was exactly where I was meant to be. "If you've missed me this much in two weeks, I can only imagine what you'll be like when we see each other in a year."

"Who are you, friendly one? And what did you do with Sonnet?" His fern-colored eyes crinkled with his smile—just like the first time I'd kissed his long-ago ancestor. My body thrummed. I would see Rapp again next summer. A promise I tucked deep into the folds of my plunging-in-heart.

CHAPTER THIRTY-TWO

—

Emma
1895

The hour was late, and Emma knew if her father closed the study door, he wanted privacy. Before, she would have crept back to her room, but tonight she knocked anyway. She had one more indulgence to ask of him, but this time it did not concern her. "It's Emma, Father."

"Yes, dear? Come in." He sat behind his massive desk amid a pile of paper. On his face were small spectacles, something she had not seen on him before. Or maybe she had never noticed.

A single log in the fireplace sent just enough heat into the room to chase away the evening chill. The old grandfather clock announced itself with steady reassuring beats. It had been a feature in the house her father grew up in and now had sat in every one of his Sweetwine homes. The antique would go to one of her brothers someday and become an unfaltering fixture in his home. And time would then carry it off to one of his sons—and certainly on from there. Emma thought in those terms now.

"May I speak to you on a subject that has importance to me? I ask one more favor of you before I leave, father."

"How can I help?" He cleared away papers and took off his spectacles. A sign of courtesy she was still getting used to from him.

"Kerry's four-year contract comes to an end on the first of November. I would like you to release her two months early so she has the ability to leave before the snow falls. She has been a faithful employee. There are more opportunities for her in a city. And she is sixteen now, almost seventeen, and must find a husband."

"Why are you discussing this with me? Your mother—your aunt—takes care of domestic affairs."

"Having you on our side will avoid trouble. She will go along with you. She may fight Kerry. And she will certainly fight me. Kerry has been faithful and true. We owe her this, father."

"And a replacement? Rose may be more amenable if there is someone waiting in the wings to take over with the boys."

"Precisely. The seamstress here in town, a Missus Love, has an assistant by the name of Goldie. And Goldie has a young sister who desires to go into service. She comes highly recommended by Missus Love who has had Anna assist her with sewing projects. The family lives right here in Monte Cristo."

He sat back in his chair and turned to the burning log. Embers popped and played a rhythm with the deep ticks of the clock. Emma knew he was considering his wife and his sons and the distress this would cause.

"Invite Anna and have her bring a member of her family,

preferably her father, to the house tomorrow evening after supper. Have her bring a letter of recommendation from Missus Love and anyone else who has used her services. I will handle any difficulties. If she can start right away, Kerry can train her before she leaves."

Emma went around the desk and put her arms around his neck. She kissed his cheek. This time there was no stiffening, no resistance. "Thank you, Father. And you will get used to affections from me. Your daughter has changed in every way and is eager to show you her love."

"THE madam thinks we have all conspired against her and she had no say in the matter," said Kerry. "She would not acknowledge me this morning and handed the boys' apparel around me straight into Anna's hands."

"Well, what she thinks is true. We *did* conspire against her. And now we will both have our freedom."

"Sweet freedom. I am ready for that, miss."

"And I, too." Emma's eyes sparkled over the trunks at Kerry. "Please, will you do me the honor of calling me Emma?" She thought Kerry might fight her. But she only smiled.

"I will."

"Okay?"

"Hey, Emma. No problem. *Okay!*"

They laughed at each other for a long moment. Kerry had learned modern-speak, too, a secret language all their own. Their divergent lives were now very much the same, touched by good people from a faraway place. They both knew their ordered world would soon tumble headlong into a time of human intermingling, where a concept called diversity would allow Emma and Kerry and Maxwell to be friends. The new realm would be built on competence, not breeding. She and Kerry had been taught well.

Together they burrowed into the clothing, rescuing fine dresses from their tissue-wrapped layers. They set aside the school uniforms and spread eight new gowns on the bed. The red velvet slipped like the finest suede across Emma's face. She let the cool material hang for a moment across her cheek and then considered its form, seeing where it could be altered to make it more presentable in a less fashionable society. Seattle was still a pioneer town, an outpost, not a sophisticated city like Baltimore. Not yet anyway.

She studied the rest. The white silk with the gold embroidery was a fancy she would never wear. The fine dresses were meant to entice a man to marriage and she would have no need of that.

They combed through Emma's too-small and worn garments that had been left hanging or sitting in piles in the wardrobe. Most were still in good condition. Emma gave Kerry all her old clothes and then set the embroidered silk dress on top. "A white dress for your wedding day. With altering, it will fit you beautifully."

Kerry laughed. "I'm only off to be a nanny somewhere. And a bride with no groom does not a marriage make."

Even in her shapeless uniform, Kerry presented grace and timelessness in a freckled sort of way. Her childish body belied her quiet inner strength and bravery, capable of handling anything life threw at her. She would be as much a prize as any other woman in Seattle. A man would be lucky to have her.

"You will be a bride someday, Kerry. And you will have family that will stretch out far behind you. I believe that is your destiny. And if I am lucky, that will be my destiny, too."

Kerry opened the stuffed pillowcase she had carried with her into the room and drew out a stack of freshly laundered clothes and a pair of turquoise tennis shoes. She bent and spread them out across the bottom of the biggest trunk. "You just never know when modern attire might come in handy."

Emma clapped her hands together and laughed, tickled to the heavens. *Yes. You just never know.*

THEIR fussing over the dresses done, Emma closed the door behind Kerry, unlocked her writing drawer, and retrieved Sonnet's unopened letter. She plucked the book, *Little Women*, off the fireplace mantel. Opening it, she slid the letter between the pages.

CHAPTER THIRTY-THREE

—

Sonnet
2015

I'm just glad your parents are meeting you in London and flying back to Cape Town with you," said Aunt Kate. The Macadangdang family had walked the McKay kids through SeaTac Airport as far as they could without airline tickets of their own. The security maze came next, and then the long trek to their international gate.

"It's not that big of a deal," said Evan, laughing. "It's not like we haven't already flown a million times by ourselves."

"Millions and millions of times. Tough guy, huh?" Uncle Vince threw a fake punch at Evan and then grabbed him around the neck, giving him a tight squeeze. "I'm going to miss you kids. The house will be too quiet."

"You know, your dad and mom have been trying to get us to come visit for the last couple of years. We've been talking about it . . ." Aunt Kate gazed at Uncle Vince. "Since you're leaving South Africa next summer, we thought we might come for Christmas vacation. Wouldn't that be fun?"

I twirled around amid the screams and took Lia's arms,

shaking them. "Oh, we'll have a good time. You'll love Cape Town. We can ride horses around. Have some crazy fun."

"Right. Crazy fun—just what we need," she said, laughing.

"No, just normal-crazy fun. Go on a safari and see the animals. Swim in our big pool at night. You can meet my friends. It's *your* birthday next, Lia. We can celebrate while you're there."

Uncle Vince took his phone out of his pocket. "Time for you guys to go. Let me snap a couple of photos first. I'll forward them to Terry and Pam—let them know their kids are on the way. They'll be happy to know we had a nice couple of weeks without them. Parents can be such worriers."

Niki and Lia in their tank tops, shorts, and flip-flops, and Jules, Evan, and I in our traveling clothes, lined up against a wall tiled in swimming salmon. We hooked our arms around each other's, big secret smiles on our faces, bound accomplices in our clandestine, top-secret adventure—lips sealed—always and forever.

"LET me switch, Evan," said Jules. The usual flying arrangement had Evan between Jules and me. Today she wanted Evan out of the way. He set his pillow up against the window, wiggled around for a minute, and fell asleep.

Jules said, "We really didn't talk. As usual, Lia kept hogging you."

"That's rich coming from you, girl-conjoined-at-the-hip-with-Niki."

Jules laughed and shrugged. "You have a point. Anyway, we were all so worried about you. After we figured out what happened I thought I'd never see you again. It was really scary. In fact, I have never been so scared in my entire life."

"I was pretty scared, too. I can barely stand to have it in the pondering part of my head, yet."

"You know what I think? Emma went back and hid the photos and the receipt for the Baltimore school so we could find them. I mean, really, how else would those things just happen to be there? I'm not sure about the tin soldier, though."

I thought about Jacob and Miles and the tin soldiers. I would miss them, my little brothers who had worshipped me. "The soldier in the fireplace grate might just stay a mystery."

"Why were you chosen to go there?"

"Chosen? How would I be chosen, Jules?"

"I don't know. By the gods or Great Spirit or something. You got picked to go on that great escapade."

"You're funny. It just happened. Nothing or nobody chose me. Destiny just happens."

"You just always seem so lucky, though. You get to be the smartest. You get to be one of the fawned-over twins. And now you travel back in time."

My mouth hung open. "You're envious . . . of me?"

"Well, you have a lucky charm that I don't have."

"You're the beautiful one that all the guys fall in love with. I'd be happy with just that."

"You are the smartest, Sonnet. And you do have the best hair. It's way thicker than mine."

Remarking positively on someone's looks was the greatest compliment Jules could give. I took it in the spirit it was intended. "Okay. I will admit I do have good hair."

"What happened to Emma? Did she get with Tor and live happily ever after?"

"Yes. I'm sure of it." I hoped so with all my heart.

"Which might make Rapp related to Emma, too."

I nodded. And related to Jacob and Miles and John . . . and even Thorn. The very idea I had been wondering about all along.

"Uncle Jack said he'll start checking into their Loken genealogy. We'll have news the next time we come back. And then you can write a book, 'cause it would make a good story, maybe even have it made into a movie. If you ever tell us your side of it. Too bad you didn't keep a journal."

I didn't need a journal. The past weeks were seared into me forever. "I'll write about it eventually. I'm still dealing with it now. It was semi-terrifying."

"And semi-what else?"

"Semi-heaven. You know, meeting awesome people. Going around to amazing places. And then just regular stuff in between. Like eating and sleeping and hanging around the bedroom."

"Life in 1895 sounds just like life in 2015."

"Pretty much." The plane had jolted us up through the clouds and was now gliding smooth and fast toward Europe and Africa and home. I held the armrest between our seats and turned to face Jules, and she did the same to me, reaching out her hand and running her finger across my birthday ring's sheen. Her eyes—Kerry's eyes—stared back at me for a moment before they closed.

I twisted my ring around my finger as a star-filled sky sped by out the window past my brother's sleeping head. Jules had called the last couple weeks a great escapade, but they felt more like a precious gift to me. I was grateful for every bit of my time in Monte Cristo, grateful for every moment that had bounced me like a ball between sweet pleasure and cutting pain.

That quiet place between darkness and dreams tugged me in. Floating free, as if a scarred and callused hand let go of mine, I drifted up like the wispy clouds hugging Simeon's mountain, gliding on a jasmine-scented breeze above giant trees and cliffs painted shades of dark emerald and stone. A grand home sat alone in a clearing. Its giant wood-whorled clock bonged twice.

A hot Chinook wind whipped at my hem and blew me toward the heavens. Too far, too fast, I felt myself slip-sliding away. Someone caught my arm and pulled me close as we tumbled back to earth, splashing down into a mighty river.

She wore what I wore, was a mirror image of me. She had been with me from the beginning. How had I not known?

We swam together through clear, green water, dodging speckled fish and skimming over river rocks and nuggets of shiny gold.

She smiled at me, and I knew I was forgiven.

And then Emma let me go.

CHAPTER THIRTY-FOUR

—

Emma
1895

*E*mma waded through the meadow to her hiding place . . . a hollowed-out area of the hill, close to the gravel road and just up the slope from a gnarled tree where tiny red birds hopped and chirped. Dense bushes, heavy with late August blackberries, hid her from the mansion's many windows and the eyes that peeked for her. She lay back on the flower carpet, putting her nose close to an orange blossom, fragrant like honey.

In her hands was *Little Women*. She opened its worn leather cover and flipped through the pages, blurring the words of the loving March family, characters she had adored since she was small. It was only fitting that very same book now held a secret message for her.

The envelope felt as light as a puff of smoke, surely not weighty enough to hold the words of a girl who had traveled to 1895 from the future. A girl who, for a short time, lived as "Emma." Who had come to her home and changed her life forevermore.

The day she and her Seattle friends had found the boarding school receipt in her mother's closet, Emma had told them she would run away before getting on a train to Baltimore. But she knew in her heart of hearts it would have been impossible with her old way of thinking. Her old way of being. Where Sonnet had seen family when she looked at Kerry and Maxwell, Emma would have only seen a yawning gulf. An impassible divide. She would not have had the help or have known how to ask for it. She would not have had the courage to fight for herself or the wisdom to know what to do.

If not for Sonnet, she would have been on that train to Baltimore, and any chance for a life with Tor snuffed out.

Emma Sweetwine. Pressed with force, Sonnet had formed the script in bold, up-and-down block letters, so unlike the ornamental, flourish-prone handwriting of the Victorians. The difference in methods summed up the dissimilar worlds more than Emma could do with the spoken language. She would keep this letter close and practice hers and with time she would make her own writing stronger.

The envelope crackled open.

Emma,

I'm leaving soon for the Ice Caves Fair. I won't come back to this house to live. Whatever happens, it's impossible for me to be here any longer with Rose. I've caused trouble for you and I'm sorry for that.

I want to thank you for allowing Tor in my life. I know you didn't give your permission— I just took it. But I couldn't have survived this without him. He is a good guy, Emma, and he loves you so much. By helping me, he helped get you back. And for Tor, that was really all he ever wanted.

Because for him, I was you, Emma. I was always just you.
You are my forever sister.
Love,
Sonnet

The paper fluttered to her waist.

Except for a few white clouds hanging from Foggy Peak, the afternoon sky was as clear and blue as Emma had ever seen it. The shadows thrown from the tall evergreens were cooler now. It would soon be fall and with that the weather would change. Rain would come and then snow. The gold mining town would be buried for months under a white-blue carpet of snowflakes. Emma would be gone from here, living a life in Seattle. A life that would burst with the kind of freedom she had found on Lake Washington with her beloved tribe.

And Tor would be there, too, building a future for them with his hammer and nails.

A rush of flapping shook the loftiest branches in front of her, trembling pinecones to the ground. She lifted her eyes to the eagle, its feathered black wings stretched like arms ready to embrace a luminous world. The regal bird soared away into the sun's fading rays and led her thoughts to a boy with dark shaggy hair. This time, instead of pushing Rapp away, she let the idea of him sit there in all its handsome wonder. She turned it around and around in her mind and nudged at it from every angle.

Tor's progeny, most certainly. And hers, most probably. Emma's heart expanded at last with simple understanding.

There was a reason for everything, under the sun.

"Thank you, forever sister," Emma whispered to the mountain wind. It was too small a gesture for all the gratitude she had welling inside—but there would be a lifetime to show appreciation for the path Sonnet had laid out before her.

"Where are you, Emma? Come push us!"

Emma nestled the precious letter back in its envelope and then again between the pages of her favorite book. Holding it tight against her heart, she strode away from the twittering red birds and the sweet smell of blackberries toward her brothers' waving hands.

In the distance, the Sweetwine mansion, whom some knew as Sylvia, stood pleased before a green arc of towering trees. Her pastel beauty lit up the land and the people she touched, reflections from the dying sunlight of a most perfect Monte Cristo day.

ACKNOWLEDGMENTS

This book came to me like a sandstorm, blasting me on a scorching August day, literally a hair-on-fire day, as I lounged around my Bahraini home trying like the devil to cool off. I was imagining rain-drenched ferns and mossy logs and the deep, dark shade of a majestic evergreen tree. Suddenly I was fifteen years old again and, with my parents and four brothers, hiking through a forest in a ghost town called Monte Cristo, an abandoned gold mining town in the North Cascades. That "what if" thing started happening and a full-blown story came tumbling into my mind. A genre, a plot, a Victorian mansion. And characters with names. Sonnet and Emma were more than two teenagers on a page. They were every girl I had ever known, including me. *But Not Forever* was born.

I want to thank those parents, Fib Peterson and Kathleen McLoughlin, for taking me on hikes in Monte Cristo. And of course, my brothers—Jer Peterson, Kirk Peterson, Kris Peterson, and Karl Peterson— for scaring the bejesus out of me on those hikes, without them this story would have never happened.

Along the way I had all sorts of help, usually doled out from a very long distance— virtual critiquing, hand-holding, hugging, and humor. In no particular order, here you are. Thank you all from the bottom of my heart: Geri Peterson, Bonnie Unsell, Nancy Bardue, Tami Scheibach, Joanne Peterson, Kris Barrows, Maddy Brindle, Marny Lund, Dottie Perkins,

Michael and Sam Morton, Brent Hartinger, Anne Clermont, Mary Kole, The Bahrain Writer's Circle, P4S, Brooke Warner and Lauren Wise at SparkPress, and Crystal Patriarche and Madison Rowbotham at BookSparks.

Finally, for putting up with this new obsession called writing, I want to especially thank my husband, Greg Von Schleh, and my biggest fans, Damon and Terry Siguenza. This book would not have been possible without your support, wisdom, and love.

Jan Von Schleh is a third-generation Seattleite who has lived and worked around the world in fascinating places including Zimbabwe, Nicaragua, Democratic Republic of Congo, Turkmenistan, and the Kingdom of Bahrain. When she's not writing, she likes to explore ancient buildings wherever she can find them and wonder about the stories they would tell—if only they could talk. She is sure that whatever those stories are, they most probably have to do with love.

SELECTED TITLES FROM SPARKPRESS

SparkPress is an independent boutique publisher delivering high-quality, entertaining, and engaging content that enhances readers' lives, with a special focus on female-driven work.
Visit us at www.gosparkpress.com

Tree Dreams, Kristin Kaye, $16.95, 9781943006465. In the often-violent battle between loggers and environmentalists that plagues seventeen-year-old Jade's hometown in Northern California, she must decide whose side she's on—but choosing sides only makes matters worse.

The *Alienation of Courtney Hoffman*, Brady Stefani. $17, 978-1-940716-34-3. When fifteen-year-old Courtney Hoffman starts getting visits from aliens at night, she's sure she's going crazy—but when she meets a mysterious older girl who has alien stories of her own, she embarks on a journey that takes her into her own family's deepest, darkest secrets.

Running for Water and Sky, Sandra Kring. $17, 978-1-940716-93-0. When 17-year-old Bless Adler visits a local psychic, the woman describes a vision of Bless's boyfriend, Liam, lying in a pool of blood—sending Bless on a 14-block sprint to reach Liam before she loses the only person she's ever opened her heart to.

Wendy Darling Vol 1: Stars, Colleen Oakes. $17, 978-1-94071-6-96-4. Loved by two men—a steady and handsome bookseller's son from London, and Peter Pan, a dashing and dangerous charmer—Wendy realizes that Neverland, like her heart, is a wild place, teeming with dark secrets and dangerous obsessions.

Blonde Eskimo, Kristen Hunt. $17, 978-1-940716-62-6. Neiva Ellis is caught between worlds—Alaska and the lower forty-eight, white and Eskimo, youth and adulthood, myth and tradition, good and evil, the seen and unseen. Just initiated into one side of the family's Eskimo culture, she must harness all her resources to fight an evil and ancient foe.

Within Reach, Jessica Stevens. $17, 978-1-940716-69-5. When 17-year-old Xander Hemlock dies, he finds himself trapped in a realm of darkness with thirty days to convince his girlfriend, Lila, that he's not completely dead—even as Lila struggles with a host of issues of her own.

About SparkPress

SparkPress is an independent, hybrid imprint focused on merging the best of the traditional publishing model with new and innovative strategies. We deliver high-quality, entertaining, and engaging content that enhances readers' lives. We are proud to bring to market a list of *New York Times* best-selling, award-winning, and debut authors who represent a wide array of genres, as well as our established, industry-wide reputation for creative, results-driven success in working with authors. SparkPress, a BookSparks imprint, is a division of SparkPoint Studio LLC.

Learn more at GoSparkPress.com